THE SECRET SOCIETY
of the
Pink Crystal Ball

RISA GREEN

sourcebooks
fire

This book is for everyone who has ever been afraid to believe in something.

Especially yourself.

Published by Sourcebooks Fire, an imprint of Sourcebooks, Inc.
P.O. Box 4410, Naperville, Illinois 60567-4410
(630) 961-3900
Fax: (630) 961-2168
teenfire.sourcebooks.com

Library of Congress Cataloging-in-Publication data is on file with the publisher.

Printed and bound in Canada.
WC 10 9 8 7 6 5 4 3 2 1

One

Things About Me That Might, in Some Alternative Universe, Be
Interesting Enough for the Committee of Tenth Grade Teachers to
Pick Me for the AP Art History Trip to Italy

● I have the highest GPA in the tenth grade.

● I can recite the periodic table in alphabetical order to the tune of
the disco classic "YMCA."

● In fifth grade, I won a silver medal in the New York Times
Crossword Puzzler contest, junior division. And I would have won the
gold, if I had not been competing against a nine-year-old prodigy from
Ohio who knew that a beast with twisted horns is called an eland.

● When I was five, I had an extra row of bottom teeth. Like a shark.

● I am so flat-chested that they do not make a bra in my size. Not
even a training bra.

● I play a mean game of Rummikub.

● According to family history, I am a distant relative of Susan B.
Anthony, the first women's suffragist in the United States.

● I am most likely the only person under the age of forty who has
attended a Barry Manilow concert.

● Did I mention that I have the highest GPA in the tenth grade? My God, am I boring...

⌒✳⌒

I jump nearly a foot off of my bed, startled by a roar of thunder.

Lindsay and Samantha, my two best friends, are lying on the floor, flipping through last week's issue of *Teen People*. But either a) they both have been cleverly hiding from me the fact that they are completely deaf, or b) they are simply too engrossed in the trials and tribulations of young Hollywood to have noticed that the sky almost just completely broke in half.

Finally, after another heavy rumble, Lindsay drops the magazine and rolls over onto her back.

"I'm so tired of this rain," she complains to no one in particular. "I don't understand how I'm ever supposed to get my driver's license if it keeps pouring like this. My dad won't let me practice if it's even overcast outside, let alone if an eighth ocean is falling from the sky. I mean, enough already. It's been almost a week."

Samantha grabs the magazine off the floor where Lindsay left it, and brings it close to her face to get a better look. I have no idea why she obsesses over these magazines the way she does. Samantha is effortlessly attractive and by far the best-dressed girl in the whole school, probably even the whole county.

She has perfect, wavy dark blond hair, a tall slender body that most people would have to work out four hours a day and only eat wheatgrass to attain, and her mother's entire designer wardrobe at her disposal. (Did I mention that her mother used to be a model? Did I also mention that Samantha totally inherited her legs?) Plus, she's got an innate sense of style that most celebrities have to hire Rachel Zoe to achieve. I mean, have you ever seen anyone wear Commes des Garçons with Converse? (Actually, have you ever seen anyone wear Commes des Garçons? So. Weird.) But seriously, she could easily be *in* one of those magazines. Of course, if you ask her, she'll say, "I hate the way I look." She isn't fishing for compliments either. It's still something I've never figured out about her.

"God, what is up with those lashes?" she asks aloud. "This model looks like she has spiders crawling out of her eyes." Samantha puts the magazine back down on the carpet and turns to look at Lindsay. "FYI, it's all our parents' fault. If they hadn't spent the '80s running around with aerosol hair sprays and insecticides and Styrofoam cups, we wouldn't have any of this extreme weather today."

"My dad probably did it on purpose," Lindsay remarks. "I'll bet you he *only* used products with CFCs in them, in the hope that one day his actions would prevent his future daughter from ever getting behind the wheel of a car."

"Mmm-hmmm," I say, half ignoring them—because Lindsay always complains about not having her driver's license and Samantha always blames her parents for everything—but also because I am too busy staring at the fluorescent yellow flyer that Mr. Wallace gave to everyone in my AP Art History class today. At the top, it implores us to PAY ATTENTION! And besides, there's no point in telling either of them that chlorofluorocarbons were banned from aerosol sprays in 1978, or that Styrofoam has nothing to do with extreme weather patterns. They wouldn't listen anyway.

Suddenly, a flapping mass of paper hits me in the face. I look up from the handout that I've tacked to the bulletin board next to my bed.

"Ow," I say, rubbing my forehead and laughing in spite of myself. "Why'd you throw that magazine at me? And don't blame one of your celebrity crushes."

Samantha arches her eyebrow. "You've been completely ignoring us since we got here, and I, for one, am starting to take it personally. What's going on in that genius-girl head of yours?"

With a sigh, I pull the tack out of the handout and hold it up for them to see. I do my best to appear nonchalant. "It's a contest. Mr. Wallace announced it today in AP Art History. The district was given a grant to send five kids to Italy for two weeks this summer, so that they can study great works

4

of art. And the district pays for everything. Plane tickets, hotels, food, even admittance to the museums." The inside of my stomach dances around just thinking about it.

"Let me see," Lindsay demands. She gets up from the floor and flops down next to me on my bed, taking the flyer. I peer over her shoulder, rereading it for the millionth time today as she reads it aloud to Samantha.

PAY ATTENTION!

AN UNFORGETTABLE SUMMER EXPERIENCE!

Five lucky students will be chosen to travel to Italy with Mr. Wallace, where they will study works by the great Italian masters in Rome, Venice, and Florence.

To be eligible to apply, you must:

- Be a student in AP Art History, with a grade of at least an A-.
- Write an essay explaining why you should be chosen to go on this trip.
- Applicants will be judged on their essays, as well as on their personalities, outside interests, and strength of character, as determined by a Committee of Tenth Grade Teachers.
- Applications are due to Mr. Wallace by 5:00 p.m., next Thursday!

"So what's the problem?" Lindsay asks brightly. "You've never gotten anything less than an A in your life, and you're great at writing essays. Of course they'll pick you." She hands the flyer back to me with a sigh. "That is so cool," she says, shaking her head wistfully. "The smart kids always get the best stuff."

"Trust me," Samantha says, "it's not that great. My parents have dragged me to Italy five times, and the place is so over-rated. I mean, really, you've seen one Jesus picture, you've seen them all. Although, I will say, the boys are totally hot."

I smile. I've got to hand it to Samantha, she's got the blasé, I'm-a-rich-kid-whose-parents-totally-ignore-me thing down pat. She even got herself kicked out of boarding school just to get back at them—something to do with a missed curfew, condoms, and a banana, though the story changes a tiny bit every time she tells it—so now she's stuck going to Grover Cleveland High with the rest of us lowly peons.

I'll never forget the first time that Lindsay and I met Samantha. It was seventh grade, the first day back from winter break, a few minutes before first period. Lindsay and I were in the girl's bathroom right outside of the foreign language classrooms. We always met there in the morning to compare outfits and catch up on anything that had happened between the time we got off the phone or computer the night before and the time we got to school in the morning. The bathroom was on the far side of the school, away from where all of the homeroom classes were, so most days Lindsay and I had it to ourselves. But when we walked in that morning, we were surprised to find a girl we'd never seen before.

I sucked my breath in when I saw her: she was wearing a long, sheer black tunic with strips of black fabric hanging from the sleeves, layered over a bright green tank top and jeans, with three-inch purple wedges. Her blond hair was long and tousled in a good way, and there were gold necklaces of different lengths in a mess around her neck. She was gorgeous and perfect and like nothing I'd ever seen before, at least not in person. Lindsay and I just stared at her as she hunched over the sink, applying black eyeliner and seven coats of mascara to her already long lashes, the delicate strips on her sleeves hanging precariously over the wet sink.

"My mom wouldn't let me wear eyeliner this morning," she explained, her mouth slightly open in that I'm-trying-not-to-poke-myself-in-the-eye way that people have when they're putting on makeup. She looked us over in the mirror, and I remember feeling self-conscious about my straight brown hair that just hung there, about the jeans that my mom had bought for me at the Limited Too, about the big red zit in the middle of my forehead. But she wasn't looking to be judgmental. She seemed to be looking for something else.

"Do you want some?" she finally asked, holding two eyeliners out toward us.

They were Chanel. I knew you weren't supposed to share eye makeup with other people because of the risk of transferring bacteria and getting an infection, but I also knew that if we said no, she would walk out of the bathroom and our chance of becoming friends with this beautiful eccentric girl would be gone forever. Lindsay and I glanced at each other, and then we each grabbed an eyeliner and joined her at the mirror. She smiled. Actually, it was more of a smirk.

"I'm Samantha," she said. "And you should know—I've never been good at sharing until right now."

The three of us have been inseparable ever since.

Two

So I take it you want to be one of the lucky five?" Lindsay asks with a smile, revealing the giant dimple in her left cheek that she hates.

I sigh. "I would kill to be one of the lucky five. Do you have any idea how good this trip would look for college? Plus, I'd get to go to Italy without my parents. How cool is that?"

Samantha shrugs. "It would be cooler if you didn't have to go with dorks from AP Art History. So what are you going to write about for your essay?"

This is the problem. I've been staring at that flyer the whole day, trying to think of a compelling reason for the Committee of Tenth Grade Teachers to pick me. But, so far, I haven't been able to come up with anything even remotely interesting about myself. Except for maybe the thing about my two rows of teeth. People always wanted to see them. I even thought about turning it into a business opportunity and charging fifty cents to take a look. It was that cool. At least, it was until I had to get them pulled, and then it just sucked.

"I have no idea," I admit. "Let's face it, you guys—I'm boring. I've never had anything happen to me. My parents aren't divorced, they're not immigrants, and both of them have medical degrees. Nobody in my family has ever had a debilitating disease. I've never had an eating disorder, a crack addiction, or autism. I've never broken a bone. Not even a toe or a finger. I don't have exciting hobbies. I mean, what do I like to do? I like to read. And do crossword puzzles. And Sudoku. And last summer, did I do community service in Africa, or volunteer at Children's Hospital? No. I did normal things. I worked at Gap Kids. I went to a Barry Manilow concert. I—"

"That's not normal," Samantha and Lindsay interrupt at the same time.

I purse my lips while they giggle. "Whatever. I'm telling you, I am the most boring, normal, regular girl with the most boring, normal, regular life ever. I mean, *look* at me."

I glance at myself in the full-length mirror on my closet door and take myself in: straight, super-fine brown hair that refuses to hold a curl (or a style) no matter how many layers I have cut into it; thin, unexciting lips; plain brown eyes; a regular, normal-sized nose; and, of course, an average height, thin, curveless body. I'm not being modest either. I know I'm not ugly or unattractive. There's just nothing special about the way I look. I have no defining characteristics, like Samantha's hair, or Lindsay's dimple.

I turn back to them. "The truth is, the only reason I even want to go on this trip is because I feel like it might make me a little bit more interesting, so that when I apply to colleges, I'll at least have something to actually write about and not have to make up a bunch of BS. But it's not like I can *say* that."

Lindsay and Samantha both nod in agreement. I love that they don't argue with me or try to convince me that I really am interesting. I'm not being sarcastic either. I really do love that about them. Honesty is the mark of a true friend.

"Well, at least you're not tortured every day by Megan Crowley," Lindsay offers, trying to cheer me up. "I'd give anything to be boring enough for her to leave me alone."

Megan Crowley is what Hollywood or certain clueless grown-ups would call a "mean girl" or a "queen bee." Translation: she's an insecure bitch who makes fun of other people so that nobody will make fun of her. And Lindsay just happens to be her favorite target.

It all started when we were in third grade. You see, back then, Lindsay used to be kind of mean too. Which is hard to believe, because now she's, like, the cheeriest, most harmless person on the planet. Samantha can't even picture it, not even if she closes her eyes and tries really,

really hard. She says she just can't get past the dimple, or maybe it's the peace-loving hippie vibe that Lindsay gives off, but either way, I see her point. It *is* tough to imagine. And yet, it's true. Lindsay *was* mean. Not to me—we've been best friends almost since birth—but, you know, to other people.

If I had to psychoanalyze the situation, I would say that Lindsay was probably going through some sort of sibling jealousy phase brought on by the births of her two younger sisters when she was four and seven, respectively, which then manifested in the form of meanness toward other girls at school, since school was the only place where she was able to attract attention anymore, even if it was negative attention. But that's just my opinion.

Anyway, back in third grade, Megan Crowley peed in her pants at Charlotte Reese's birthday party, and tried to pass off the huge wet spot on her crotch as spilled water. Everyone probably would have believed her too, only Mean Lindsay was sitting next to her when it happened, and she knew that Megan didn't spill any water. But rather than just letting it go, Mean Lindsay yelled out, "*She did not spill water! She peed in her pants! I saw it happen.*" And then Megan Crowley burst into tears and Charlotte Reese's mom had to take Megan upstairs to shower off, and Megan had to borrow a pair of Charlotte's underwear and a clean pair of Charlotte's pants. Which would have been bad enough, except that Megan is really tall, and Charlotte Reese is what people politely call "vertically challenged," and so poor Megan looked like she was wearing lederhosen for the rest of the afternoon.

Meanwhile, somewhere around fifth grade Lindsay totally mellowed out and became, like, the Nicest Girl Ever, while Megan has morphed into a full-fledged villainess/varsity cheerleader (which, I think an argument could be made, is really the same thing). And when you take into account the fact that Megan has never forgiven Lindsay for the pee incident, well…if you have ever watched any teen movies at all, then you know that this is not a good combination.

To make a long story even longer, what happened was that, in eighth grade, Lindsay accidentally passed gas in the girl's locker room after gym class, and she had the unfortunate luck of being right next to Megan when it happened. Instead of ignoring the perfectly human function the way any polite person would do, you guessed it, Megan made a whole big deal about how disgusting and gross Lindsay was, and she began calling her Fart Girl. And the name stuck. So now, even though it's been two entire years since it happened, whenever Lindsay walks into a room, Megan inevitably comments, "Watch out everybody, it's Fart Girl." Ha, ha…not.

But the worst part is, lately, Megan's been getting even meaner. A few months ago, Lindsay found a can of beans sitting on her desk when she walked into homeroom, and just last week, there was a huge picture of Supergirl taped onto Lindsay's locker, but with a big F written on her chest in thick, black Sharpie and wavy lines coming up from her butt…as if to depict, you know, a wafting odor. And everyone is so afraid of becoming Megan's next victim that people who used to be friends with Lindsay just stay away from her now. Even boys have been avoiding her. Samantha and I are the only stalwarts. Lindsay and I have been best friends since preschool, and I'm not about to abandon her because of an idiot like Megan Crowley. And Samantha… well, Samantha just doesn't care. She thinks that everyone at our school is a loser anyway.

But it's a shame, because Lindsay is really cool and funny—not to mention super-cute. (Just don't ever call her that to her face, because she'll launch into a diatribe about how "cute" is not exactly a compliment, unless you're a puppy or a newborn baby.) She's short (though she prefers the term "petite"), but she's got a great body and she already wears a size 34C (okay, I'm jealous). She has thick, perfectly straight chestnut-colored hair with natural red highlights that never frizzes, not even in the middle of August, and she's got crazy blue eyes that are so blue that strangers sometimes stop her to ask if they're real or if she's wearing colored contact lenses. And that dimple, of course. You could bury treasure in that dimple, it's so deep.

If Megan had just been absent that day in eighth grade, or standing on the other side of the locker room, I know Lindsay would be way popular now. Although, the truth is, I'm not really complaining. I know it's selfish, but I kind of like that Samantha and I have her to ourselves.

A long, thin finger of lightning cracks open the sky and, for a moment, my room lights up like it's the middle of the day in August. I realize that I'm going to have to ask my mom to give them a ride home. I can't let them go out on bikes in this kind of weather.

"Oh, I totally forgot!" Lindsay suddenly announces. "Speaking of Megan Crowley, wait until you guys see what I bought." She goes over to her backpack which she dumped next to my door and pulls out a brown paper bag. "I know this is going to work. I just know it. It's *the* top seller for eradicating evil."

Samantha and I roll our eyes at each other. That's the other thing about Lindsay: ever since this feud with Megan started, she's gotten progressively more new agey on us. First it was protective healing crystals and sacred essential oils, and then it was tarot cards and runes, and God only knows what she's discovered this time. She found this place in town called Ye Olde Metaphysical Shoppe (yes, its real name) and whenever Megan Crowley does something really mean, Lindsay goes there and blows her entire allowance on whatever the crazy lady behind the counter says will help. Samantha and I are both convinced that Lindsay and Lindsay alone is keeping Ye Olde Metaphysical Shoppe from filing for ye olde bankruptcy. But hey, whatever works.

Lindsay opens up the paper bag and pulls out a small doll made from what appears to be old dishrags. It has blond hair made from yellow string, it's wearing a badly sewn, miniature replica of a GCHS cheerleading uniform, and its eyes have been sewn shut with black thread in the shape of small *x*'s. "What is that?" I take it from her and turn it over in my hands.

"It's a voodoo doll," Lindsay answers excitedly. "Of Megan. I sewed her eyes shut so that she can't see me coming. And now," she pulls a small pin cushion out of the paper bag and removes a sewing needle from it, "I'm going to stick this in her mouth, so that her tongue will hurt whenever she's about to say something mean." She pushes the needle through the doll's red lips, and it emerges out the back of its head. "There," she says, smiling with satisfaction. "Take that, biyatch."

Samantha and I both laugh.

"Okay, really, that is the most ridiculous thing I've ever seen," I tell her. "Please tell me that you don't really think that this is going to work."

Lindsay lets out a heavy sigh, as if I'm the one who needs to be reasoned with. "You're so closed-minded," she says. "Why can't you just accept that there are things in this world that aren't concrete? Veronica says that people like you are just threatened by the idea that you can't control everything." (Veronica being the crazy lady behind the counter who, apparently, has received her Ph.D. in armchair psychology.)

"I'm not threatened," I tell her. "I'm logical. And sane. You should try sanity some time. It feels pretty nice."

Lindsay pretends not to hear me, gazing into the *x*'s where the doll's eyes used to be.

"Let me see that," Samantha says, reaching out for the doll. She takes the pin out and sticks it through the top of the doll's head. "Oooh," she says, in a falsetto, Megan Crowley voice. "It's a good thing I don't have a brain, or that might have hurt!"

Lindsay and I giggle. Samantha tosses the doll back to Lindsay, who carefully removes the needle and puts it back through the doll's mouth.

"Lindsay, you should talk to my mom. She's becoming more and more like you every day," Samantha says, flopping down on my bed. "Seriously, did I tell you? She just started seeing a psychic. Madame Gillaux. She does readings for all of these celebrities and socialites, and my mom flies her down from New York every other week. Because, you know, why give your money to starving children in Africa when you can spend it in so many other, more important ways? Anyway, last week, Madam Gillaux said she saw a baby in our family's future, and my mom totally freaked out and made me go to the gynecologist, and now I'm on the pill." Samantha tosses her hair back. For a second, she seems a lot older than sixteen.

"Really?" Lindsay asks, laughing. "But you don't even have a boyfriend."

"Thank you, Lindsay, for reminding me," Samantha groans. "But don't worry. I will. Aiden is going to see the light and dump that fleabag slut of his one of these days. And when he does, I will be ready. And, thanks to Mommy Dearest, protected from unwanted pregnancies."

I shake my head. Aiden Tranter is a somewhat popular junior—emphasis on "somewhat." In my opinion the only reason that Samantha is even interested in him is because he has absolutely no interest in her. In fact, he totally hates her. Ever since he got his license last year, his mom has been forcing him to drive Samantha to school every day, because Samantha's mom doesn't want to have to get up at the crack of dawn to drive her own daughter herself. (Or, as Samantha would say, she needs to get her ugly sleep.)

The thing is, Aiden lives two blocks from school and Samantha lives in this fancy, gated neighborhood that's, like, fifteen minutes in the other direction. So Aiden has to get up extra early in order to pick up Samantha and make it back by 7:30 a.m. It's a completely ridiculous arrangement; there are tons of other kids who live closer to Samantha, not to mention tons of boys who would gladly drive three hours every morning for the chance to sit in a car with her for twenty minutes. But Aiden's mom is a social climber, and she desperately wants to join the snotty, exclusive country club that Samantha's parents belong to. So Samantha got her mom to promise Aiden's mom that if Aiden would drive Samantha to school every day, she would put in a good word with the membership committee.

Meanwhile, Samantha turned sixteen three months ago. But she keeps failing her driving test on purpose just so that she can continue to get rides with Aiden. Which only makes Aiden hate her that much more.

Personally, I don't see what the big deal is about him. He always looks like he just rolled out of bed, even when he's trying *not* to look rumpled. And he's got to be dumb because there's no way that even a remotely smart person could tolerate his girlfriend, the aforementioned "fleabag slut," for more than five minutes. Her name is Trance Jacobs. (Yes, really. Trance. And this just occurred to me: Maybe she should get a job at Ye Olde Metaphysical Shoppe?) I tutored her in math last year. The girl just could not understand the concept of a fraction unless I put it in terms of sale prices at Wet Seal. "You should get a voodoo doll of Trance," Lindsay suggests. "Or else a love potion! If you can get three drops of Aiden's sweat, you can do the one that activates his pheromones. Veronica swears that after any guy has drunk her famous love potion, he will never look at another girl ever again."

Three

The phone rings before Lindsay has a chance to slay us with another one of her Veronica-isms, and I lunge for it.

"Hello?" I say into the receiver.

"Is this Erin?" asks an unfamiliar woman's voice on the other end.

"Yes. Who is this?"

"I'm a friend of your aunt Kate's," the stranger informs me. "Could I please speak to your mother?"

My aunt Kate. Now there's a name I don't hear very often. Aunt Kate is my mom's younger sister, and they have what my mom describes as "a complicated relationship." Complicated as in they haven't spoken to each other in over a year.

According to my parents, when I was a baby I couldn't say the word Kate, so I called her Kiki instead, and that's what I've called her ever since. Even today, I would never refer to her as my aunt Kate. She will always be Kiki. Although my dad calls her my aunt Kooky, because she's always doing weird things like running off to live in an ashram or becoming a vegan or joining a Native American tribe and changing her name to She Who Communes with Water.

Still, she's fun to hang out with. Or at least, she used to be, back when she and my mom were still on speaking terms. In the summers, I used to go to her house in the afternoons, and we'd spend hours on the porch, working on the *New York Times* crossword puzzle together. She's the one who taught me how to do them in the first place. She used to say that I'm a lot like her, even though everyone else says that I'm exactly like my mom. Smart. Rational. Black and white. Stubborn as hell. Actually, come to think of it, my aunt Kiki is stubborn as hell too. I guess it runs in the family.

"Yeah, hold on a second," I say to the woman on the phone. I open the door to my room. "Mom," I yell. "Phone's for you." I deliberately leave out the part about Kiki because I don't want to get into a whole explanation when I have none.

"I'll be right there," my mom yells back.

When she picks up the phone, I hang up and stand at the top of the stairs, hoping to eavesdrop a little on the conversation.

"Yes?" I hear her say. And then she says it again, but this time her voice is tight and tense. "Is something wrong?" she asks.

By this time, Lindsay and Samantha have come out to join me in the hallway and they nod as I put a finger to my lips.

"What?" Her voice is filled with alarm. Suddenly, I'm nervous. Lindsay looks at me and I shrug. I can only imagine what Kiki did this time. I just hope she didn't get busted for smoking peyote again, because the judge warned her that he wouldn't be so lenient if he ever saw her in his courtroom again.

Then my mom starts to cry.

Now I'm officially freaked out. Mom never cries. Ever. She's a pediatrician. She sees sad, sick kids every single day, so she's trained herself not to get emotional about anything.

Example: when I graduated from preschool, our class sang "The Circle Game" by Joni Mitchell. If you don't know the song, the chorus goes like this: *The seasons they go round and round/*something, something, *up and down/We're* something, something, something, *time/ We can't return, we can only look behind*. Okay, so maybe I don't remember all of the words, but my point is, imagine a group of five year-olds singing some sentimental song to their sappy parents while wearing tiny little mortar board hats. I'm telling you: Mom had the only dry eye in the house.

"Okay," she whispers. "Thank you." I hear a beeping noise as she hangs up the phone, and then a heavy thud.

23

Four

When I get downstairs, I find my mom lying in a crumpled heap on the kitchen floor.

"Mom! Mom, are you okay?" I check to see if she's breathing, which she is, and just as I shout for someone to call 9-1-1, she lifts up her hand.

"No, don't. I'm fine. I mean, I'm not fine, I'm just...you don't need to call an ambulance." I'm not sure if she hit her head when she fell, so I check for signs of a concussion, just the way she taught me.

"What's your name?" I ask her. "Are you nauseous?"

She pushes herself into a sitting position, then waves me away. "I didn't hit my head. I just, I just, oh my God! Kate!" She starts to sob, right there on the floor.

"What happened? What did that woman say?" But my mom just shakes her head. Now *I'm* the one who's starting to feel nauseous. I've never seen my mother act this way. "Mom, come on. Tell me what happened."

"She's gone." The words stick in her throat.

"What?" My heart is pounding, working overtime as my

brain tries to comprehend what she's telling me.

"They found her outside in a field, with a metal umbrella. The lightning…" she lets her sentence trail off, but I don't need for her to finish it. I get it. My aunt was struck by lightning, and now she's dead.

In freshman science we learned that in just the few milliseconds that a lightning strike lasts, it delivers four hundred kilovolts of electricity. In other words, if it hits you, nine times out of ten, your heart is going to stop immediately. And if you do somehow manage to survive, you'll have deep burns at the point of contact, as well as a host of medical problems ranging from respiratory distress to brain damage.

I picture my aunt's body being electrified. I wonder if she was afraid. I wonder if she even had time to think about being afraid.

"What was she doing in a field?" I hear myself ask. Aside from a swimming pool, the dumbest place to be during a thunderstorm is in an open field. And the dumbest thing you can do while in an open field during a thunderstorm is carry a metal object. Everybody knows that.

Mom just shakes her head. "I don't know. Her friend didn't tell me much. She just said that they found her about an hour ago, and that the EMT declared her dead when the ambulance arrived. She wanted to be cremated, and there's going to be a memorial service on Wednesday."

Lindsay and Samantha clear their throats uncomfortably and I spin around. I had completely forgotten that they were there.

"Dr. Channing, I'm so sorry," Samantha says.

"Um, Erin, I think maybe we should go," Lindsay adds.

"No," I shout, not really meaning to raise my voice. "You can't ride your bikes home in this. Especially not after what just happened. Please, my dad will be home any minute. He can drive you. Just wait for him."

Lindsay and Samantha look at each other, and Lindsay bites her lower lip, just like she always does when she's about to agree to something she doesn't want to do. My eyes are welling up with tears and I open my mouth to say something, but I don't know what to say. All I can think is, *How is this happening? How can Kiki be gone?*

The garage door opens with a low rumble.

"There," I say, feeling relieved that I have something else to focus on for a minute. "See? He's home. Come on, let's go upstairs and get your stuff."

We trudge up the steps in silence, the three of us wincing as we hear my dad opening the door, and then my mom telling him what happened. She's crying again.

"This is so crazy," Samantha whispers, putting her arm around my shoulder. "Are you okay?"

I nod, even though I'm not. It all feels surreal, like it's

happening to someone else. Someone in a movie that I'm watching. A bad movie.

"I...it's just, I haven't even seen my aunt in almost a year," I stammer. My throat is clogged. "It's just weird, though. It doesn't make any sense. I mean, Kiki was a lot of things, but stupid wasn't one of them. Why would she go out into an open field, with a metal umbrella, when there's been thunder and lightning going on for days?"

Lindsay starts to say something, but then hesitates.

"What?" I ask.

"Nothing," she says. "It's totally inappropriate under the circumstances."

"What?" I ask again. "Just say it. It's me."

"Okay, well, I was just thinking that it's kind of a coincidence, how you were just saying how boring your life is and that nothing ever happens to you, and now, you know, just out of the blue, this happens."

I tilt my head, unclear as to where she's going with this. I notice that Samantha does the same thing.

"So what's your point?" I ask.

"I don't know. I'm just saying, like...maybe you conjured this," Lindsay mumbles. "It's all very strange and mysterious. Maybe you conjured the whole thing. Like... maybe this happened so that your life could become more interesting."

I glare at her. I know she meant for that to come out differently, but still. I try to swallow, but the golf-ball-sized lump in my throat makes it difficult.

"So, you're saying that I'm responsible for my aunt's death just because I happened to mention that I think my life is boring and that I can't come up with a good reason for why I want to go to Italy this summer?"

She opens her mouth and closes it.

"You're right," I snap, and I can feel my eyes stinging. "That was totally inappropriate. Do me a favor? When you're in the car, don't say anything like that to my father, okay?"

Lindsay nods apologetically. "I got it," she says. She pulls her fingers across her lips as if to zip them, then throws away the imaginary key. "Not a problem. I'm sorry."

I know that she really *is* sorry, and when she reaches out to hug me, I hug her back, holding on for longer than I mean to. I sniffle into Lindsay's shoulder, and she pats me gently on the back.

"I'm sorry," she whispers. "I know you really loved her."

I wipe my eyes as I finally pull away from her. I notice that Samantha is looking at me now, in the same hesitating way that Lindsay did.

"Now what?" I ask.

"Well, um, do you think it would also be inappropriate if I asked your dad not to play his Barry Manilow CD in the car?"

We all laugh—even me.

"Are you sure you're okay?" Lindsay asks one more time before heading down the stairs.

"I'm fine," I lie, trying to reassure her. Samantha cocks an eyebrow at me in disbelief. "I'm *fine*," I say again. "Now go on, go, my dad's waiting."

The two of them disappear down the staircase, and as soon as they're gone, I run into my room, fling myself onto the bed, and silently sob into my pillow.

Five

I can't sleep at all. Every time I close my eyes, all I can see is my aunt: her skeleton lit up from inside her body, her hair standing on end, like something out of an old *Tom and Jerry* cartoon. I toss and turn for a few hours, listening to the rain beating down on the roof above me and watching the clock change from eleven to twelve, and then from twelve to one in the morning. All the while, my brain is racing. Why did Aunt Kiki and my mother stop talking? And why didn't she ever call me? How come I don't know more about her life, other than the bad, silly messes she always found herself in?

I sit up and throw the covers off of me. This is useless. I'm never going to be able to sleep.

The light is on in the kitchen. When I walk in, I find my mother at the counter, sipping a cup of herbal tea.

"Hi," I say.

"Hey," she says back. "Can't sleep?"

I shake my head.

"Me neither. Want a cup of tea? Or I could heat up some milk for you."

I look at the floor. "Could I have some tea milk?" I ask sheepishly.

When I was little, like four or five, I used to have these crazy scary nightmares—like *Friday the 13th* kind of stuff (even though I had never seen it or watched anything like it)—and my mom would give me a drink she called tea milk to calm me down. It's half tea, half milk, and a ton of sugar. Now that I think about it, it's basically the same thing as those chai lattes that I get from the Coffee Bean. Only, a chai latte costs four bucks and sounds a lot cooler than tea milk.

"I haven't made that for you in years." Mom reaches out her hand to smooth my hair down. "I would love to make you some tea milk."

I watch her as she goes about the process. From the back, she looks a lot like my aunt. Same height, same build, same hair color. I can feel the tears welling up again, and I reach across the counter to pull a tissue out of the box. When I sniffle, my mom turns.

"Oh, sweetie, I know this is hard." She hesitates. "You know…I can never decide if it's better for the family for a loved one to go suddenly or for it to be long and slow. Because when it's long and slow, you get to tell them all the things you need to say, but then you have to watch them suffer. And when it's sudden, there's no suffering, but then you don't—" Her voice breaks, and she starts to cry again before she can finish her sentence. She takes a deep breath and recovers. "There are just so many things I never got to say to her."

"What happened between the two of you?" I ask. The question tumbles out of my mouth before I can stop it.

Mom puts my tea milk down in front of me and then sits down with a sigh.

"I'm not sure. I just always felt like she refused to grow up. She never got a real job, she never got married, never had kids. She just lived her life without any responsibility. Which is fine, but...she didn't have any regard for anyone else. And I felt like I always had to clean up her messes."

I nod. I've heard the stories a million times before. But Mom wants to tell them again, and for once, I don't want to stop her. All I want to talk about is Aunt Kiki right now. If venting about her helps Mom to feel better too, then I'm all for it.

"When she got arrested for peyote possession, I bailed her out. When the Chinese government kicked her out of the country, I was the one who arranged for her transportation home. When she got bitten by a monkey in Costa Rica, I was the one who called the hospital and made sure that she got all of the shots she needed. But it didn't go both ways—" She pauses and manages a sad smile. "You know all this."

"It's okay."

"But it wasn't," Mom counters. "Kiki never did anything to help *me*. Do you remember when grandma broke her hip a few years ago? I had to take care of her for three months, even though I have a full-time job and a family. And Kiki...she was off doing yoga at an ashram in India, and she was completely unreachable. It was infuriating."

"But you always fought about things like that," I remind her. "What happened to make you stop speaking to her?"

She sighs and puts her hand on top of mine. "Oh, Erin. I didn't stop speaking to her. She stopped speaking to me. One day I called her and she just never called me back. I left her message after message, and I emailed, and I sent her a letter. I even tried to go over there a few times to see her in person. But she refused to see me. And I have no idea what I did. It's like one day she just decided that she didn't want anything to do with us anymore. I never told you because I didn't want you to be hurt. I know how much you loved her."

What? I am horrified. I had always just assumed that it was all Mom's fault. But for Aunt Kiki to stop calling us... calling *me*? To just cut off contact like that for no reason? I can understand why she might not want to talk to Mom—God knows, I have been on the receiving end of my mother's nagging. But Kiki always told me that she loved me like I was her own daughter, and I believed her.

This changes everything, though. Now I don't know what to believe.

Six

I've never been to a memorial service before, but I can tell you with the utmost confidence that this memorial service is not normal. I mean, we are talking freak show here. We are talking Weirdness with a capital W.

First of all, my parents and I and about fifty other people are sitting in my aunt's living room. Which would be fine, except for the fact that all of the furniture has been removed and we're sitting on the floor. In a circle. *Holding hands.* And to make it even creepier, the lights have all been turned off, the curtains have all been drawn, and there are candles in all four corners of the room. In the middle of the circle sits the urn holding my aunt's ashes. All they need is dry ice and the sounds of chains clanking and people moaning and it would be an awesome setting for the B-movie version of a haunted house.

On one side of me is my mother, and on the other side of me is a man who is a dead ringer for Jerry Garcia. He's wearing a black leather motorcycle vest with a Hells Angels patch on it. And did I mention that we are holding hands?

My father, who is on the other side of my mother, is holding hands with a woman dressed in a flowing, flowery sleeveless number. The woman has a giant graphic tattoo on her arm of a mother breast-feeding two babies at the same time.

Then there's the woman leading the service. She's wearing a long black robe, her eyes are abnormally large, and her gray wiry hair is sticking up everywhere—as if *she* were struck by lightning. (Sorry. Bad joke.) She could pass either for a judge hopped up on amphetamines or a substitute teacher at the Hogwarts School.

I'm also really uncomfortable (physically, that is), because my mother said that I had to wear a dress and high heels, and now. I'm having a hard time figuring out how to sit on the floor without flashing my underwear to the man sitting across from me in the circle (who, incidentally, has a gray ponytail and is missing four fingers on his left hand).

But the worst part is that I'm too distracted by the oddity of it all to feel anything.

The lady in the robe keeps talking about my aunt Kate, saying really nice things about her…and I keep glancing over at my mom to see if she's going to start crying again. But she doesn't, and I wonder if she's feeling the same way I am. I look past my mom over to my dad, but I have to turn away because I can tell that he's trying really hard not to crack up—and I know that if he catches my eye, we'll both burst out laughing. I don't want to be disrespectful. Although, Jerry Garcia's palm is really sweaty, and I am wondering if it would be considered disrespectful if I were to let go of it and wipe my hand on my dress.

"Will everyone now please rise," says the lady in the black robe. "One at a time, take your turn to speak to our beloved Kate. Tell her whatever you need to. Help her in her journey into death."

Jerry Garcia smiles at me and drops my hand as he stands up. *Oh, thank God.* I notice, however, that he has tears in his eyes, and I wonder how he knew Kiki. Actually, I wonder how *any* of these people knew Kiki.

The lady in the robe approaches the urn and kneels down next to it.

"Kate," she says to the urn, "I wish you peace in the afterlife. May you be reborn into a better world." She walks over to an empty spot on the floor and sits down, cross-legged. I notice that under her black robe, she's wearing jeans and Birkenstocks. Her toenails are yellow, gnarled, and unpolished, and I'm sorry that I even looked at them.

Everyone else has stood up and is now in line, waiting to talk to my aunt's ashes, except for me, my mom, and my dad. I started to stand up when the lady in the robe said that we should, but my mom gave me a look of death, so I sat right back down. Now she's staring straight ahead.

Her teeth are gritted and her face is a deep shade of red. I recognize that face. It's the same face she made when I was ten and I captured a squirrel and brought it into the house because I wanted it to be our family pet.

"What do we do?" I finally whisper to her.

"We sit here," she hisses. "And when this ridiculousness is over, we will take my sister's ashes, and we will go home and have a proper memorial service for her. In a church. With chairs."

So *that's* what's bothering her. It isn't the ceremony itself, it's that she's not in charge. Out of the corner of my eye, I see that Jerry Garcia is next in line. When he kneels down to take his turn, I strain to hear him. There are obviously a lot of things about Kiki that I didn't know, but I can't really imagine her as a bad-ass motorcycle chick.

"Kate," Jerry Garcia says, dabbing at his eyes. "I will never forget how good you were to my Sadie. When she was a kitten and she broke her little paw…" His voice breaks, and the guy behind him pats him on the shoulder. "You just fed her from that eyedropper and you were so patient." He pauses again to get control of himself. "We're really going to miss you. You were a very special lady."

He stands up and hugs the guy behind him, sobbing into his shoulder. *Huh*. I definitely was not expecting a kitten story from the Hells Angels guy. That'll teach me to judge a book by its cover.

I listen to a few more people talk to my aunt—

"Kate, I hope they have tofurkey bacon in heaven, I know how much you loved it…"

"Kate, thank you for showing me that meditation can give me a better high than mushrooms, or even LSD…"

"Kate, if you ever want to send a sign that you're with me, just blow out three candles, and that way I'll know it's you…"

—but then I tune them out and focus instead on trying not to let my empty stomach grumble too loudly.

Finally, when everyone has taken their turn and sat back down in the circle, the lady in the robe stands and moves back to the middle.

"Journey on now, my sister Kate. We will follow when we can. May you be born again at the same time and in the same place as those you knew and loved in this life. May you know them again and love them again."

She lights a candle resting on a tall pillar, and then she picks up the urn and walks slowly out of the room. When she's gone, everyone else stands up and follows her, except for me and my parents. We just look at each other, not quite knowing what to say.

"Even for Aunt Kooky, that was pretty out there," Dad finally mutters.

My mom takes a deep breath, trying to steady herself. "She's dead, Peter. Must you keep calling her that?" Then she straightens out her jacket and dusts off the back of her skirt. "I'm going to get my sister's ashes," she says with resolve. "I'll meet you at the car in twenty minutes." She walks out of the room, leaving my dad and me there by ourselves. I look at my watch. It's almost 3:00.

"I'm starving," I say to him. "Do you think there's food out there?"

"Tofu, maybe," he says, sulking a little after getting yelled at by my mom. "But I don't know if there's any food."

Seven

As soon as we step into the dining room, my father is surrounded by a group of people who want to hear stories about my aunt Kate from before they knew her. I somehow manage to slip by unnoticed. I wander over to the buffet table to see if there's anything I can scarf down quickly before my mother comes back and drags us to the car by our hair. I do a quick scan of the table: carrot sticks, celery sticks, some fruit, aha! Bagels and cream—no wait, that's tofu cream cheese. Whatever. I'm so hungry right now I would eat a tofu horse if that's all there was.

I scrape some of the faux cream cheese onto my plate, and as I reach for a bagel, I notice the picture hanging on the wall above the table. It's a poster of a Thomas Hirschhorn sculpture titled *Camo-Outgrowth*, my aunt's favorite work of art. The piece is made up of about fifty or sixty globes, sticking out horizontally from the wall, each one partially covered in camouflage. It's always hung there, but with the furniture all moved around, it looks strangely out of place. I stare at the poster, and for the first time today my throat tightens and my eyes begin to sting. I remember when Aunt Kiki bought it, right after the piece had been installed at the county art museum. She'd said it was "haunting her." So she went back and bought the poster, and every time I came to visit her she had come up with another explanation for what it was supposed to mean. I must have spent a good twenty hours of my life talking about that poster with her. In fact, it was the sole reason why I decided to take AP Art History this year.

Someone taps my shoulder, startling me.

When I spin around I find a thin, petite woman with very pale skin and very dark hair standing in front of me. Her eyes are red-rimmed and swollen, but her face is otherwise pretty. She's older, but not as old as my mom. Mid-thirties, maybe. She's holding a small, brown cardboard box.

"Sorry," she says. "I didn't mean to scare you." Her voice is calm and steady, and I recognize it instantly. She's the one who called the other day.

"That's okay," I tell her. "I'm Erin," I announce, holding out my hand.

"I know. I'm Roni." She shifts the box to her left hand and shakes my hand with her right. Her skin is smooth and cool. "I'm very sorry for your loss."

"Thanks." I hesitate for a moment. "Were you and my aunt close?" It's obvious that they were, but I don't know what else to say to her. It's not like I can be all, *Hey, was that the weirdest freaking memorial service you've ever been to or what?*

"Kate was my best friend," Roni says, her eyes beginning to water again. "She loved you very much, you know."

I want to ask Roni, *Then why didn't she call me for an entire year?* But I'm worried that if I open my mouth, I'll cry too, and I won't be able to stop.

She holds the box out toward me. "She wanted you to have this."

"What is it?" I manage to croak, without taking it from her.

"You'll see," she says. She reaches out and places the box in my hands. "Just please, don't open it until you're alone. It was very important to Kate that you not open it until you're alone."

I shrug. "Okay. Um…thanks."

She attempts a smile, but it comes out as more of a grimace. As if even her mouth muscles are too sad to make the full effort. "And here," she says, taking a piece of paper out of the back pocket of her jeans. "This is my phone number. Call me when you're ready."

"Ready for what?"

"When you're ready, you'll know." With that, she turns around and walks back into the crowd.

I look down at the piece of paper she handed me.

Roni, 555-9436. When you're ready.

At that moment, my mother comes barreling toward me, with my father following behind. Her face is even redder than before, and I can tell that she's been crying.

"Come on," she says, grabbing my arm. "We're leaving."

"Can I just eat my bagel?" I ask. "I'm starv—"

"Take it in the car," she orders. "Now." She pulls on my arm and I have to almost run to keep up with her.

"Where's the urn?" I whisper loudly as we snake through the crowd of people toward the front door.

"They won't let me have it," my mother states. Her voice is even and matter-of-fact. She's gone into doctor mode. "Apparently, Kate instructed in her will that her best friend was to keep it. They even had a lawyer here, ready to stop me in case I tried to take it." She swallows hard. This is hurting her. A lot. What was my aunt so angry about? Why did she want it to be this way?

When we get to the car, I realize that I'm still holding the box. My parents are so upset that neither one of them even notices. I slide into the backseat and place it on the floor next to me. I'm tempted to open it now during the drive home. But then I remember what Roni said. I look at it again. It's just a plain old, regular cardboard box. There's no writing on it, no label, nothing to give me a clue as to what is inside.

I guess it can wait.

Eight

A piece of paper folded into a tiny square lands on my desk about seven minutes into homeroom. I glance around to see if Mrs. Schroeder is looking, but she's too busy inhaling her daily piña-colada-flavored yogurt to notice. Samantha swears that she actually has a piña colada in there, and that the yogurt container is just for show. I have to say, it would explain a lot.

Keeping my hands below my desk, I unfold the paper and read the note. It's from Samantha, via Lindsay.

Aiden is going to see the Flamingo Kids at the Corridor this weekend. You guys have to come with me. This is my chance to show him that I am not just a dumb girl he drives to school, but a hot woman whom he intensely desires. And actually has a brain, unlike Trance. Pass to Erin when you are done.

Samantha talks a big game, because in spite of her hotness, Lindsay and I both know that she has kissed a total of three boys in her life, and one of them is her cousin. I turn the piece of paper over and read Lindsay's response.

Sorry, Sam. I am at my dad's this weekend. But let me know if you want that love potion. You can slip it in his drink when he's not looking! xo L.

I take out my pen and write my answer under Lindsay's.

I think you have mistaken me for someone who enjoys going to concerts. Sorry! xoxo E.

I fold the paper back up and discreetly toss it onto Samantha's lap. I watch her as she opens it up and reads our answers. She frowns, then takes out her pen and writes something else. A minute later, the square lands back on my desk.

You should try to live a little. No wonder you have nothing to write about for your essay. L S.

Mr. Wallace is standing by the blackboard, his brown goatee freshly trimmed, his black, plastic emo glasses resting comfortably on his nose. His whole look is so entirely "art teacher" that it's almost as if he's wearing a costume. He picks up a piece of chalk and writes *1/3* on the board in massive numerals.

"Your final project for the year will be a team project. Each of you will be assigned a partner, and each team will be given a topic. Teams must visit the Museum of Art together at least three times, and then each team will give an oral presentation to the class, reporting their findings."

He lifts his left arm and points to the fraction he's written. "This project will represent one-third of your final grade, and you will have one week to complete it. For those of you who are planning to apply for the trip to Italy, your grade on this project will count in your application."

This trip is going to be the end of me, I think.

I had completely forgotten about it after the memorial service yesterday, but then Samantha so nicely reminded me this morning in her note. Now I've been thinking about it all day again. That and, of course, what's hidden in that little cardboard box Roni gave me. When we got home from the memorial service last night, I thought about opening it, but I was so tired and I had a ton of homework to do, and I just wasn't in the mood for any big surprises or family revelations. So I'd left it sitting on my desk…

Whatever. I *really* need to figure out what I'm going to say in that essay.

Mr. Wallace picks up a piece of paper and starts reading off the teams. I listen intently for my name. I just hope he puts me with someone good, because I do not want to get stuck doing all of the work on this project. I do a quick calculation of my grade in this class so far: A-. Which means that I need to get at least a B+ on this project in order for me to be eligible for the trip. I glance around the room, searching for potential partners. Emily Gardner would be good. She's smart, and she works hard. Or maybe Phoebe Marks. I've seen the outlines she makes when she's studying for a test, and they are *sick*. My gaze stops, however, on the seat two rows up in front of me. Just not *him*. Please, do not let my partner be Jesse Cooper—

"Emily Gardner will be with Phoebe Marks," Mr. Wallace announces.

My heart sinks as the two girls smile at each other across the room. *That's okay*, I think, trying to stay positive. There's still Jack Engel, or Maya Franklin. Even though Maya is a bitter and jealous girl who has been trying to oust me from my place as number one since the day they began tallying class ranks, she still would be better than Jesse Cooper. "Jack Engel will be with Carolyn Strummer. Erin Channing will be with…" I hold my breath. *Please say Maya. Please say Maya—*

"Jesse Cooper."

Oh God. I sink down in my seat.

This is a nightmare. How could Mr. Wallace be so dumb? Has he not noticed that Jesse Cooper is the one person in the entire class that I never speak to? I sit back up, and I focus on the back of Jesse's head. His jet black hair is standing up, like, two feet. Okay, not really—but still, he's going for a spiky punk rock thing that seems thirty years too late and might have been hot once but now is just…confusing. He's got a tiny silver hoop hanging from his left ear, and he's wearing a yellow Volcom T-shirt and black jeans. (To his credit, not too tight and actually pretty normal looking, aside from the holes.) I look down at his shoes: black Converse high tops. The bottom of his foot is lifted off of the ground, so that only his toes are touching the floor. I notice that there's thick, black writing on the bottom of his left shoe, and I lean forward to try to read it.

I see you looking.

I can feel my face turn red. I quickly look back at Mr. Wallace. A few seconds later, I glance at Jesse's shoe again. Now it's flat on the floor. Did he do that on purpose?

What happened to him? I wonder for the zillionth time.

Jesse Cooper didn't used to be this way. In fact, up until the beginning of ninth grade, he was one of my closest friends. When we were in middle school, we had almost all of our classes together, and we ate lunch together almost every single day. He was smart and funny and flirty. And yes, he was my first kiss. (And so far, shamefully, my last.)

It happened at an eighth-grade graduation party at Jeff DiNardo's house. Jeff's parents were upstairs in the kitchen and a group of us were hanging out in the rec room, when somebody suggested that we play a game of Seven Minutes in Heaven. We were using a spinner from Jeff's sister's Twister game, and when it was my turn, the spinner landed on Jesse. Which I will admit, I had sort of been hoping for, because I guess I might have had a little crush on him back then. Emphasis on the "might have."

But anyway, we went into the closet, and he asked me if I wanted to kiss him, and I said I guess so, and we kissed. But it wasn't just like, a little peck on the cheek or anything. It was a real kiss. With tongue. It surprised me at first, that he opened his mouth and everything, but I kind of liked it—okay, full disclosure, I liked it a lot—and before we knew it, the seven minutes were up, and people were opening the closet door. And I remember being disappointed because I didn't want it to end, and all I wanted for the rest of the night was to take another turn and have that spinner land on Jesse again, so that I could go back into the closet with him and stay there forever.

Okay, so maybe it was more than "might have."

But then, just a few days later, his father had a heart attack and died. It was awful. His dad was young and healthy. He exercised and ate right. After we heard about it, I remember my mom saying that you just never know what's lurking in your genes. I also remember being really angry with her for saying that, even though she hadn't said anything wrong. And then right after the funeral Jesse's mom sent him off to some art camp for the summer, and I didn't even get to say good-bye to him, or to tell him how sorry I was about his dad. And then, when he came back, he wasn't the old Jesse anymore. He was, well...he was like *this*. With the hair and the shoes and the earring. Soon he was hanging out with this whole new group of artsy/punk rock kids, and we just sort of stopped talking. I mean, yes, it was weird in the beginning, because we had been really good friends, and then we just weren't. And to be honest, I was angry at him for not opening up to me. There he was, three months after the most tragic event of his life, spending time with all of these kids he's never even talked to before, and he doesn't even call me? So we went our separate ways, and that was that. Or at least, it was, until Mr. Wallace took it upon himself to force us back together again.

Like I said, this trip is going to be the end of me.

Jesse is waiting for me in the hallway when class is over.

"So, cool topic, huh?" he asks in an impossible-to-read tone.

On our way out, Mr. Wallace handed us all papers with our topics on them. Ours is to look at one work of art from each of three different time periods and to discuss how spirituality is represented in each. I'm not sure that I would describe it as "cool," though. Spirituality isn't exactly my thing. But I'm also not sure if Jesse is being sarcastic or serious, so I don't answer him.

Maya Franklin walks over to us, and she's giving me the evil eye. *Now what did I do?* I wonder.

"Sorry we're not partners, Jesse," she says. "I think we would've made a good team." Wait a second, is she flirting with him? Does Maya Franklin have a thing for Jesse Cooper? Ew. Just thinking about her liking a boy gives me the creeps, let alone thinking about her liking Jesse Cooper.

"Um, yeah," Jesse says, looking confused. "Good luck, I guess."

Maya flashes a fake smile at me and walks away. Weird.

"*Anyway,*" I say, choosing not to comment on the bizarreness of that exchange, "we don't have a lot of time, so we should figure out a schedule for going to the museum."

He thinks for a second. "You know, they're open late on Thursday nights. Do you think you could go tonight? Like, around 6:30?"

Wow. He really has changed. The Jesse I knew was a total procrastinator. There's nothing I'm supposed to do tonight—aside from some science and math homework, my schedule is wide open. I think of Samantha and Lindsay's note again. My life *is* boring, isn't it?

"Sure, I can go tonight," I say. I notice that he has a small tattoo on the inside of his left wrist—though from this distance I can't quite make out what it is. My mind starts racing with questions. When did he decide to commit so permanently to this look of his? Does he think that this is at all weird, because he's acting like we were never good friends and then not friends? Why does he act like that kiss in the closet never even happened? Maybe he's had so many kisses since then that he doesn't even remember?

"Great," he says. "I'll see you then." He chews his bottom lip, and staring at those lips, I feel my face get hot. I turn away before he sees me and think for the hundredth time in a very short while: *God, I am so lame.*

Nine

Thanks to Jesse, I had almost forgotten about the box.

When I arrive home from school today I'm surprised for a second to see it there, sitting on my desk.

I glance at my watch. Lindsay and Samantha are going to be here any minute. Normally, I would wait for them and make them open it with me, but there's just something about the way Roni said those words—*it was very important to Kate that you not open it until you're alone*—that makes me think I should do as she said.

Moving quickly, I slit the packing tape open with my house key. I don't know what I'm expecting, exactly. Pictures? Letters? Some sort of explanation? My stomach flutters nervously and I hold my breath as I pull open the top flaps and look inside. It's…

It's a pink, plastic ball. Well, technically, it's a Pink Crystal Ball; just the type of retro-kitsch toy that never ceased to amuse my Aunt Kiki. You ask it a question and shake it, and then a silly, new age-y answer floats up to the surface. It's supposed to tell the future like a crystal ball, except, you know, it's plastic. And pink.

I reach inside and remove it from the box. The ball itself is actually clear, but it's filled with a pink, glittery liquid that's reflecting the sunlight and scattering tiny dots across one wall of my bedroom. The bottom of it is flat, so that it can rest on a plastic, silver pedestal, which, I notice, is also inside the box. I pull it out and examine it. Someone etched "RC 52" onto the underside of the base, but otherwise, it looks just like every other Pink Crystal Ball that has ever graced the shelves of Toys"R"Us.

So that's it, then? My dead aunt left me a fake crystal ball? *That's* the big secret that I needed to be alone to see? I'm starting to wonder if maybe my dad is right. Maybe she really *was* kooky. What am I thinking? Of course she was! That memorial service was like a circus sideshow gone horribly wrong.

I look inside the box again to see if there's anything else, and I notice an envelope taped to the bottom, as well as a thin, rolled-up scroll, tied with a piece of raffia. I untie the scroll first and unroll it, hoping for some sort of explanation. But it's just a long list of names. Names I never heard of except for the very last one, Kate Hoffman—written in my aunt's handwriting. Seeing her signature there like that creeps me out, and I look at the goose bumps that have suddenly appeared on my arms. I roll the scroll back up and carefully untape the envelope from the bottom of the box.

This has to be it. This has to be the letter from her, explaining why she wanted us out of her life so badly.

But when I open it, I'm disappointed to see that it's a not a letter at all. It's just a list that she wrote that makes absolutely no sense whatsoever.

* Absolute knowledge is not unlimited; let the planets be your guide to the number.

* There are 16 ways to die, but four of them you will never see.

* The future belongs to you alone. Other voices will be disappointed.

* One rotation is as far as you can see. Only uncertainty lies beyond.

* You will know all when no more is known; then it is time to choose another.

That's it. That's all it says.

Wow, Aunt Kiki, I think bitterly. *Thanks so much.*

Lindsay and Samantha burst into my room just as I'm putting the paper back inside the envelope. Lindsay immediately notices the ball and snatches it off of my bed.

"Oh, my God!" she squeals. "A Pink Crystal Ball! I love these!" She shakes it and looks up at the ceiling as she asks her question.

"Is Megan Crowley going to suffer from a long and painful bout of chicken pox that will leave permanent scars on her face?" She looks at the ball for an answer. "'Your future is obscured. You must ask again.'" She shakes it a second time. "Okay, how about…is Megan Crowley going to get stood up at prom and become the laughingstock of the whole school?" She looks down at the window. "'Your future is obscured. You must ask again.'"

"Let me see that," Samantha says, grabbing it out of Lindsay's hands. "Does Aiden Tranter want to devour me like the men in those cheesy romance novels that my mother hides under her mattress?" She looks at the ball expectantly. "'Your future is obscured. You must ask again.' Ugh, forget it." She hands the ball to me. "Here, you try. You're the genius, maybe you can figure out what's wrong with it."

I shake my head. "No thanks. You know I don't believe in that kind of stuff."

"Oh, please," Samantha says. "Don't be ridiculous. You don't have to believe in anything to play with a Pink Crystal Ball. It's just for fun. Come on, ask it a question. You know you want to. Ask it if Spencer Ridgely thinks you're smexy."

I roll my eyes at her. "Spencer Ridgely is, like, the hottest guy in the whole school. Possibly even the whole world. And he's a senior. He doesn't even know who I am."

"Not the point," Lindsay says, jumping on Samantha's bandwagon. "Come on, just do it. It's not that hard. Repeat after me. 'Does Spencer Ridgely think I'm smexy?'"

"What is 'smexy'?" I ask, immediately wishing I hadn't.

Samantha rolls her eyes at me this time. "It means smart and sexy, stupid. God, you need to hang out in some classes that aren't AP. Maybe you'll actually learn something useful. Now would you stop stalling and just ask the question already?"

"Fine," I say, succumbing to their peer pressure. I pick up the ball and shake it. "Does Spencer Ridgely think I'm smexy?" I ask, not even trying to hide my annoyance. I peer into the plastic on the flat side of the ball. It takes a second for the message to come up.

Yes, your fate is sealed.

"Well?" Lindsay asks.

I frown. "It says, 'Yes, your fate is sealed.'"

She claps her hands excitedly and Samantha laughs.

"Give me that thing," Lindsay demands. "I want to try it again." I hand it to her, and this time she shakes it extra hard. "Is Megan Crowley's boyfriend going to cheat on her with a slutty girl from St. Joseph's and give her a raging case of syphilis?" Her lips twist in a frown. "'Your future is obscured. You must try again.' This thing sucks," she says, tossing it back onto the bed. "Where did you get it, anyway?"

"My aunt left it to me. Her friend gave it to me at the memorial service yesterday. It came with these." I show her the paper and the scroll.

"I thought crazy aunts were supposed to leave people gobs of money that nobody knew they had," Lindsay says, half to herself.

"Hey, that would be a great T-shirt," Samantha interjects. "'My crazy aunt died and all I got was a fake crystal ball.'"

Even I have to laugh at that one. To be honest, it feels good. It hurts less to think of Kiki as just some "crazy aunt" who didn't have a grip on reality. Before the laughter fades, Lindsay says that she can't stay. She just stopped by to see how I was doing. She promised her mom that she would help her move some stuff out of the garage.

Poor Lindsay, I think. Ever since her parents got divorced, she's become the man of the house. She takes out the trash, hangs pictures, helps with moving heavy stuff. I always tell her that, one day, she's going to make some guy a fantastic husband.

"Have fun," I say.

"Oh, don't worry, I will. This is Mr. Lindsay Altman, signing off." She gives us a salute and then bounces out of my room and down the stairs.

"I should go too," Samantha says. "My mom is having a dinner party tonight for some really important clients of my dad's, and I need to be home so that I can totally ruin it."

"Ha! Nice attitude."

She shrugs. "Hey, it's quid pro quo in my house. She makes me miserable, I return the favor. Not all of us are lucky enough to live in a sitcom family like you." She pauses suddenly, as if she might have said too much, then quickly smiles. "Cue laugh track here." She grabs her black Prada backpack and disappears out the door.

Alone again, I take the paper out of the envelope again and stare at it, trying to make some sense of the words. What does that mean, "There are sixteen ways to die"? And what's "the number"? Why did she leave all of this for me? Why was it so important to her that I have it?

There's got to be something I'm missing.

My stomach lets out a deep rumble, and I realize that I haven't eaten anything since lunch today. Dinner isn't for another couple of hours, so I walk out of my room and start to head downstairs to get a snack. But before I make it to the bottom, I overhear my mom talking on the phone. From her tone, I can tell that she's upset. It must be about Kiki. I walk back up a few steps so that she won't see me, and I listen.

"Why would she do that?" Mom yells, her voice breaking. *Who is she talking to? Dad?* "I don't know why," she goes on. "I have no idea. Ask those lunatic friends of hers." She's quiet. And then she starts to yell again. "No. No way. She was a lot of things, but she was never suicidal. No, it's *not* a possibility!"

Okay. It's definitely *not* my dad.

"You know what? Thank you. I think I'll find someone else." I hear the beep as she presses the end button, and then she slams the phone down onto the counter.

I stand there for a few seconds, trying to process what I just heard. So, the person on the other end of that line thinks that Kiki was out in that field on purpose. Which would make sense, if you didn't know Kiki. But I'm with my mom. Kiki was so in love with the world; her crazy lifestyle was testimony to that fact. Mom is right. It's *not* a possibility. But then, why? It suddenly occurs to me that maybe Kiki was attacked. Maybe some random attacker threw her in the field, unconscious. And maybe that's when she got struck…*Oh my God—*

There are so many questions.

But like the T-shirt will say, all I've got is a fake crystal ball.

Ten

The girl at the ticket desk has red hair and really pretty green eyes, which perked up as soon as Jesse and I walked through the huge bronze double doors of the otherwise empty museum.

It must be so boring to work here; no wonder she keeps staring at us. She must be trying to figure out why two normal (okay, one normal, one with ridiculous hair) young people would choose to come here of their own free will.

As we approach her desk, I notice that she has a psychology textbook spread out in front of her, and I realize that she must be a student at the university, which is affiliated with the art museum. She's probably eighteen or nineteen, and now that I'm this close to her, I can see that she has a tiny gold stud pierced into the side of her nose, and her cleavage is spilling out of her dark green V-neck T-shirt. Her skin is perfect and she's got a full pouty mouth like Angelina Jolie's, glistening with pink lip gloss.

Okay, I think to myself. *When I grow up, I want to look like that.*

Jesse, however, seems unfazed by her hotness. He barely even looks at her as he flashes his Grover Cleveland student identification card and holds up two fingers.

"Two, please," he says quickly.

The girl raises her eyebrows, an amused look on her face. "Is this a date?" she asks playfully.

Jesse squirms uncomfortably in his black Converse and I am caught between a) thinking that she's completely out of line for asking two total strangers whether they're on a date, and b) wondering how Jesse is going to respond.

He responds with a sigh. "Cut it out, Kaydra, would you? We're not on a date."

Kaydra? Wait a second, he *knows* her? So now he's hanging out with artsy punk rock types *and* hot college girls? *Ugh*. That is so typical. And how perfect is it that her name is Kaydra? That's almost as good as Trance.

Kaydra grins and bats her eyelashes, her green eyes flashing in the overhead lighting. "Oops, sorry. Well, come on, then, Jesse, aren't you going to introduce me to your not-a-date?"

Oh my God, she is totally *flirting* with him. It occurs to me that maybe *they've* dated, or possibly even hooked up. I stare at her cleavage again. No wonder he doesn't remember kissing me.

Jesse looks down at the floor as he mumbles an introduction.

"Kaydra, this is Erin. Erin, this is Kaydra. We're working on a project together for school. The teacher assigned us to teams."

Oh, right, how nice of him to point out that the *teacher* assigned us to work together. Because, clearly, he would never have chosen to work with a slightly awkward, completely flat-chested, gangly girl with boring brown hair and boring brown eyes, who is wearing a boring Abercrombie T-shirt and little gold hoop earrings that she actually wears in her ears, and not in some other body part where earrings don't technically belong. I might as well change my name to Just a Boring Girl from AP Art History Class with Whom Jesse Is Being Forced to Work. Doesn't have the same ring as Kaydra, but what does?

"Nice meeting you, Erin," Kaydra says as she hands us each a ticket. "Have fun working on your project." On the word *project*, she winks at Jesse.

I half-smile and lie that it was nice meeting her too. I can feel her eyes on our backs as we walk away. And just because she didn't make me feel insecure enough, I accidentally trip over the front of my sneaker and almost wipe out on the black and white tiled floor. Thankfully, however, Jesse doesn't notice. Or at least, he pretends not to. Though he's probably cracking up on the inside, where he apparently keeps all the rest of his emotions too.

Once we're out of earshot of the ticket desk, I try to be all nonchalant about it.

"So, how do you know Kaydra?" It's not like I'm jealous or anything. Because I'm so *not* jealous. I don't care who he makes out with. I'm just curious how he knows her. I mean, it's not normal for a high school sophomore to just know insanely beautiful, pouty-lipped college girls, is it?

Jesse shrugs and gives me a funny look. "From here. I know everyone here."

He knows *everyone* here. Hmm. Would he care to elaborate on that? I glance at him, but once again, his eyes are focused on the floor, as if he's been hypnotized by it.

"So, what, do you come here a lot, then?"

"Yeah."

That's all? Yeah? Nice. I. Too. Can. Play. The. One. Syllable—Oh, forget it.

I give up trying to fill the many awkward silences between us and follow Jesse into the European gallery. I recognize a few names and paintings from class as I glance around at the walls: Botticelli, Caravaggio, Bosch.

Spirituality, I say to myself, thinking about our topic. *Look for spirituality*.

I wander over to a Botticelli called *Saint Mary Magdalene Listening to Christ Preach*, circa 1484. The greens and oranges of the robes worn by Jesus and the people surrounding him are still surprisingly bright for paint that's over five hundred years old.

"What about this?" I call out to Jesse, who's on the other side of the room. "It's Mary Magdalene listening to Jesus preach. That's spiritual."

"It's really not," he says, turning around to look at me from across the room, but, I notice, not even glancing at the painting. "If you really look at it, you'll see that it's all about the architecture." He walks over and stops so close to me that I can smell his…well, I'm not sure if it's his soap or one of what must be his many hair products, but it smells clean and citrusy, like a freshly peeled orange. He reaches his arm out toward the painting, accidentally brushing me on the shoulder with his hand. I look at him to see if he noticed, but he's gazing appreciatively at the painting, waving his fingers up and down in front of it.

"Just look at these columns," he explains. "It's a perspective piece. A very technical one too." He glances at me quickly and then looks back down at the floor. "You have to be careful. Just because a painting has Jesus in it doesn't necessarily mean that it's spiritual."

Well, la-di-da. Look at the art expert over here. I deliberately do not act impressed with him, even though… well, it is kind of impressive. What's even more impressive is that he can pull off a line like that without sounding pretentious. How does he know so much, anyway? We never learned anything like that in AP Art History class. Suddenly, an image of Jesse and Kaydra strolling through the museum, holding hands, flashes through my head, and I think I have a pretty good idea.

"Fine," I say, rolling my eyes at the back of his dumb hair as he walks to the other side of the gallery. "So what's your suggestion, then?" I follow him and stop next to where he is standing. Directly in front of us is an enormous painting of a naked man, his wrists chained to a rock. On top of him, a massive eagle is ripping out part of his insides with its beak. I look over at the gold plate on the wall: *Prometheus Bound, Peter Paul Rubens,* circa 1611–1612.

"I'm sorry," I say. "But what is so spiritual about a man getting eaten alive by a bird?"

Jesse points to the gold plate. "It's Prometheus," he says matter-of-factly, as if that is supposed to explain everything.

"Yeah, I know. I can read. But what's your point?"

He gives me a sideways glance. "I thought you'd remember it from when we learned Greek mythology."

I stare at him blankly. We learned Greek mythology?

"Eighth grade," he reminds me. "In Mrs. Deerfield's class?"

Mrs. Deerfield was our English teacher, aka the Teacher Most Likely to Put You into a Coma from Which You Will

Never Awake. I don't remember *anything* from that class. I shake my head at him.

"Sorry," I say. "Mr. Prometheus is not ringing a bell."

A brief look of—I can't tell if it's disappointment or annoyance—flashes across Jesse's face, which infuriates me. I mean, is he seriously annoyed that I don't remember the story of Prometheus when he doesn't even remember that we kissed in a closet for seven entire minutes? Honestly, what is his deal?

"Okay, well," he says. "Zeus wouldn't let mortals have fire, so Prometheus stole it and gave it to them. When Zeus found out, he chained Prometheus to a rock while an eagle ate his liver. And then every night his liver grew back, and every day the eagle ate it again, over and over, for all of eternity."

Oh, wait a second. I actually do remember that story. In fact, Jesse and I made a poster together about that story. It was our end-of-the-year project, and we worked on it in his bedroom, just a few weeks before we kissed. What I remember most was feeling nervous about being alone with him, in his room, even though I'd been alone with him in his room a dozen times before and had always felt fine about it. I sneak a look at him; is that why he was annoyed? Because I didn't remember making the poster with him? He really is the most confusing person I have ever encountered.

"Okay," I say. "That's a nice and also kind of disgusting story, but I still don't see what makes it spiritual."

"It's an allegory," Jesse explains. "When Prometheus stole the fire, he changed humanity. People went from being at the mercy of the gods to being in control of their own destinies. Prometheus represents the triumph of the human spirit over those who try to repress it. He *is* spirituality."

Oh.

"All right," I say, shrugging my shoulders as if that wasn't a totally brilliant interpretation of Prometheus. "I guess that sounds fine. But I still think one of the others we choose should be a religious painting. You know, just to have a more traditional take on it too."

"Yeah," he sighs. "I figured you would choose something traditional."

I glare at him. "What's that supposed to mean?"

"Nothing. Just forget it."

"No, I am not going to forget it. You can't say something like that and then not tell me what you mean."

He looks down at the floor. Again. "It's just that, you know, you never were someone to think outside the box much."

I raise my eyebrows, offended. Could he be any ruder? "That is not true," I huff. "Just because I don't have a tattoo or, or," *or cleavage, or pouty lips, or swingy red hair,* "or a nose ring doesn't make me 'in the box.' I think outside the box plenty." But I can feel my face turning red, the way it always does when I'm embarrassed, or when I lie. Or both. I mean, come on, who am I kidding? I've never thought outside the box in my life.

I look at Jesse, and I can tell that he's trying not to laugh. I keep forgetting how well he knows me.

I smile—I can't help it—and then I roll my eyes and cross my arms in front of my chest in mock defiance. "Okay, fine. I don't think outside the box. But it's not my fault. Both of my parents are doctors. How am I supposed to be creative with that kind of genetic hard-wiring?"

Jesse chuckles and gives me a sympathetic look. "Look, I'm sorry," he says. "I wasn't trying to make fun of you. It's just that this project is really important to me. I am dying to go on that trip to Italy, so we have to get an A on our presentation."

"*You* want to go on the trip?" I blurt out, not meaning to sound quite so shocked. It hadn't even crossed my mind that he might want to go to Italy too. Suddenly, my stomach feels all queasy and anxious inside. What if he gets picked and I don't? I can just picture myself sitting on my bed, rationalizing it to Lindsay and Samantha. *I didn't really want to go, anyway. I mean, could you imagine having to travel for two whole weeks with Jesse Cooper?* But then again, what if we both get picked? There goes my stomach again, but this time it's a different kind of queasy. An excited queasy. I mean, could you imagine, traveling for two whole weeks with Jesse Cooper?

Jesse's face is lit up like a sky full of fireworks. "I want to go on this trip more than anything I have ever wanted," he answers. His openness about it surprises me, and for a second, it's almost like we're back in middle school again. Just Erin and Jesse, hanging out. Except I don't remember his eyes being so blue when we were in middle school. Or maybe they just stand out more against his hair, now that he's dyed it jet black.

"Wow," I remark. "How come?"

He blushes a little when I ask him, and his face immediately changes back to the way it was before, as if he realized that he'd let his guard down, and he needed to put it back up again.

"Oh, I don't know," he says, trying to sound ambivalent about it. "Lots of reasons." Aaaaand now we're back to high school, which is good, because I was really starting to miss those vague, short answers of his. "What about you?" he asks, obviously trying to change the subject. "Do you want to go?"

"Yeah," I admit. "I haven't been able to stop thinking about it since Mr. Wallace handed out those flyers."

Jesse puts his hands in his pockets and nods. I search his face for a clue as to how he feels about this. Is he happy that

I want to go? Or does he see me as competition? As usual, he's completely unreadable.

"There's just one problem," I tell him. His eyes snap to attention.

"What's that?"

"I don't know if they'll let me take my box on an airplane. And I won't be able to think if I'm not inside it."

A slow grin spreads over his face, and he punches me lightly on the arm. "Come on. We should get back to work," he says. "The museum closes in twenty minutes."

Eleven

"Jesse Cooper is just an impossible person. That's all there is to it."

Lindsay and I are waiting in line in the cafeteria, and I've been venting to her for the last six minutes about how rude Jesse was to me at the museum last night, with his one word answers and his "you're so in the box" comment. Lindsay gives me a devilish grin, her dimple slowly revealing itself, like a girl at the beach who's reluctant to remove her cover-up.

"I think you like him," she teases.

"Oh, okay. Let's just say that I like him about as much as you like the Unabollmer."

The Unabollmer is actually a kid in our grade named Chris Bollmer who's obsessed with Lindsay. He's some kind of computer-y science genius, and a lot of people say that he's completely antisocial, but I don't necessarily agree. I think he's just a really smart guy who doesn't know how to relate to people who care about things like sports, or who will become the next American Idol, or whether Dana

Peterson got a nose job over the summer, and is therefore totally misunderstood by high school society. I mean, if he were truly antisocial, he wouldn't spend so much time trying to come up with any excuse to talk to Lindsay, and he certainly wouldn't have emailed her a virtual bouquet of flowers on Valentine's Day, along with a poem that said, "Roses are red, violets are blue, you hate Megan Crowley and I do too."

Which I thought was kind of funny and weirdly sweet. But Lindsay, not so much. In fact, the only time that Lindsay ever shows even a shadow of her former mean self is when it's got something to do with Chris Bollmer.

Lindsay frowns. "Oh, please, don't even say that. I think the only thing worse than having nobody at school talk to me is having nobody at school talk to me except for him."

"What about me and Samantha? We talk to you."

"Okay, fine. The only thing worse than having nobody at school talk to me except for you and Samantha is having nobody at school talk to me except for you and Samantha and the Unabollmer. Is that better?"

"Much. Thank you."

The nickname comes from an incident in third grade, when Chris happened to notice that one of the manhole covers on his street had been left unscrewed. He went down into it and began fooling around with the electrical system and pulling out wires. But he must have pulled on the wrong wire, because the manhole exploded while Chris was still inside, and he ended up almost killing himself. He spent two months in the hospital being treated for burns, and he had to get a tattoo to fill in a big chunk of his left eyebrow where the hair got singed off.

Anyway, when Chris came back to school in the beginning of fourth grade, he was, like, a *persona non grata*. Everybody would whisper whenever he walked into a room, and although the official story was that he had gone into the manhole looking for wires for a robot that he was building, a rumor started going around that he had actually been building a bomb, which he was planning to use to blow up some kids in his neighborhood who used to tease him.

He pretty much kept to himself after that (further fueling his antisocial image), and after a while, most people just forgot about the whole thing. But then a couple of years ago some kid at school learned about Ted Kaczynski— that crazy Unabomber guy who in the '90s sent bombs to people in the mail, until the FBI caught him and sent him to prison for the rest of his life—and that kid started calling Chris "the Unabollmer." People thought it was funny, the name caught on, and suddenly, after being ignored for years, Chris Bollmer was actively considered a freak again.

But the point is, Lindsay was never friends with Chris Bollmer. Not before he blew himself up, and not after. She'd never even spoken to the guy. Not once. Not even a hello when she passed him in the hallway. But when all of this craziness with Megan started, Chris decided that he would be the one person (besides me and Samantha) who would dare to be friends with Lindsay. I don't know if he felt a sense of solidarity with her because they both had horrible nicknames, or if he felt some kind of connection because they both shared the same social outcast status, or if he just has a major crush that he couldn't contain any longer.

Whatever the reason, he suddenly started talking to her at school and sending her emails, as if they've been friends for years. Poor Lindsay tries to be nice to him, but sometimes she gets fed up and snaps at him like an angry turtle. Not that I blame her. I mean, it does not help her cause in any way to be seen talking to the Unabollmer. Especially not right now, in the middle of the cafeteria.

"Oh boy," Lindsay says as the two of us spot him making a beeline toward us. "Here we go again." She puts her hand up over her face and turns her back to him. But Chris just walks right up and taps her on the shoulder.

"Hi, Lindsay," he says, really loudly. In the line behind us are three kids from my physics class: Lizzie McNeal,

Cole Miller, and Matt Shipley, a trio known for being more gossipy than Perez Hilton. They stop talking as soon as Chris opens his mouth, no doubt hoping to pick up a juicy tidbit or two to spread around later on. Reluctantly, Lindsay turns around.

"Oh. Hi, Chris," she says.

"Um, yeah, I just wanted to tell you good luck on the English test today. It's a big one."

I feel kind of sorry for him. I mean, you just know that he sat in his room for hours last night trying to come up with a reason to talk to her, until he finally hit on *good luck on the English test*. I brace myself as I wait for Lindsay to react—will she tolerate him today, or will she go all Teenage Mutant Ninja Lindsay on him? I exhale with relief as she kind of half-smiles and pretends that wishing someone good luck on a test is not a totally pathetic pretext for making conversation.

"Thanks, Chris. You too. It's going to be a hard one."

Lindsay and I both glance back at Lizzie, Cole, and Matt, who are holding their hands in front of their mouths and whispering to each other already. Lindsay looks desperately toward the front of the line, and I know she's praying to get out of this situation before it turns into the top news story of the day. But then Megan Crowley appears out of nowhere, smiling her wicked, evil, torturous smile.

"Well, well, well," Megan says. "What do we have here? Is it Fart Girl *and* the Unabollmer? Together? What a cute couple!"

Megan is surrounded by her usual flunkies—Brittany Fox, Madison Duncan, and Chloe Carlyle—three dumb, cookie-cutter fellow cheerleaders who follow Megan around and do whatever she says. No exaggeration, just as if they walked straight out of a teen movie. A *bad* teen movie. The pathetic thing is, they're so stupid, they don't even realize how cliché they are.

Lindsay lowers her eyes to avoid having to look at Megan, but Chris stares right at her, practically daring her to start in on them.

"Just stop it, Megan," Lindsay says softly.

"What was that? Did you just tell me not to talk trash about your boyfriend?"

"He's not my boyfriend," Lindsay insists, louder this time. She glances at Lizzie, Matt, and Cole, who are watching the whole thing unfold, wide-eyed.

"What?!" Megan screams. "You lost your virginity to him? Oh my God, you guys, Fart Girl and the Unabollmer are having sex!" Megan and her groupies crack up and everyone in line around us snickers. "I wonder what kind of baby they would have. Wait, I know. What do you get when you cross Fart Girl with the Unabollmer?"

"What?" asks Brittany.

"A stink bomb!" shouts Megan. "Get it?"

Brittany and the others are suddenly in hysterics—obviously forced and fake—but somehow that makes it even worse. I glance over at Lindsay, whose eyes are welling up. I take her by the arm.

"Come on," I whisper to her. "Let's get out of here. Don't let them see you cry."

I start to lead her out of the line, in the opposite direction from Megan and her cronies. But Chris puts his arm out in front of us, blocking the way.

"Come on, Chris, let us by," I say to him in a low voice. But he ignores me and continues to stare at Megan. The cafeteria, which is normally so loud that a band could start playing in the corner and nobody would notice, is now so quiet that it's almost eerie. At that moment I realize that it's not just Lizzie, Matt, and Cole who are watching us. Rather, three hundred pairs of eyes are all glued to the small space that Lindsay, Chris, Megan, and I are occupying.

"I hope you're enjoying this," Chris says in a loud, steady voice, "because one day, you're going to be a fat ugly housewife who peaked in high school."

"Yeah, and I still wouldn't be interested in you, bomber boy." Madison, Chloe, and Brittany giggle at Megan's stupid comeback (I'm sorry, but did she not just *agree* that she would become a fat ugly housewife who peaked in high school?), while Chris gives her the finger, then extends his index finger so that the two together make a V. He points them at his eyes, then at Megan, then back at his eyes.

"I'm watching you," he says, then turns on his heels and strides out of the cafeteria.

Lindsay makes it as far as the hallway, and then she bursts into tears.

"I hate her," she sobs. "I wish she would get run over by a car."

"I know," I whisper. I've learned by now that when Lindsay is upset about Megan, the best thing to do is to just agree with her. Telling her that she does not actually wish that Megan would get run over by a car will only prolong the agony.

We sit down in the hallway with our backs against the wall, and Lindsay splays her feet out in front of her. But I'm in a miniskirt, so I lock my knees together and tuck my legs to the side. The last thing I need right now is to be flashing the whole school my day-of-the-week underwear. Especially since I'm wearing the wrong day.

"Oh no," Lindsay says. She straightens up and wipes at her eyes, then runs her hand over her hair to smooth it out.

"What?"

"It's Spencer Ridgely," Lindsay whispers. "He's walking straight toward us."

I turn my head slowly, so as not to be too obvious. Sure enough, there he is: all six feet, two inches of total hotness. I stare at his dark wavy hair, his bright green eyes, his *GQ* cheekbones. He really is ridiculously good-looking. What do people that good-looking even think about? Not us, for one thing. Which is a relief, in a way. Especially right now, when Lindsay is still all splotchy from crying.

"Lindsay, please," I say. "He doesn't even—"

"He's staring at your thighs," she breathes.

I whip around to see what she's talking about, and my boring mud-brown eyes lock with the most spectacular emerald-colored irises I've ever seen. I'm too stunned to move or speak or even to look away, and Spencer Ridgely— yes, *the* Spencer Ridgely—flashes me a cocky, lopsided grin.

"Smexy," he comments, looking my legs up and down appreciatively.

Lindsay and I both stare at him, our mouths agape.

"What did you just say?" Lindsay asks.

"I said 'smexy,'" he repeats, without a hint of embarrassment. "You know. Smart and sexy. Like a hot librarian. In a good way." He smiles again, as if amused by our adoration, and then continues his stroll down the hall. "See ya," he calls out over his shoulder.

"Did you…" Lindsay asks, still too stunned to even finish her sentence.

"Yeah." I know what she's thinking. And even though my instinct is to start screaming and jumping up and down because Spencer Ridgely just commented on my appearance—"in a good way"—I have to put that instinct on hold for a second in order to set Lindsay straight. "It's a coincidence," I say sternly. "That's all it is."

Before Lindsay can argue with me, Samantha comes walking up from one of her illegal, off-campus lunch excursions. Only juniors and seniors are allowed to leave school during lunch period, but the rent-a-cop who's supposed to check school IDs in the parking lot is totally in love with her, and he lets her go out whenever she feels like it. Most days, she'll flirt with a dorky junior who has a car, and she'll get him to give her a ride to wherever Aiden is going for lunch that day. Then she'll sit across the room and make seductive eyes at him while he ignores her and makes out with Trance. Or, at least, that's what I've heard. From Lindsay, of course—although, come to think of it, how would *she* know?

"Oh my God, you guys," Samantha gushes. "I just heard the greatest story about Chloe Carlyle." Samantha is wearing black leggings with a long hot pink T-shirt and her mother's black Dolce & Gabbana motorcycle boots. Her hair is in a ponytail and little pieces have fallen out around her face, framing it perfectly. As usual, she looks like she's about to strut down a catwalk.

"So Brittany and Megan were in the bathroom and they didn't know I was in there, and Brittany was telling Megan about how Chloe sang the national anthem at her little brother's hockey game or something last night, and Chloe didn't know the words. She sang, 'the lambs that we watched were all gallantly screaming.' And everyone was laughing at her and saying she was stupid, and I guess Brittany was there too for some reason, and Chloe made her swear not to tell anyone about it. But of course Brittany went straight to Megan and blabbed the whole thing. Isn't that awesome?"

She looks down at us, and I wonder how it is even possible that she just said all of that without taking a single breath.

"Wait a minute, what are you doing sitting on the floor?" She glances at Lindsay and crinkles her nose. "And why is your face all splotchy?"

"We were in the cafeter—" I start to explain, but Lindsay interrupts me.

"You are not going to believe this," she gasps. "Spencer Ridgely just walked by, and he told Erin that she's smexy."

Samantha's mouth drops open. "Nuh-uh," she says. She blinks at me. "Really?"

I nod at her and, I'll admit, I'm having kind of a hard time containing my excitement. I mean, hello, Spencer Ridgely just noticed me. *Spencer. Ridgely.*

"'Like a hot librarian' were his exact words! Can you believe that?" I'm about to give her a play-by-play of the entire encounter, from him staring at my thighs to our eyes locking to the casual *see ya* over his shoulder, when I suddenly realize, that in all of my excitement, I've forgotten to be the rational one. So instead I let out a little fake cough, put my serious face back on, and try to act like it was no big deal. "I mean, yes, he did say that. But, as I was just saying to Lindsay, it's a coincidence. It doesn't mean anything."

Lindsay is grinning from ear to ear, as if the whole thing with Megan and Chris Bollmer never even happened. Or maybe she's just really happy to have something else to think about.

"No way," she argues. "That was no coincidence. That was magic. That crystal ball of yours is magic. For real."

Twelve

Samantha, Lindsay, and I are all sitting around the kitchen table, finishing our homework. They agreed to come over tonight to help me with my Italy essay because I still have absolutely no idea what to write about. Although, come to think of it, I didn't even ask them to help me.

We were in free period this afternoon—it was sixth period, after we had all calmed down from the Spencer Ridgely hysteria—and when I mentioned that my parents were going out tonight, Samantha said that she and Lindsay would be over at five. Which normally would have been great, but I kind of hemmed and hawed, and finally I told them that I didn't think it was such a good idea, because as much as I would love to hang out with them and watch a movie, I really *do* need to get started on this essay, and I have a feeling that it's going to take a while since I have no clue what I'm going to say. And that's when Lindsay suggested that she and Samantha could help. Which was really sweet and quite a relief, actually, because at this point, I need all the help I can get.

I hear shoes clacking on the hardwood floor—I can tell by the sound of them that they're not heels, but rather the ugly, practical, orthopedically correct black flats that my mother always wears—and then she appears in the kitchen. She's wearing a black knee-length sheath dress, and I think she's even got some makeup on—if "makeup" could be defined as a little bit of ChapStick and some under-eye concealer. And she's wearing perfume. Hanae Mori, to be exact. It's my mom's favorite (also her only), and she only wears it when she has somewhere really important to go. Unlike Samantha's mom, who wears perfume to the market or to play tennis or even just to sit around the house. Samantha's mom says that she doesn't feel like she's fully dressed unless she's wearing an *eau de toilette*—she actually says that, *eau de toilette*, and she says it with a perfect French accent. When she was modeling in Paris in her twenties, she taught herself to speak the language. And just for the record, Samantha's mom also does not feel fully dressed without mascara, eye shadow, lip liner, lipstick, heels, and, I've heard, a thong.

Samantha would kill me for saying this, but it's not hard to see where she gets some of her habits. Although, I guess the same could be said for all of us, for better or worse.

My mom takes her wallet out of her purse and places two twenties on the kitchen counter. "Girls, I'm leaving you cash for dinner, and there are takeout menus in the drawer. Tip the delivery guy fifteen percent, and when he rings the doorbell, make sure you ask him for identification. There are all kinds of crazy people who go around impersonating delivery men."

Samantha, Lindsay, and I all roll our eyes at each other. We've been through this drill a million times with my mother.

"Got it, mom," I groan. "We'll ask for ID. Promise."

"You look nice, Dr. Channing," Lindsay says, changing the subject. "Where are you off to?"

My mom blushes. "Oh, it's just a charity event for the hospital where I work. I'm getting an award. It's really nothing."

"It's not *nothing*," my dad counters as he walks into the kitchen. "She's getting the award for pediatric doctor of the year. It's the hospital equivalent of a Best Picture Oscar." He's wearing the same black suit that he wore to Aunt Kiki's memorial service last week, but with a light blue tie instead of his grey funeral one. His thick brown hair is slicked back and, if I squint, I can kind of see how my mom thinks that he looks like Mel Gibson. But I have to squint really, really hard.

Samantha clears her throat. "You know, since you're getting an award, I could fix your hair for you. We could put it up in a French twist—just a little sexy for evening, but still very professional. And we could put some color on your cheeks, and maybe a little bit of lip gloss?"

My mom smiles. "Thank you for offering, Samantha, but I'm afraid that I'll have to pass this time. We're already late as it is."

Samantha has been trying to make over my mom since she first laid eyes on her, but every time she offers, my mom finds an excuse for why she can't do it. I've tried to tell Samantha that she shouldn't take it personally. But of course Samantha always pouts, just a little.

When my parents are finally gone (after reminding us three more times to ask the delivery guy for ID), Lindsay rifles though the takeout menus.

"I'm *starving*," she announces. "What about pizza? Or there's that sandwich place that delivers. They have the best chicken parm hero. Yum."

"Sorry," Samantha says, plucking the menus out of her hand. "But I wasn't planning on gaining five pounds tonight. Do you have any idea how many calories are in a chicken parm hero? It's like a fat suit on a plate."

Lindsay giggles. "Well excuse me, Jenny Craig. What did you have in mind? And don't say salad. I want real food."

"Do you guys trust me?" Samantha demands, suddenly serious.

At this, Lindsay and I exchange worried glances. The last time Samantha asked us that question, we ended up hiding in a bush in front of Colin Broder's house, looking out for the police while Samantha wrapped toilet paper around a tree in his front yard. He was a senior, she was a freshman; he said he would meet her at the movies and he never showed up; she found out the next day that it had all been a joke, and that he had a girlfriend who went to a private school a few towns away. Moral of the story: Samantha does not do well with jokes. At least, not when they're at her expense.

"Um, no, not really," I say. But she just rolls her eyes at me and picks up the phone.

"Who are you calling?" Lindsay asks, as Samantha begins to dial.

"Ahn's Market. It's in Chinatown." Lindsay and I glance at each other again, and Samantha catches us. "Honestly, you two should be more appreciative, because I'm about to order dim sum that will change your lives forever."

Samantha is right. This dim sum *is* life-changing. I don't even know what it is that I'm eating, I just know that I want to it eat every day for the rest of my life. Although that is unlikely, because in addition to being insanely good, it's also outrageously expensive. The forty dollars that my mom left us didn't even begin to cover it, so Samantha put it on her mom's house account and gave the cash to the delivery guy. (And yes, we asked him for ID. Although I can't really imagine that there are that many serial killers out there impersonating small Asian men in gray flannel pants and moth-eaten green wool cardigans.)

"Okay, Erin," Lindsay says seriously, once we've devoured every last morsel of food. "It's time to get to work."

"I *know*. I have got to figure out what I'm going to say in this essay. And by the way, I am totally open to suggestions. Just throw out any ideas you have…"

Samantha and Lindsay look at each other and both of them burst out laughing.

I'm confused. "What?"

"Did you really think that we were going to help you work on your Italy essay?" Samantha asks.

My eyes narrow. I should have known that this was too good to be true. Lindsay maybe…but Samantha? Helping me with an essay? I am such an idiot.

"Okay, fine. I knew it was weird. So why are you really here?"

"Where's the ball?" Lindsay asks.

"What ball? What are you—" And then I realize that she's talking about the Pink Crystal Ball. And just like that, I know that there is no way that I am going to be working on my Italy essay tonight.

Thirteen

* Absolute knowledge is not unlimited; let the planets be your guide to the number.

* There are 16 ways to die, but four of them you will never see.

* The future belongs to you alone. Other voices will be disappointed.

* One rotation is as far as you can see. Only uncertainty lies beyond.

* You will know all when no more is known; then it is time to choose another.

"It still doesn't make any sense," I finally say, after staring at the list for the hundredth time. "Nothing is going to change that."

"Well, it has to mean something," Lindsay answers. She and Samantha are sharing my desk chair, doing a Google search for "Pink Crystal Ball."

"There must be a reason why your aunt gave it to you," Samantha adds.

"You know," Lindsay interjects, "this ball is a perfect example of 'low' magic because you use it to bring about changes to the self instead of the world in general. It's also called practical magic. It's so funny, I was just reading about this the other day."

Samantha snorts. "I'd say it's more like plastic magic in this case."

The two of them laugh at Samantha's little pun, but I am not amused.

"Listen, I know you guys want to believe that this thing is magic, but it's not. It's just a gimmicky toy."

"Oh really," Lindsay says. "Then how do you explain what happened with Spencer Ridgely today?"

"I'm sorry," I say, beginning to feel insulted, "but is it really so hard to believe that Spencer Ridgely would notice me without some sort of magical intervention?"

Samantha and Lindsay both turn around and give me identical, who-are-you-kidding looks. "Uh, yeah," they both say at exactly the same time. Then they laugh.

I have to laugh myself.

"Come on, Erin," Lindsay adds, "It's also *what* he said. It can't be a coincidence that he called you 'smexy.'"

"Yes it can," I argue. "'Smexy' is a popular word. Lots of people are using it. He just as easily could have said that I was hot or smokin' and you wouldn't have thought anything of it." But I'm grinning as I say it, and laugh again in spite of myself.

"He didn't, though," Samantha reminds me, serious again. "He said you were *smexy*. And by the way, the word is not all that popular yet. I just happen to be on the cutting edge of the lexicon. You didn't know what it was, remember?"

"Okay, okay," I grumble. "Fine. It was magic. You win." Samantha flashes me a victory smile and turns back to the computer. "Even though it wasn't," I add, under my breath.

"I heard that," they both say—again at the same exact time.

A second later, Lindsay sits straight up in my desk chair. "Oh my God," she whispers. "Did you read that?"

Samantha nods excitedly. "Erin, come here. You have to see this."

I roll my eyes at them. "What? Let me guess, a magic Ouija board?"

"No, seriously, come here. Look what Lindsay found." I get up and go to the desk, then lean over Lindsay's shoulder to read what's on the screen.

The origins of the Pink Crystal Ball toy are based in the Spiritualist community of the 1940s, which popularized the use of séances to communicate with the dead. Robert Clayton was the son of a renowned clairvoyant in Baltimore, whose weekly séances drew crowds from all over the eastern seaboard.

Observing the popularity of his mother's services and how the children in the audience would often imitate his mother afterward, Robert came up with the idea to create a toy that could predict the future. After a few unsuccessful attempts (including a Magic Bowling Ball, a Magic Fortune Cookie, and the unfortunately named Magic Pig Ball), Clayton hit on the idea of creating a plastic version of a crystal ball, which he aptly named the Plastic Crystal Ball. His toy manufacturer, however, suggested that Clayton fill the ball with a pink liquid to better appeal to a female demographic, and the name of the toy was changed to the Pink Crystal Ball. The design turned out to be a monstrous hit, inspiring legions of would-be psychics for generations to come.

In 1952, the year the Pink Crystal Ball was first sold to the public, Clayton brought one home to show his clairvoyant mother, who by this time was on her death bed. Legend has it that his mother took the toy into her hands and immediately fell into a psychic trance from which she never awoke. Moments after Clayton removed the ball from her hands, his mother died. It is believed that while holding the toy in her last moments, Clayton's mother endowed it with truly mystical, fortune-telling properties.

The toy was thought to have been destroyed in a fire at Clayton's home in the late 1960s, but some claim that Clayton never had possession of it for more than a few months. Instead, many believe that the toy has been passed around the world, working its magic only for those who have been chosen to receive it.

Lindsay and Samantha both turn around to watch me as I finish reading. Their eyes are wide, and I can tell that they believe every word of it.

"It's an urban legend," I say with a shrug. "Like the one about those guys in Mexico who steal people's kidneys and then leave them sitting in a bathtub filled with ice. Look it up on Snopes," I suggest. "I'm sure it's there."

Samantha shakes her head. "It's not. I already checked."

"Well, whatever. It's not real. First of all, there is no such thing as a clairvoyant. Those people in the '40s who held séances were all scam artists. It's a known fact."

Lindsay gets up out of the desk chair. "Let me see the ball."

"What? Why?"

"Just let me see it," she insists.

"Okay." I retrieve the cardboard box from the top shelf of my closet, then take the ball out and hand it to her. She turns it over, examining the inscription scratched into the base.

"RC 52," she says, tapping her chin. "RC 52," she repeats. She looks back at the screen to reread the paragraph.

"Oh my God," she says suddenly. "RC 52! Of course! Robert

Clayton, 1952! This is the one, you guys. This is *the* mystical Pink Crystal Ball!" She picks it up again and gently shakes it. "Are you Robert Clayton's ball?" she asks. She looks down at the window, then looks up at me, triumphantly. "'Your future is obscured. You must ask again.'" She smiles like someone who just solved a Rubik's Cube for the first time.

"Why are you smiling?" I ask. "If it was really mystical, it should have said yes."

Lindsay shakes her head, still smiling. "No. It doesn't work for me. And it didn't work for Samantha either. It's like the website said: it only works its magic for those who have been chosen to receive it. Don't you see? Your aunt chose you to receive it, so it only works for you. That's why she left you the ball. That's why it was so important to her!"

I think about this for a minute. I think about the scroll with all of those names, and my aunt's signature right there at the end. I think about that bizarre memorial service, and about Roni handing me the box, and instructing me not to open it until I was alone. I think about the ball, and the legend, and the "RC 52" inscribed into the paint.

"You're right," I hear myself say to Lindsay.

"I am?" she says.

"She is?" Samantha asks, sounding even more shocked.

I nod. "Yes. You're right that my aunt must have believed that this ball was magical, and that's why she made such a big deal of leaving it to me. It makes total sense. I mean, she ate this kind of stuff up, you know? Of course she believed it."

"But what about you? Do you believe it?" Samantha fixes me with a meaningful stare. I stare back at her as if she's lost her mind.

"Sam, it's a plastic toy. Somebody probably bought this at Toys'R'Us and made up the legend as a joke. It's like a chain letter, only worse." I pick the ball up and snort at it. "Come on. It's totally ridiculous."

Lindsay is giving me a horrified look that I instantly recognize. Long-forgotten memories from grade school come flooding back to me.

March 2000. Lindsay and I are six years old.

Me: *The tooth fairy isn't real, Lindsay. It's just your mom coming into your room at night and leaving you a dollar while you sleep.*

Lindsay: *Silence. Horrified look.*

September 2004. Lindsay and I are ten.

Me: *Mermaids aren't real, Lindsay. They're just something that bored sailors made up in order to pass the time when they were...you know, desperate.*

Lindsay: *Silence. Horrified look.*

Thank God I wasn't the one who told her that Santa Claus wasn't real. Although, I'm sure whoever it was got the same exact look.

Lindsay crosses her arms in front of her chest. "Remember how you told me that Jesse Cooper said that you never were an out-of-the-box kind of thinker?"

"Yeah," I say, my heart sinking at the very thought of it.

"What?" Samantha exclaims. "He did? How come I didn't hear about this?"

I scowl at Lindsay. "Because I told Lindsay not to mention it to you, because I knew you would use it against me for the rest of my life."

Samantha laughs. "You're so right. I totally will."

"Hello?" Lindsay says, interrupting us. "Remember me? The girl trying to make a point?"

"Yes, sorry," Samantha says, still laughing to herself. "Please, continue making your point about how Jesse Cooper told Erin that she's not an out-of-the-box kind of thinker." I glare at Samantha, and she puts her hands up like she's totally innocent.

"He was right," Lindsay continues.

"What?" I exclaim. "Now you're turning on me too? Come on, Lindsay. Just try to look at this from a rational point of view. A plastic crystal ball that can actually tell the future? It's...*absurd*."

"No, it's not." She arches an eyebrow. "What's absurd is your inability to consider anything that doesn't come with its own geometric proof."

"What are you talking about? What does that even mean?"

Lindsay throws her arms up in frustration. "It means that the world is not all protons and—what do you call 'em—ions."

As soon as she says it, I purse my lips together, trying to stifle a laugh.

"What?" she asks, annoyed by my amusement.

"It's protons and neutrons. And also electrons. They're the basic particles of an atom, which is what all matter is comprised of. So technically, the world *is* all protons and neutrons. And electrons, of course."

The left side of Samantha's lip curls up in exasperation. "Listen to yourself."

"That's my point," Lindsay explains.

"Your point is that I'm a geek?" I ask, uttering the unspoken word. (Though I prefer Spencer Ridgely's "hot librarian.")

"No," Lindsay says. "My point is that the world is *not* just comprised of matter. Sometimes you have to believe in things that don't have a scientific explanation."

"Yeah," Samantha adds. "But you are kind of a geek."

No, I think to myself. *No, you don't have to believe that.* But I don't dare say it. I can tell that Lindsay is on the verge of getting upset (for real), and there's no reason to antagonize her. So when she picks up the ball and holds it out to me, I don't argue.

"Here," she says. "Ask it a question."

"Okay, fine. Will I get picked for the Italy trip?"

Samantha scoffs, "Wow. For someone who doesn't believe, that's a pretty intense question."

I roll my eyes and look down at the ball. "'The beyond eludes me at this time.'" I give Lindsay a smug look. "See? It doesn't know anything."

"Not necessarily," she counters. "Maybe it just doesn't know that. Come on, ask it something else. Something specific, so we'll know if it's the ball making it come true."

I sigh. "Okay. Okay, I have a good one." I shake the ball. "Will Mr. Lower say that the English paper I wrote was well researched and insightful? Because it was," I add, glancing at Lindsay. She waves her hand to tell me to hurry it along. I look at the window again, and the pink liquid inside seems to part down the middle as the white, plastic triangle appears. "'Yes, it is written in the stars,'" I read.

Lindsay beams. "Perfect," she declares.

"Perfect?" Samantha yells. "Are you kidding me? You have this thing…this, this…crystal ball, that potentially could make happen anything that you want to happen, and you ask it about an *English paper*? For real? That's like getting a wish from a genie and asking it for world peace. I mean, Jesus, Erin. Use your imagination. Ask it if Bill Gates is going to name you as the sole beneficiary of his estate. Ask it if Zac Efron is going to show up at school tomorrow and announce that he must have you as his child bride. Come *on*. Ask it something good. The Italy trip was a start, at least..."

The look on Samantha's face is so serious and agitated that Lindsay and I both start to laugh again.

"Seriously, it's a good thing that I'm the chosen one and not you, or every hot guy on the planet would be showing up at school tomorrow," I tell Samantha.

"Damn straight," she says. "Now come on. Ask it something better than whether your teacher liked your paper."

"Okay," I say, thinking. I'm so bad at this kind of stuff. I feel like it's my birthday and I have to hurry up and think of a wish before the candles run out of wax. "Okay. I've got it." I shake the ball. "Will I get into Harvard and discover a cure for cancer and win the Nobel Prize and marry a smexy scientist who looks amazing in a lab coat?"

Samantha smiles approvingly. "Much better. What does it say?"

I stare down at the ball, and I'm surprised to feel butterflies dancing in my stomach. What if this really is possible? What if I just laid out all of my dreams and they really will come true? The pink liquid clears and I stare at the answer...

"'The beyond eludes me at this time,'" I read, trying to hide the disappointment in my voice. "You see?" I say to Lindsay.

"No, come on," she replies. "Maybe that was too much, or too distant. Try it one more time. Ask it something more immediate. Like…like…will your boobs grow? That's a good one."

Actually, it is a good one. I've been praying to the boob gods every night since I was twelve years old anyway, so asking a Pink Crystal Ball doesn't seem so far-fetched.

"Okay," I agree. I shake the ball again and look at it intently. "Will my boobs get bigger? I mean, just a little bit bigger. I don't want to look like I had a boob job or anything, I just want to be able to fill out a bra. You know, I'd like a little cleavage. But not too much."

Samantha rolls her eyes at me. "Could you *be* more neurotic? Come on, what does it say?"

I stare down at the ball. It says…*It is your destiny*.

Well, okay. I'm definitely not going to argue with that.

Fourteen

Mom!"

The word is a shriek. I am standing in front of the full-length mirror on my closet door, still wearing the size XL Barry Manilow T-shirt (to be used as sleepwear *only*) and a pair of old sweatpants that my cousin sent me years ago from Penn State. Panic sets in. Either circus clowns came into my room in the middle of the night and switched out my regular mirror for a fun house mirror, or there is something seriously wrong.

"Moooooooom!" I yell again, more urgently.

"What?" she yells back. I can hear the sound of her bare feet slapping on the wood floor, and then she opens the door to my room, still tying her robe around her waist. "What is wr—" She stops mid-sentence to take me in. "Oh my God, Erin, what happened to you?"

"I don't know…I just woke up and when I looked in the mirror, I looked like…like this!" I lift my swollen fingers up toward my swollen face. It looks like it's been injected with whatever it is they use to put the puff into corn puffs.

My mom comes closer to examine me. She touches my cheeks, she makes me stick out my tongue, she presses on my lips (which, I will admit, look kind of sexy and Kaydra-ish).

"Lift your shirt up," she instructs.

"Mom," I protest.

"Erin, I'm a doctor. And your mother. There's no need to be modest."

Fine. I lift up my shirt and stare straight ahead while my mother pokes my abdomen.

"It looks like you're having an allergic reaction to something," she concludes. "Did you use a new soap or lotion yesterday, or did you eat anything different?"

I take a second to think about yesterday. Yesterday, yesterday…I went to school, I had a sandwich, I came home, Lindsay and Samantha came over, we ordered dinner…oh my God. *The dim sum.*

"We had Chinese food last night. Samantha ordered it. She told us to trust her. I have no idea what was in it."

My mom gives me her you-should-know-better-than-to-trust-Samantha look. "Well, whatever it was, don't eat it again. I'll get you some Benadryl and you should be back to normal in a few hours."

"A few hours! I can't go to school looking like this."

She stares at me. "You don't have a fever. You're not missing school just because of a little swelling. End of discussion. Now get dressed." She tries to hide a smile, then gives up. "And anyway, look on the bright side—you went up about three bra sizes overnight."

I stop in my tracks. "What did you just say?"

But she's already out the door.

I pull my shirt off and stand sideways in front of the mirror. Whoa…They really did get bigger. I glance at my swollen arms and my swollen feet. It's just too bad the rest of me did too. I look over at the ball, sitting innocently on top of my desk.

"Okay," I say to it, "if this was your doing, it was not exactly what I had in mind."

Jesse Cooper is fifteen feet down the hallway, heading straight for me and my swollen self. I look around, hoping to discover a heretofore secret passageway or a vortex to another dimension—preferably one in which I do not resemble a female counterpart to the Pillsbury Doughboy. (Although, I wouldn't mind keeping the lips. And, of course, the boobs.) Unfortunately, however, I am surrounded by nothing but closed lockers and unflattering overhead lighting. And since I was late for school as a result of my impromptu appointment with Dr. Mom this morning, the hallway is also completely devoid of people. Except for me. And Jesse Cooper.

"Erin?" he asks tentatively, as he gets closer. "Oh…hey?" It still sounds like a question.

"Hey," I say back to him, as casually as possible. In all of my excitement about the fact that I could actually fit into a bra, I decided I should flaunt it for the few hours that it's going to last. So I went deep into my closet and pulled out every single item of clothing that I own (also a contributing factor to my lateness), and settled on the tightest, lowest-cut top that I could find: a bright red V-neck sweater. At home it made me feel like a 1950s Hollywood starlet. But now that I am here in an empty high school hallway, face to face with Jesse Cooper, I'm feeling less Marilyn Monroe and more Trashy Ho.

"We need to go to the museum again," he says. "Do you think you could go today? After school?" I notice that he's trying to keep his eyes from looking anywhere but at my sweater, and I wonder if this is what it's like all the time for girls who have boobs. I can see how it might get annoying on a daily basis. But as a first timer, I'm kind of enjoying it.

"Today?" I ask. "Hmm, yeah, I don't think I can go today."

This is a total lie. I could easily go today, but I don't want him to think that I have no social life (even though I don't). I mean, he shouldn't assume that I just sit around at home every afternoon (even though I do), or that I'm available whenever it's convenient for him (even though I am). Also, I am a little anxious about how long this puffy-coat of an allergic reaction is going to last (Mom says longer than twenty-four hours and she's taking me to the hospital). "What about the day after tomorrow?" I ask.

He thinks for a minute. "Could you go tomorrow? My band has practice the day after…" He doesn't finish.

I raise my eyebrows at him. His band? I didn't know he was in a band. I didn't even know he played an instrument. When did that happen? "Yeah…I mean, I guess I could move some stuff around. That's fine."

"Cool. Well, I'd better get back to class."

"Yeah, okay. See you tomorrow."

"Right. See you tomorrow." I'm about to start walking again, but he hesitates.

"Hey, what, um, what happened to you, anyway? Your face is like…" I can tell that he is searching for a word that won't offend me, and I feel bad watching him struggle. If Samantha were in this situation, she would just stand there and let him suffer.

"I had an allergic reaction to some Chinese food," I explain. "But my mom said I should be back to normal in a few hours."

He nods, then glances at my sweater again.

"That's good. I mean, not that you look bad or anything," he says, his cheeks flushing red. "You just, you know, you look better the other way."

Fifteen

I find Lindsay and Samantha in the hallway as soon as class is over. Lindsay is in her usual school attire: a long sweater, skinny jeans, Converse slip-ons (no laces). Then there's the ever-present "healing crystal" on a red leather string that she got from Veronica at the Metaphysical Shoppe. Samantha, meanwhile, is decked out in a gray loose-fitting belted dress over black jeans and green suede high-heeled shoe boots.

"There's something you need to see," I whisper. I grab them both by the arm and lead them around the corner, to where the tenth grade lockers are located.

"Um, hello, we're not blind." Samantha smirks at my sweater.

"Oh my God!" Lindsay shrieks. "Look at them! They're huge! I mean, okay, they're not huge. They're still probably an A cup, but they're huge for *you*. Oh my God! I knew it! I knew that crystal ball was really magic!"

"Shhhh!" I hiss. "It was an allergic reaction. To the dim sum," I add, glaring at Samantha. "And anyway, I am not talking about my boobs."

Samantha cocks an eyebrow. "Really? Because everybody else is. Lizzie McNeal and Cole Miller are practically foaming at the mouth." She turns to Lindsay. "I wonder what Jesse Cooper thinks of them. It seems that he and Erin had a little tête-à-tête in the hallway this morning."

I have to laugh. "How do you even know about that? It just happened, like, half an hour ago."

Samantha smiles. "I'm an information ninja, people. You'd be shocked at the things I know."

"Okay, well, I bet you don't know about *this*." I reach into my backpack and pull out my English paper. I turn it to the last page and hold it out for them to see.

Excellent work, it says, in Mr. Lower's red scrawl. *Well researched and insightful.*

Samantha shrugs. "I'd rather talk about your boobs."

"Come on, you guys, don't you remember?" I ask them. "Those are the exact words that I used with the ball last night."

Lindsay squeezes my swollen arm. Her eyes are wider than I've ever seen them. "You're starting to believe it, aren't you?"

I look down at the floor. I spent all of English class struggling with that very question (that is, when I wasn't replaying my run-in with Jesse). I mean, I am not the kind of person who believes in things like this. I'm just not. It's how I define myself. The logical one. The rational one. The one who believes in math and physics, not magic and psychics. But

109

at the same time, I can't explain it. Really, how many coincidences can there be? So, do I? Do I believe that this ball is really magic? And more importantly, if I do, then does that mean that I have to change my whole definition of myself?

I shake my head. "I don't know," I admit. "Maybe."

Lindsay smiles and puts her arm around my shoulders. "Welcome," she says. "I knew you'd come around one day."

I shake her arm off of me. "Okay, just so you know, I draw the line at the ball. I still do not believe in your voodoo doll, or your crystals, or any—"

"Whatever," Samantha interrupts. "Can we focus on what is important here? I mean, do you guys understand the power that we have with this thing? Do you realize what you can do with a *magic* Pink Crystal Ball? You could ask it to make every guy in school only want to date the three of us. You can ask it for straight As. You can ask it for a new car—"

"You can ask it to make me popular," Lindsay interrupts, in a voice so quiet we can barely hear it—and quickly follows up with a "Kidding."

"Wait, you guys," I say. "I don't know about all that. It doesn't always work when I ask it things, remember? We have to figure out how to use it." I pause. "You know, I was thinking about it in English class before…and I think that the list my aunt left me is really a set of instructions. Or clues, maybe. I don't know. But you're right, Lindsay. It has to mean something. Why else would she have written it? Until we figure out what it all means, though, I don't think we should ask the ball anything serious."

"She's right," Lindsay agrees. "Remember in *Back to the Future*, when Michael J. Fox started changing his parents' story, and then his brother and sister disappeared from the picture he had in his wallet? It could be like that—"

The warning bell rings before either Samantha or I can laugh.

"To be continued," I tell them as I slam my locker door shut.

All three of us jump when we see that Chris Bollmer is standing there. He's wearing the same thing he always wears: jeans, a T-shirt, and a black long-sleeved hoodie. Not that I pay that much attention to Chris Bollmer, but I don't think I've ever seen him *not* wearing that black hoodie. I once overheard someone say that he wears it because it covers the burn scars on his arms from when he blew himself up in that manhole.

"Jeez, Bollmer," Samantha mutters. "You almost gave me a heart attack."

Lindsay glares at him. "Were you eavesdropping on us? How long have you been standing there?"

"I wasn't eavesdropping on you. I've only been here for a couple of seconds."

I study his face. I'm not sure I believe him. He looks like

he's telling the truth, but then again, he always looks like such a lost little puppy when he's near Lindsay, so it's kind of hard to know what's really going on in that head of his.

"Then what do you want?" Lindsay demands.

Samantha and I exchange glances. But I wonder what Samantha's thinking. I know what I'm thinking: I'm relieved I've never had a stalker.

"I just need to know why," Chris says.

"Why what?" Lindsay asks.

"Why do you let Megan treat you the way she did yesterday? Why don't you ever stand up to her?"

She furrows her brow, and then lets out a laugh. "Are you kidding me? Stand up to her? That just makes her want to do it more. *You* should know that. Look, I appreciate that you want to help me, Chris, I really do. But unless Megan Crowley moves or gets kicked out of school, she is never going to stop picking on me. If I just lay low and stay out of her way, I can manage. And that is why I don't stand up to her. I'm sorry if that's not what you want to hear, but that is the truth."

"No," Chris argues. "You're wrong. If you roll over every time she starts in on you, she'll never stop. But if you show her that you're not going to take it, she'll back down. I'm telling you."

As Chris is saying this, people start spilling into the hallway before the next bell. Lindsay's eyes are darting around in all directions, and I know she's checking to see if Megan or any of her cronies are around. She's too late, though. Out of the corner of my eye, I spot Megan at the other end of the hall, and she's strutting toward us with her *well, well, well, what do we have here?* look on her face. I swear, it's like Megan can smell when Lindsay is vulnerable.

"Aw, look at this," Megan announces in an extra-loud voice. "Are we having a lover's quarrel?" She inserts herself between them, putting an arm around each of their shoulders. "You know, if you're having problems, all you have to do is kiss and make up." She puts her hand on the back of Lindsay's head and pushes it toward Chris's face, but Lindsay ducks out from under her arm. When she stands back up again, her face is bright red and her eyes look wild, as if she's been possessed.

"Don't you touch me!" Lindsay screams. She hesitates for a split second, then stands up tall and gets in close to Megan's face. "Are you still peeing in your pants, Megan? Because they make diapers for grown-ups, you know. I'd be happy to pick some up for you the next time I'm at the drugstore."

Megan's face flushes, and the corners of her mouth turn up in a snarl. "You do *not* want to start a war with me, Fart Girl."

Lindsay laughs, even though her eyes are daggers. "You started one a long time ago, Soggy Bottoms."

A small crowd has gathered around us. Megan glares at

Lindsay as people laugh out loud at her joke. Samantha and I exchange a secret smile.

"You have no idea what you're in for," Megan growls. "I'm gonna make you sorry you were ever born." She spins around on one heel, elbowing people out of her way as she storms off.

Lindsay slumps back into the lockers behind her, looking shaken and pale. Her hands are trembling. "Are you happy now?" she hisses at Bollmer.

"Yes," he says, oblivious to how upset she is. "You were awesome. Are you kidding me? Soggy Bottoms? That's like, the greatest line ev—"

"Chris," I say, putting my hand up. "Just stop."

Lindsay's eyes start to tear up. She's going to lose it any second. Samantha reaches out to try to calm her down.

"Linds, come on. Let's just go to class."

But Lindsay ignores her and looks Chris right in the eye. When she opens her mouth to speak, her voice comes out choked, and so soft that it's almost a whisper.

"You always say in your emails that you just want to help me, right?"

Chris nods. "I do want to help you, Lindsay. You don't deserve to be treated this way."

"Then the best thing that you can do for me is to stay away from me. Okay? Just stay away."

Sixteen

I can't find Lindsay anywhere for the rest of the day, and when I get home from school I call her house to see if she's okay. And to let her know that I have (half sadly, half to my huge relief) depuffed. Everywhere.

Her mom picks up on the second ring. "Oh, hi, Erin. Actually, Lindsay is sleeping. She came home from school early today because she wasn't feeling well. She said she had a headache. I would think you would've known. Aren't the two of you joined at the hip?"

I let out a polite laugh. "Yeah," I say. "I knew she wasn't feeling well, but I didn't realize she'd gone home."

I want to tell her that Lindsay didn't have a headache at all. I want to tell her all about Megan Crowley—and how, as Lindsay's mother, she needs to step in and do something. She needs to go talk to the principal and make him put a stop to it, because God only knows what Megan is going to do to her after what happened in the hallway today.

But I can't. Lindsay hasn't told her mom about any of it. Between work and kids and trying to get over the fact that her husband left her for a twenty-six-year-old dental hygienist, the last thing Lindsay's mom needs is to be worried about Megan Crowley. You'd think she'd notice that something is wrong, though. I mean, Lindsay comes home with an awful lot of headaches. But no. It's like one of those reality shows: a divorced mom, doing the best she can to work and raise three kids at the same time, yet totally clueless about the fact that one of them is shooting heroin, or puking in the bathroom after every meal…or, well, being verbally abused and spending all of her money on voodoo dolls.

"Okay, well, will you just tell her that I called?"

"Sure. I'll let her know. Oh, and Erin…how are you? Lindsay told me about what happened to your aunt. It's just awful. I'm so sorry."

"Oh…thanks." I swallow.

"How's your mother taking it?"

"She's doing okay. She's my mom. Not really one to get all emotional."

"Yes, well, tell her I was asking about her, would you? And I'm very sorry for your loss."

"Thanks, I will. Bye."

We hang up the phone, and I stretch out on my bed, staring up at the ceiling. The truth is my mom is *not* okay. Of course, she's pretending—going to work, getting dressed up for award ceremonies at the hospital, acting like none of this bothers her—but I know that it's all an act. When my dad is asleep and she thinks that I'm asleep, I hear her opening and closing drawers, rifling through pictures, and sometimes, I hear her crying.

Damn, Aunt Kiki, I think angrily. *What kind of a mess have you left this time?*

I get up and take the letter Kiki left me out of my desk drawer. I promised myself that I was going to start working on the Italy essay today. But ever since I got my English paper back this afternoon, I can't stop thinking about the crystal ball. I stare at the list again, and suddenly, I have an idea.

What if I tackle this the way I would tackle a math problem, or a science project?

I grab a pencil and a piece of paper, and I write down the first question that pops into my head.

What are the properties of a Pink Crystal Ball?

Actually, it's not a bad question. I mean, I have no idea how this thing is constructed. I pick up my pencil again.

Glittery liquid—what is it?

What are the answers written on? How does it work?

Okay, I think. I can do this. *This* is how I roll.

I go over to my computer and type "Pink Crystal Ball" into the Google search bar, just like Lindsay did yesterday. I can feel my pulse racing with excitement, the way it always does when I'm about to figure out an answer to a complex problem. I can't believe I didn't think of this sooner.

I find a bunch of websites advertising Pink Crystal Balls for sale, and a couple that manufacture Pink Crystal Balls with custom answers on them...and then, finally, I come across a site put up by a guy who tried to dissect a Pink Crystal Ball with a rotary drill.

Hmmm. That's my kind of guy. I click through the site, reading his commentary but skipping over the pictures of him drilling (unfortunately, he's old, and not at all cute), and then finally, I find what it is I'm looking for.

With the innards of the ball exposed, the answer mechanism is finally revealed. The device is actually an octagonal dipyramid made of clear acrylic, with a different message on each face. The dipyramid is hollow, enabling it to fill with liquid to minimize floating. It is comprised of two pieces held together by clips.

An octagonal dipyramid? We learned about a lot of shapes in geometry last year, but this is a new one for me. I go to Wikipedia and do a quick search for "octagonal dipyramid."

In geometry, a dipyramid is any two pyramids placed base to base symmetrically. An octagonal dipyramid contains sixteen faces and ten vertices with each face in the shape of an isosceles triangle. More commonly, it is also known as a sixteen-sided die.

A sixteen-sided die. I grab the paper and quickly scan over it.

There are sixteen ways to die, but four of them you will never see.

That's it! Sixteen ways to die. Sixteen answers on the die inside the ball.

This is a puzzle, I think to myself. *Aunt Kiki left me a puzzle.*

It's all starting to make sense now. I look at the letter again, and suddenly I get it. Aunt Kiki didn't just write a letter to go with the ball. She wrote *this* letter for *me*, specifically. I look at the first clue again. *Four of them you'll never see.* What does that mean? I think for a minute, tapping the end of my pencil on the desk.

What are all of the answers on the die?

I think back to the answers that Lindsay and Samantha and I have gotten from it so far, and I write them all down.

Your future is obscured. You must ask again.

Yes, your fate is sealed.

The beyond eludes me at this time.

Yes, it is written in the stars.

It is your destiny.

I start tapping my pencil again. That's only five answers. What are the other eleven? I pick up the ball and shake it once, then again, then a third time, but each time, the die fails to float up. There has to be an easier way. I go back to the computer and type "Pink Crystal Ball answers" into the Google search bar, and sure enough, up comes the official Pink Crystal Ball website with a list of all of the answers, which are still the same as the ones on the original ball made in 1952. I scan through them and do a quick count. Eight of them are yes answers, four are no answers, and four are uncertain.

I look back over the answers that I've already received: three yeses, two uncertains. *Four of them you'll never see.*

I close my eyes, and I can picture myself and Aunt Kiki sitting on the porch outside of her house, both of us hunched over the *New York Times* Sunday crossword. She used to make fresh lemonade. I can almost taste the perfect mix of tart and sweet hitting my tongue; I can almost feel the cool summer breeze coming in from the side of the porch.

Don't make assumptions, Kiki used to say. Her deep, raspy voice rings in my head. *Read every word carefully. Sometimes, what the clues don't say is just as important as what they do say.*

My eyes fly open and I smile: I've got it. It doesn't say that four answers will *never* be seen. It says four of them *you'll* never see. Meaning me, the one who was chosen to receive the ball. She must have known I would find that story about Robert Clayton on the Internet. She must have known that I would figure out that the ball only works for me. And if the ball only works for me, then it should always do what I ask it. Which means that the four answers that *I* will never see have to be the no answers.

I put my pencil down, triumphantly, on the desk.

And then I pick it up again.

But if the ball does what I ask, then why do I also get uncertain answers?

I chew on the end of my pencil as I think about it. Wasn't there something in the clues about uncertainty? I pick up the paper again and I find it. Clue #4.

One rotation is as far as you can see. Only uncertainty lies beyond.

It must have something to do with this. But what is one rotation?

One rotation. Rotate the ball?

As I'm writing this, I hear the *ding* of an email arriving in my inbox. I glance over at the screen.

jcoop88

It's Jesse. There's no subject heading.

I think back to our conversation in the hallway this morning and I feel my cheeks turn hot. It was weird the way he kept staring at me, and then that comment, about how I look better the other way…I've been dissecting it, and I *think* it was a compliment. On the one hand, he might have been saying that he likes the way I look when I'm not a 3-D puffy sticker version of myself. But on the other hand, maybe he was only saying that I don't look so great as a 3-D puffy sticker version of myself, and not really commenting on my normal-looking self at all. Which could be why he's emailing me.

Maybe he realizes that he's been maddeningly vague and obtuse over the last few days, and he wants to clarify himself. Or, maybe seeing me all bloated this morning made him realize that he's actually superattracted to me when I'm not bloated, and so he's emailing to let me know that he's had some time to reflect, and he's come to the conclusion that he much prefers boring, mousy-haired, gangly, flat-chested girls over voluptuous, green-eyed, nose-pierced, swingy red-haired college girls who flirt with total abandon. It's possible.

I click on the message.

> Just FYI: when we go to the museum tomorrow, it's your turn to choose the painting. So make sure you're prepared, okay?

Or not.

I roll my eyes at the computer. He really *is* the rudest person ever. I love how he just assumes that I wouldn't be prepared. I shoot back a message.

> FYI to you: I am always prepared. g2g. c u tomorrow.

I hit the send button, and I'm immediately sorry that I

wrote "g2g" and "c u tomorrow." It's so girly and mainstream. I'll bet Kaydra doesn't use text abbreviations in her emails.

I sigh to myself. Of course I'm not at all prepared. It hadn't even occurred to me that I would need to choose a picture at the museum tomorrow. But I suppose I need to step up. I mean, it wouldn't be fair to make him do all the work just because he knows every picture in the museum by heart.

I put the ball on my nightstand and fold up the paper on which I wrote my notes. As if I don't have enough on my mind already, now I need to pick out a painting that's sufficiently out-of-the-box to impress Jesse Cooper.

4:07 a.m. I bolt upright in bed like I've been shot out of a cannon. My desk light is on and there are art history books all over my bed. I rub my eyes, confused, trying to recall what it was in my dream that freaked me out so much. But it's too late—I've lost it. All I can remember now are fleeting fragments. A giant set of Picasso-style walking boobs... Chris Bollmer running down the street with an umbrella... a torrent of ten-dollar bills falling from the sky...

I'm starting to think that I might need some serious help.

I push the books off of my bed and turn out the light. I can hear the drawers opening and closing in the guest room, and I roll over and put a pillow over my head to try to block out the sound.

Seventeen

I slide my left hand under my desk and sit back in my chair, adjusting the angle of my hand so that I can get a clear view of my cell phone. My heart pounds as Mrs. Cavanaugh, my AP Physics teacher, drones on about how to calculate the index of refraction for a rectangular slab of glass.

Cleveland High has explicit rules about texting in class. First-time offenders get a warning, second-time offenders get detention, and third-time offenders have to do an extra ten hours of community service. But the worst part is that if a teacher catches you, they're allowed to confiscate your cell phone for a week. They even make your parents sign a contract in the beginning of the school year agreeing that this is okay with them, and that they won't call to argue about it if and when it happens.

Usually, I just leave my cell phone in my backpack all day—that way I'm not tempted, and my friends know that I'm not going to get their texts anyway, so they don't even bother. But today, I'm making an exception.

I slip my right hand under the desk when Mrs. Cavanaugh turns around to write on the board, and for the first time ever, I notice that half of the class does the same thing. Moving my fingers as quickly as I can, I type a message to Samantha and Lindsay.

> Figured it out. They r clues. 16 ways 2 die = 16 answers on the die. Lots more 2 tell u. g2g.

I pull my hand up to the desk and grab my pencil just as Mrs. Cavanaugh turns around. Trying to appear innocent, I make the mistake of meeting her eyes.

"Erin, can you tell me which of these equations on the board solves for the wavelength of yellow sodium light in a vacuum?"

My face flushes. I have no idea what she's talking about.

"Um, I'm sorry, can you repeat the question?"

Mrs. Cavanaugh flashes me a disappointed look, as if to say that she thought I wasn't like the others. "Maya, which of these equations solves for the wavelength of yellow sodium light in a vacuum?"

"The first one. Five point eight nine times ten to the minus seven m," Maya responds.

"Correct," says Mrs. Cavanaugh.

Maya flashes me a smug smile.

I resist the temptation to stick my tongue out at her. Her GPA was something like two tenths of a point lower than mine at the end of last year, and she's just dying for me to mess up so that she can overtake me. But still, even though I can't stand her, I can't help thinking that it would have been much easier if Maya had been my partner for the Art History project instead of Jesse.

If Maya had been my partner, I wouldn't have spent half the night poring through the museum's online catalog in search of an out-of-the-box picture. I wouldn't be so tired today that I can hardly see straight. And what was that crazy dream about? If I close my eyes, I can still see the boobs—they were blue and attached to a pair of legs (long, shapely, nice legs, the kind that belong to cancan dancers, or the Rockettes…or Samantha)—and they were walking toward me lifelessly…zombie boobs. Actually, now that I think about it, they were probably more Salvador Dalí than Picasso.

A reply from Samantha pops up on my phone.

> Wth r u talking about? And since when do u txt in class?

A second later, a text appears from Lindsay.

I told u it meant something! U r going 2 get me in trouble. Been busted txting 2x already. Don't want commty srvce!

I'm slightly relieved, I admit. I finally spoke to Lindsay last night, and she seems better about the Megan/Bollmer debacle in the hallway yesterday. Veronica, the nut job from the Metaphysical Shoppe, sold her some kind of protective crystal that works like an invisible force field to keep evil at bay. Or something like that.

Samantha chimes in again.

Oh! R we talking about the ball? U figured it out???

I wait for Mrs. Cavanaugh to turn around again, and then I slip my hand back under the desk.

Duh J Will tell u l8r. Don't go out 2 lunch 2day.
Meet us in the caf.

Mrs. Cavanaugh glances in my direction. This time I grab my pencil and pretend to take furious notes.

"So in this problem, who can tell me what the angle of incidence is?" I look up at the board. It says:

$n_1 \sin \theta_1 = n_2 \sin \theta_2$

I have no idea. I flip through the pages of my textbook, skimming for the answer.

"Erin?" Mrs. Cavanaugh asks cautiously, giving me a second chance.

"Ummmm, oh-one?"

She raises her eyebrows then frowns. "Yes, oh-one is correct. Lucky guess."

Maya and a few other kids giggle while I smile awkwardly. I'm not used to being the butt of teachers' jokes in class. When she turns around again, I glance down under the desk to read Samantha's reply.

> Ugh. Fine. But it better b gud. Aiden is going 2
> Wendy's & u know I luv a salad bar.

I flip the phone closed and slide it into my backpack, then turn my full attention to learning how to measure the speed at which light moves through various objects.

When the bell rings, Mrs. Cavanaugh asks me to stay. Uh-oh. My heart pounds as I pack up my stuff and everyone shuffles out around me. Lizzie McNeal, Matt Shipley, and Cole Miller give me knowing looks as they walk past, and I can just imagine what they're going to say about me once they get out into the hallway. When everyone is finally gone, I walk up to Mrs. Cavanaugh's desk. She's erasing the board, her back to me.

"Um, you wanted to see me?"

Mrs. Cavanaugh turns around. I've never really been this up close to her before, and I notice for the first time that she has very pretty blue eyes. Not as pretty as Lindsay's, but still…they're a deep, dark shade of blue—almost navy—and the brown eye shadow that she's wearing really makes them stand out. (Or "pop," as Samantha would say.)

"Yes, Erin, I did. I know you were texting in class today. It's not like you to do things like that, so I'm not going to file a warning with the office. I'll give you the benefit of the doubt and assume that it must have been an emergency situation."

I nod at her gratefully, unable to speak. As ridiculous as it sounds, there are tears welling up behind my eyeballs, and if I even so much as open my mouth, the levee's going to bust wide open. I hate disappointing people. When I was a little kid, my mom never had to punish me. All she had to do was say that she was disappointed in me, and boom: waterworks. I clear my throat.

"Thank you," I say in a shaky whisper. "It won't happen again, I promise."

"Good. Now go on, you're going to be late for your next class."

Samantha waltzes up to the small round table that Lindsay and I have snagged in the corner of the cafeteria. In her short, waistless purple dress and her cork-heeled wedge sandals, she looks almost waifish. She sits down with a plastic bottle of orange juice and grimaces as she eyes my chicken soft taco smothered with sour cream and Lindsay's lasagna and giant gingerbread cookie.

"I can't believe you guys eat this crap every day. It's a miracle that neither one of you is obese."

"I can't believe that I got busted texting in class," I complain. I'm really not even hungry for lunch. Ever since I left physics, I've had a pit in my stomach the size of a small country.

"Well, you can't text two-handed," Samantha explains. "Of course you're going to get caught. There's an art to it. Here, watch this." She takes a pen and her cell phone out of her bag and puts the cell phone on her lap, then hunches over the table. She holds the pen in her right hand and writes *this is how not to get caught texting* on my napkin.

"Now, check your phone."

"What? But you didn't do anything."

"Check your phone," she insists. I pull my phone out of my backpack and open it up. On the screen is a text message from Samantha.

Nxt tym skip the sour cream. It wil mak u f@.

I look up at her, amazed. "That's mind-blowing. It's really too bad there's no way to parlay a talent like that."

"I know," she laments. "If only they gave grades for dodging the system, I'd have a 4.0."

Lindsay laughs, but I just pout.

"You need to cheer up," Samantha announces. "I think you'll feel much better if you come to the Flamingo Kids concert with me Saturday night."

I roll my eyes at her. "I told you, I don't like concerts. They're loud, and people step on each other, and I've never even heard of the band so I won't know any of the songs. No thank you."

"First of all, you've never even been to a concert."

"I have too," I argue.

Samantha giggles and raises her eyebrows. "Barry Manilow with your dad doesn't count."

Barry Manilow isn't the only concert I've ever been to. I also saw Neil Diamond with my mom when I was nine. But I decide not to mention that.

"I so wish I could go with you," Lindsay sighs. "I would rather go anywhere than to my dad's house this weekend. Can you believe he wants me to meet his new girlfriend? He showed me a picture of her and she was wearing a skirt from Forever 21. I know because I tried it on. I mean, I'm sorry, but it's disgusting. She's twenty-six years old. He could be her father."

"Wait, isn't your dad forty?" I ask, quickly doing the math in my head.

Lindsay sticks her tongue out at me. "Yes, but he could have fathered a child when he was fourteen. It's not unheard of. And besides, she acts like she's eighteen, so theoretically, he would have been twenty-two when she was born."

"At least your dad wants to hang out with you," Samantha interrupts. "My dad lives with me and I don't think I've said more than ten words to him in the last five years. I swear, if he ever moved out, I would never hear from him again. I know it. And the only reason why he hasn't is because he didn't make my mom sign a prenup, and now he doesn't want to give her half of his money."

"You don't know that," I say.

"Yes, I do," Samantha answers matter-of-factly. "They got in a fight once at the dinner table, and he said it. Right in front of me and my sister. My mom told him he'd better start saving, because as soon as I go to college, she's going to take him for every penny he's worth."

Lindsay and I both get quiet. Samantha doesn't talk about her parents very often, except to say that she can't stand being around them. And now that her sister's away at college, they fight more than ever. Samantha once told me that her mom wants to file for divorce but thinks she's doing Samantha some kind of huge favor by waiting until she graduates. As if having your parents live together automatically makes for a happy childhood, even if everyone knows that they can't stand the sight of each other.

The silence lingers. I love Samantha, but she opens up so rarely that when she does say something really personal, without irony or sarcasm, I don't always know how to respond. It's easier with Lindsay. She cries and vents to me all the time. But right now I'm afraid to say the wrong thing, so I just don't say anything, and instead focus on moving the food around my plate. Lindsay, too, bends over her lunch and practically inhales her lasagna. But Samantha just sits there, sipping at her plastic bottle of orange juice from a straw.

Finally, Lindsay cracks under the weight of the silence. She glances up at Samantha. "Aren't you going to eat anything?"

Samantha sighs. "No. I decided that this would be a good time to start my juice fast, since I had to eat *here* today." She looks around, clearly disgusted by the cafeteria. "Beyoncé lost, like, twenty pounds on the Master Cleanse."

"You don't need to lose weight," I tell her. "Beyoncé's left thigh is bigger than your entire body."

"Whatever. I appear to be thin in clothes because I know how to hide my flaws, but believe me, I'm a train wreck when I'm naked."

"So what?" Lindsay asks, eating the last bite of her lasagna. "It's not like anyone is going to see you naked in the foreseeable future."

Samantha shrugs. "You never know. I could hook up with someone at the concert Saturday night."

I roll my eyes at her. I know exactly what she's thinking. "You're not going to hook up with Aiden when he's at a concert with Trance, Sam."

Samantha smiles coyly. "I would if a certain magic ball were to get involved."

Oh no. I suddenly feel like I'm going to be sick, and it's not because of the soft tacos. "I don't think that's a good idea…"

Samantha narrows her eyes at me. "Why not?"

I hesitate. I actually don't know why not. There's just a very loud voice in the back of my head, telling me that IT'S NOT A GOOD IDEA. "I just…well…I think we should figure out what the rules are first. I mean, we don't want to screw anything up, you know?"

"No," Samantha answers flatly. "I don't know. And anyway, I thought you said you figured out all of the rules."

"That's not what I said. I said that I figured out that the letter is a list of clues. But I never said I figured out what all of them are. I've only figured out one of them."

"Whatever," Samantha argues, her voice taking on an edge. "I think you just don't want anyone else to have their wishes come true besides you. You're being selfish."

"That is not true! I'm not being selfish. I just want to make sure we're using it right before we start asking it things. I mean, who knows what could happen?"

Samantha cocks her head sideways, like she doesn't believe me. "Really? Then why have you asked it things? I mean, you got to have big boobs for a day, and you got to have an A on your English paper. So why can't I get anything? Why can't Lindsay?"

I look over at Lindsay to defend me. "Lindsay, can you please explain to her that this is not a good idea? Remember what you said yesterday, about *Back to the Future*, and Michael J. Fox's family disappearing?"

Lindsay bites her lower lip, and I can tell that she's about to throw me under a bus. She is horrible at saying no to people, and to Samantha in particular.

"Well, I know I said that, but it does seem to all be working out for you. I mean, it seems like if the ball can't do something, it just tells you to ask again later or it says it can't tell you now. I don't think there's anything dangerous about it."

Samantha smiles victoriously. "You see? Our resident expert in all things weird and metaphysical thinks it's fine."

The voice in my head is screaming now, insisting that this is THE WORST IDEA EVER. But I don't know how to explain it to them. If I say that it's a gut feeling I'm having, Samantha won't believe me. She'll think that I'm just trying to keep the ball for myself.

"Okay, fine. I'll do it. I'll ask the ball for you." As soon as I say it, the voice inside my head stops screaming and lowers itself to a whisper.

You'll be sorry, it says.

Yeah, I think. *No kidding*.

Eighteen

This one," I announce as I stop in front of a gigantic canvas. "This is it."

Jesse and I are in the Modern and Contemporary Art wing of the museum, and I am looking up at the busy, colorful, semi-abstract-looking painting hanging before me. It looks just the same as it did in the online catalog, only it's much bigger than I imagined.

Jesse stops next to me and reads the wall plate out loud. "*The City*, Fernand Léger, 1919."

As he studies it, I take the opportunity to study him.

He's wearing black jeans and his black Converse, with a light blue T-shirt that has a drawing of a horse on it, above which is a caption bubble that says, "Daytrotter." The T-shirt is kind of tight, and through it I can see the outline of his (very well-defined) chest and shoulder muscles. Which makes me wonder when he started working out (or maybe it's just genes?), because when we were in middle school he was one of those super skinny boys—the kind whose ribs you could count right through his skin—and whenever he wore shorts, the image of Pinocchio would always come to mind.

But now, the only image coming to mind is one of him with his shirt off, which I keep trying to make go away because a) he's rude and I do not get him at all, and b) I need to concentrate on our presentation and not on whether he has a six-pack under there.

Jesse turns away from the painting to look at me. "Well, it's definitely from a different time period than *Prometheus*. Maybe I'm missing something, but I'm just not seeing the spiritual." He walks closer to the painting and points at it. "I see it as an urban landscape," he explains. "These figures are supposed to be buildings and scaffolding and billboards. And this, over here—" he points to four dark gray coils in the background, "—these are supposed to be smoke from a smokestack." He shakes his head. "It's a painting that celebrates the machine age. I hate to say this, but of every painting in this entire museum, you picked the one that has absolutely nothing spiritual about it whatsoever."

I'm trying really hard to contain my glee—I'm thinking about dead puppies and starving children and even my aunt getting struck by lightning—but I just can't stop myself from grinning ear to ear like a big goofy dork. I have done it. I have out art-historied Jesse Cooper.

"I know," I say, somehow managing not to sound too smug. "That's why I picked it."

Jesse gives me a puzzled look. "But the assignment was to pick paintings from different periods and to talk about how spirituality is represented in each of them. Remember?"

"Yes, I remember. And I picked it because, like you said, it celebrates the machine age. But I think what the artist was saying is that in the modern industrial world, there's no room for spirituality. I think he was trying to say that science and technology and industry have replaced religion. That machines are the new God."

I look over at Jesse for a reaction, stifling my urge to yell, *Ha! Take that, Mr. Wrist Tattoo!*

He stares at the canvas, thinking. Then, finally, he nods his head.

"That's good," he says, turning to me with a smile. His voice sounds surprised and impressed at the same time. "That's really good. I'd never thought of it that way." He scratches his chin and peers at me as if he's seeing me for the first time. The intensity of his stare makes me blush, so I drop my eyes and pretend to brush something off of my shirt. "Maybe you won't have to worry about taking that box on the airplane after all," he says.

I smile. I don't know why his validation is so important to me, but I feel like a kindergartner who just got a gold star for cleaning up the rug. I don't say anything back to him, though. I want to seem modest while he continues to marvel at my brilliance.

But instead of more brilliance-marveling, Jesse glances at the giant black rubber watch on his wrist.

"I'm starving," he announces. "I need a snack. Do you wanna come?"

Oh my God, yes, I want to come. Between getting in trouble in physics and getting into that fight with Samantha, I had hardly any appetite at lunch, and I barely even touched my soft tacos. If I don't get something to eat, there is an excellent chance that I might die of hunger before my mom arrives at six o'clock.

"Okay," I say. "But where do you want to go? The snack shop is closed. They were locking it up when we passed it before."

Jesse waves his hand as if to say that it's no big deal. "Oh, that doesn't matter. I'm connected here, remember?"

Ten minutes later, a heavyset older man in a navy blue security guard outfit is removing the giant circle of keys from his belt and unlocking the door to the snack shop for us. He's completely bald, unless you count the white hairs that are sprouting from his ears, and he walks veeeerrrrry slllooooowwwwly, and with a pronounced limp. I'm trying to imagine how it was that he got his job here at the museum; I mean, which person met him and said, "Yes! Now *this* is the man whom I want protecting priceless works of art"?

"Thanks, Lloyd," Jesse says as he pushes the door open.

"No problem," Lloyd answers in a deep smoker's voice. As he walks out and leaves the two of us alone among the empty tables and upside-down chairs, Lloyd gives Jesse a wink. I expect Jesse to protest and to introduce me to Lloyd by my proper name, Just a Boring Girl from AP Art History with Whom Jesse Is Being Forced to Work, but he doesn't say anything. He just flashes Lloyd a crooked smile. Hmmmm.

"So they just let you hang out in here, unsupervised?" I ask.

Jesse shrugs. "They know I'm not going to do anything stupid. And I always leave money for whatever I eat." He walks behind the counter and bends down, disappearing for a moment. When his head pops back up, he's holding a banana, an orange, and bags of Fritos and SunChips. "Pick your poison," he says, holding them out to me.

I'm hungry enough to eat all three, but I don't want to seem like a glutton, so I just reach for the banana. Jesse puts back the orange, then swings himself over the counter like it's a pommel horse. Once he's landed, he digs into his pocket and pulls out a few dollars while I fumble for my backpack.

"Hold on," I say, "I have money."

He shakes his head. "It's okay. It's my treat. Consider it reparation for my having doubted your ability to choose a painting."

I think about it. He's acting so different all of a sudden. It's like I passed a test that I didn't even know I was taking, and now I've been let into the I'm Cool Enough to Be Friends with Jesse Cooper Club. Or let back into it, I should say. I glance at him again, then quickly lower my eyes to the floor.

"Okay," I decide. "But if it's reparation, then I think you should buy me the orange too."

Jesse laughs. He walks back behind the counter and grabs the orange, then tosses it to me.

I catch it with two hands and hold it up to show him. "Consider yourself forgiven."

He lifts two of the chairs that are stacked upside down on the table and places them on the floor. "Madam," he says, pointing at one of the seats with a flourish of his hand.

I sit down, unpeeling my banana, and he sits down across from me and breaks open the bag of Fritos. Then he leans his chin on his hand, his blue eyes settling on my face. "So. Erin Channing. What have you been up to the last two years?"

There's something so knowing about the way he says it, and once again, I feel myself blushing. I have no idea how to answer him though. I don't want to tell him that I've been up to absolutely nothing, and that I'm still exactly the same as I was when we were friends back in eighth grade. Especially since he's in a band, and he hangs out in a museum, and he lifts weights, and he dates college girls with nose piercings, and has completely forgotten all about the fact that we kissed, even though I still think about it…well, kind of a lot.

"Oh, I don't know. The usual. School. Friends. Family."

He nods. "Mostly school, though, right? I mean, how else could you have the highest GPA in tenth grade?"

I blush again. "I guess. But I do other stuff too. I mean, I'm not just some loser who stays home and does nothing but study all the time."

Jesse looks taken aback. "I wasn't suggesting that you are. It's just been a while since we've talked. I wanted to catch up, that's all." He finishes the Fritos and moves on to the bag of SunChips, opening it with a loud pop. "Anyway, I like the painting you chose. But I will admit, I thought you were going to go for something more obvious, like a Jesus picture or an Old Master painting with cherubs and stuff. You definitely surprised me." He stuffs a handful of chips into his mouth. "In a good way," he says, but it comes out sounding like, "iw a goow way."

143

I try to arch one eyebrow, the way Samantha does. "Yeah, well, that's me. Full of surprises."

"So what made you pick it? What made you think of that painting?" He sounds genuinely interested in knowing, and a part of me is starting to think that maybe he's not so rude, after all. I mean, he did apologize, sort of. And he did compliment me. Sort of. Maybe underneath the hair and the tattoo and the art snobbiness, maybe he's just the same old Jesse. Except with a better body. And without braces.

"I don't know," I say. "I guess…this sounds stupid, but the painting kind of reminded me of myself. It's like, even though it's sort of abstract, it's still a very no-nonsense painting. Like me. I mean, I'm not really that into the biblical stuff or the religious references. I think I relate better to buildings and scaffolding and things that are real. Things that you can see with your eyes."

He chuckles. "God, you must hate this project."

I look right into his blue eyes. "Not all of it," I say, except that I didn't mean to actually say that, I meant to just think it, and as I watch my comment register on his face, I can feel my own face heating up, and I know for sure that I am redder than a red velvet cupcake, and all I want to do is crawl under the table and die, right here in the snack shop. But seeing as how there are no weapons or long ropes at my immediate disposal, I decide instead to change the subject.

"What about you?" I ask quickly. "What do you think about spirituality?" That's right. *Deflect, deflect, deflect...*

"Me? I don't know. I guess I'm into it. I mean, not religion so much, but I believe in stuff like fate and destiny and things like that." He paused. "Like, okay. Last summer, my mom's friend asked me and my mom and my brother if we wanted to go out on a boat with them for the afternoon, and we were at the dock, all set to go, and I just had this really bad feeling about it. And I told my mom, I feel really strongly that we should not get on that boat. And so my mom pretended that I wasn't feeling well and we didn't go, and we found out the next day that they'd been in a boating accident, and that if anyone had been sitting in the seats in the back of the boat, they probably would have died. And those were the seats where me and my mom and my brother were supposed to sit. So I mean, yeah, I believe in stuff like that."

Interesting. I wonder if his dad dying so suddenly has anything to do with him believing in that stuff. I wonder if it's how he makes sense of all of it. It's funny: his story reminds me of the screaming voice inside my head this afternoon—the one that was telling me not to ask the ball about Aiden and Samantha—and I can't help but wonder if I'm not walking into the lesser equivalent of a boating accident by agreeing to this.

"What about other stuff?" I ask, feeling him out. "Like, Lindsay believes in voodoo dolls and crystals. Do you think any of that is real?"

Jesse scoffs. "I think voodoo dolls and crystals are just ways for scam artists to prey on people who are vulnerable."

"Me too," I agree. "But what about clairvoyants?" I ask, trying to be nonchalant. "Do you believe that there are people who can actually tell the future?"

Jesse looks up at the ceiling, and I presume that he's thinking about it. I suddenly realize I am staring at him and quickly turn away.

"Well," he says finally, "I know it sounds crazy, but I've done a lot of reading about ESP and precognition, and I think that there really are people who have some sort of sixth sense. I mean, look at Nostradamus. He lived in the sixteenth century, and he predicted the rise of Hitler, the atomic bomb, and the assassination of John F. Kennedy. That's weird. And did you know that fourteen years before the Titanic sank, a guy wrote a book about a huge luxury ship called the Titan, and in the book the ship goes through a dense fog and crashes into an iceberg in April, and it sinks, killing hundreds of people?" He shrugs. "I just don't know how else you explain things like that."

"Yeah," I say. "I know what you mean."

Jesse studies me for a moment. I keep my eyes on the table, uncomfortable with how intensely he's looking at me. He takes a deep breath.

"I've never told anyone this before, but after my dad died, my mom and I went to see this woman who said she could channel the dead. My mom's friend went to her after her mother died, and she said that there was no way that this woman could have known the things that she knew. She swore that it had to be real."

I look up. My eyes are wide open. I had no idea that normal people actually did things like this. I mean, I know Lindsay would do it, and I know Samantha's mom sees a psychic, but there's nothing that Lindsay or Samantha's mom could do that would surprise me. But Jesse? He's a pretty smart guy. And his mom is a Princeton-educated lawyer with the ACLU. She's not exactly flaky.

"So, was she?" I ask. "Was she real?"

Jesse shakes his head. "I don't know. She sure *seemed* real. She knew his name right away, and she knew little things that even my mom didn't know about. Like, she said my dad wanted to know if I was still planning to go skydiving, and that was something I never told anyone except for him. My mom would have killed me if she even knew I was thinking about it. But then again, maybe it was just a lucky guess. There's no way to know for sure."

"No," I agree. "No, there isn't."

"That's why I want to go on that trip to Italy, though," he admits.

"Because you want to know if that woman could really talk to the dead?" I ask, laughing in confusion.

"No," he says, cracking a smile. "Because I want to get to know my dad better. His mother's whole family is from Italy. When he was a kid he used to spend every summer there, hanging out with his cousins. So I feel like, if I go on that trip, I'll get to see the world the way the Old Masters saw it, but I'll also get to see it the way my dad saw it. I think it would give me a lot of insight into who he was."

Wow, I think. I guess he isn't going to have any trouble writing his essay. I try to tell myself to stop feeling envious—after all, I'd rather have my father than go to Italy—but still, I can't help wishing that I had a reason even a tenth as good as that one. I also can't help wishing that we could both go on this trip together, because the more time I spend with Jesse Cooper, the more I think I might like him. He's getting easier to talk to, he's smart, and he's hot—I smile to myself. *Smexy*.

Jesse crumples up the SunChips bag and tosses it four feet across the room, sinking it into the trash can.

"What about you?" he asks. "How come you want to go to Italy?"

I would make something up, but if I were able to think of anything, then I'd already have written it in my essay. Plus, it does seem like we're playing a game of truth or dare. I mean, he did just tell me that he went to see a woman who communicates with dead people.

I look past him, trying to hide my embarrassment. "It's a terrible reason, but basically, my life is boring," I confess. "And I'm hoping that if I go to Italy, it will become less boring. Pretty pathetic, huh?"

Jesse reaches out and pats my hand. I feel a tingle shoot out from the spot where he touches me, and I wonder if he feels it too. Does he really not remember that kiss?

"Nah, that's not so bad," he says, taking his hand away. "I can think of way more terrible reasons than that."

Nineteen

I just want my sister's ashes back," my mom says into the phone.

We're in the car, on our way home from the museum. She pulled up out front at six o'clock on the dot, just like she said she would. But when I got inside, the phone was pressed to her ear, and she held up one finger, signaling me not to say anything.

As we pull away, I watch Jesse walk to his car—a beat-up black 1980s Cadillac—and I find myself wishing that I were getting into that car with him instead of riding away in my mom's silver Volvo. God, I can't wait until I turn sixteen. I hate being a summer birthday. When Jesse and I were twelve, he used to lord over me the fact that he would be able to get his license a full six months before I would. I remember how he used to tease me. *"You'd better be nice to me, or I'm not going to drive you anywhere. I'll be the cool guy with the car, and you'll be the lame girl who has to have her parents pick her up all the time."*

It's so weird. I remember that like it was yesterday and now here we are. Maybe *he's* the one with ESP.

"I don't care what kind of relationship they had," my mom says, her voice beginning to rise. "She was my sister. Aren't there laws against this?" She pauses as the person on the other end of the phone responds, and then she starts to yell. "No. No, I'm not going to calm down. I want the ashes. If you can't get them for me, then I'll find someone who can. Thank you." She pushes the end button on the phone with her right hand, and I notice that the knuckles on her left hand have turned white from gripping the steering wheel so hard.

"Who was that?" I ask cautiously.

"Nobody," she says, staring straight ahead. "Just another incompetent lawyer."

So *that's* who she was talking to on the phone the other day. I wonder how many lawyers she's hung up on so far.

"You're hiring a lawyer to get Aunt Kiki's ashes back?"

"Yes. I need some closure. I can't go visit her in a cemetery. I have nothing that belonged to her. She was so selfish. This is just like her, not to think about anything but what she wanted." My mom looks up at the roof of the car. "I'm glad you were so worried about your friends, Kate, but what about me? Why didn't you worry about me?"

I glance over at my mom again. She looks...well, sad, obviously. But also maybe slightly off her rocker.

"Have you tried calling her friends?" I ask. "I mean, I know you asked at the memorial service, but if you explain the situation to them rationally, maybe they'll—"

"I tried that. But these people are not rational. They're just like Kate."

"Well, what did they say?"

My mom sighs. "They said something like 'when the time is right to have the discussion, then we'll have it.' But I'm not going to sit around waiting for them to decide that the stars have aligned or that the sun is in Jupiter's moon or whatever it is those crazy people think will be the right time."

Hmmm. That sounds familiar. I think back to the memorial service, and Aunt Kiki's friend Roni. *How will I know when I'm ready?* I had asked her. *You'll just know*, she had said.

I want to ask my mom if Roni is the friend she spoke to, but I don't feel like explaining how I know Roni, or why Roni was talking to me at the memorial service. But still…I wonder if it was her. It had to have been.

It occurs to me that maybe I'm ready now. Maybe Roni meant that I should call when my mom started freaking out so much that I couldn't take it anymore.

Well, Roni, I think to myself, *I believe that time has arrived*.

As soon as we finish eating dinner I go upstairs and head straight for my desk. I know exactly where I left the card with Roni's number on it. I hid it under the blue heart-shaped glass paperweight from Tiffany that my grandma gave me when I started high school. (My grandma, apparently, never got the memo that I stopped liking heart-shaped things when I was eight. She also must have missed the one about how nobody has used paperweights since, like, 1973.)

I deliberately picked that spot to hide it, because I didn't want my mom to see the card if she ever came in my room when I wasn't home. I lift up the paperweight...and there's the card. Without giving myself time to chicken out, I pick up the phone and dial the number. At first I felt bold about this, but now that it's ringing, I'm feeling kind of nervous. I'm not sure exactly what I'm going to say, and I'm just about to hang up when Roni answers.

"Hello?"

"Um, hi, can I speak to Roni please?" Of course I already know that I'm talking to her; I'd recognize her voice anywhere. But I just needed to stall for a minute so that I could gather my thoughts.

"This is Roni."

"Oh," I say, pretending to be surprised. "Hi, Roni. This is Erin. Kate's niece? Do you remember? You gave me your number at the memorial service?"

"Of course I remember."

"Right. Well, um, I'm calling because, um, I think I'm ready."

Roni doesn't hesitate for even a second. "No, you're not."

"Wait—what? Yes I am. My mom is freaking out over here. She really wants Kiki's ashes. She needs closure. And I can't take it anymore, with the drawers opening and closing all night. I can barely sleep."

"This isn't about your mom, Erin. This is about you, and what Kate wanted for you. Now call me back when you're ready for real." It sounds as if she's about to hang up, and I desperately want to stop her.

"Wait!" I yell. "Don't go!" There's silence on the other end of the line, but I know she's there. I can hear her breathing. "I've used the ball," I say.

This time, she does hesitate. "And?" she finally asks.

And? What does she mean, *and?*

"*And*…it's really cool?" I say, trying to guess what the right answer might be.

Roni sighs. "Like I said, call me when you're ready."

And just like that, the line goes dead.

In my inbox, there are, like, twenty-five messages from various retail establishments. The Gap, J.Crew, Abercrombie & Fitch, the iTunes store. There are also three from Samantha (1. When can we ask the ball? 2. Why are you not answering me? 3. Where are you? You can't be out. I swear, if you changed your mind I will never speak to you again.); one from Lindsay (Hi, I really hope you're not mad at me today for not sticking up for you at lunch. It's just that Samantha can be really persuasive, and you know she scares me a little when she gets that way, and I'm not good at saying no to her.); and one more from an email address that I don't recognize: theweevil26j.

The subject line reads: *I Know.*

Theweevil26j? Who is that? I mentally scan through the list of people I email, but nobody I know has an address like that. Oh, well. It must be spam. About a year ago I got forty messages a day from someone called rj69, who promised to make my penis bigger in less than ten days or I'd be guaranteed my money back. But that was before I had the filter that my dad put on my computer, after he saw one too many episodes of *Dateline: To Catch a Predator.*

Now, if anyone sends me an email, my inbox automatically sends them an email back asking them to verify who they are, and I get an alert that someone not on my "safe list" is trying to contact me. Seriously, for someone I don't know to get a message to me now, they would need to have, like, a retina scan and C.I.A. level clearance. So how did this theweevil26j person get through?

I'm about to hit delete, but then curiosity gets the better of me.

Who are you, Mr. Weevil? And what exactly is it that you know?

I click on the message to open it.

> I heard you talking yesterday. I know you have it.
> Either you make her stop, or I will.

Beneath the message, pasted into the email, is the text from the website that Lindsay found the other night, about Robert Clayton and the Pink Crystal Ball with mystical properties.

I realize immediately that it's from Chris Bollmer. It figures that he would know how to hack his way around my spam filter. I reread the message.

> I heard you talking yesterday. I know you have it.

Damn. I *knew* he heard us talking behind my locker. And now he knows about the ball. I rub my temples as I try to think through what this means.

> Either you make her stop, or I will.

Whoa. He's talking about Megan of course, but what is he trying to say? Is he insinuating that he's going to try to hurt Megan? The bomb rumor from fourth grade crosses my mind, but I quickly dismiss it. Obviously, the guy's a few Fruit Loops short of a bowl, but I don't think he's exactly a domestic terrorist.

But he knows, I think to myself.

But so what? Even if he tried to tell people about the ball, who would believe him? I'm still not even sure if I believe it. I mean, yes, it's all definitely been a little strange, but there has been a logical explanation for everything that's happened. Okay, maybe not for Spencer Ridgely, but certainly for my boobs growing. And is it really so bizarre that Mr. Lower would write that my paper was well researched and insightful? My paper *was* well researched and insightful. I knew that when I turned it in.

I hit reply.

I have no idea what you're talking about.

A few seconds later, another message appears.

Yes, you do.

Well, yeah, of course I do. But does he really think I'm going to admit it to him? In *writing*? I click on the *x* in the corner of my email screen to close it. *Later, Unabollmer. Find someone else to bother.* I suddenly feel bad for secretly thinking that Lindsay is too mean to him. The guy really is kind of creepy.

I reach across my desk and pick up the ball, turning it over in my hands, and I close my eyes. Instead of darkness, I see Jesse. The blue eyes…I shake the ball.

"Will I get picked for the Italy trip?" I ask it.

I realize that this is the first time I've asked it anything without Samantha and Lindsay there, egging me on, and for a second, I feel stupid. Do I really think that there is such a thing as a magic Pink Crystal Ball? But Jesse's voice is echoing in my head. *There's no way to know for sure.* I look down, waiting for the pink, glittery liquid (which, thanks to the guy with the rotary drill and the website, I now know will permanently stain anything it touches, including skin) to clear.

The beyond eludes me at this time.

I shake my head, bringing myself back to reality. Who am I kidding? Of course this thing isn't real.

I take out the paper with the clues on them and pick up where I left off last night. I might not believe in it, but I still want to know what Aunt Kiki was trying to tell me.

One rotation is as far as you can see. Only uncertainty lies beyond.

I take out the other paper, the one on which I had written my notes. *One rotation. Rotate the ball?*

Suddenly, I want to smack myself in the head. *It's not rotate the ball, stupid*, I think to myself. It's talking about the sun. One rotation of the sun. One twenty-four-hour period. That's as far as you can see. If I ask it anything that's supposed to happen after that, then I'll get an uncertain answer. My heart pounds as the doubt begins to creep back into my head again. This certainly would explain why it didn't answer me about whether I would get into Harvard and cure cancer and marry a doctor. And it explains why it never answers me about the trip. The teachers aren't meeting to pick the kids until next week, so it's too far in the future.

I think back to everything that's happened: all of it has occurred within twenty-four hours of me asking.

Okay, then. Let's give it one more test. Once and for all, I'm going to make up my mind about this thing. If what I ask it comes true this time, then I will officially join the ranks of the believers.

But what should I ask it for? What do I want to happen in the next twenty-four hours?

It doesn't take me long to think of something this time. I shake the ball again.

"Will Jesse Cooper ask me out on a date?" My heart pounds as I wait for the pink liquid to clear.

The spirits whisper yes.

I need to get on a three-way call with Samantha and Lindsay. Immediately.

I reach for the phone, but before I can grab it, it rings. That was weird. I pick up the receiver.

"Hello?" I ask.

"Hey."

Oh my God. It's Jesse. I look over at the ball, incredulous. *No way.*

"Oh, hey," I answer, trying not to sound like I'm completely freaking out. "How are you?

"I'm good," he says. "I was just thinking, you know, we need to plan our next museum outing."

I narrow my eyes, furious. "Um, yeah, can you hold on for a second?" I put the phone on mute and I pick up the ball. "This does not count," I say to it sternly. "Uh-uh. Asking me to go to the museum for a school project is not the same as asking me on a date. That is totally cheating. You are a cheater." I put the ball back down and pick up the phone, taking it off of mute.

"Sorry, it was my mom. Anyway, what were you saying?"

"I was saying that we need to go to the museum, to pick our last painting."

"Right," I say, attempting to keep the disappointment out of my voice. "Sure. When do you want to go?"

"Well, the museum is closed on Sunday, and even I can't get us in then. So how about Monday after school?"

he suggests. "That still leaves us Tuesday to work on the presentation and practice and stuff."

"Yeah, Monday's good for me. That's fine."

"Okay," he says. There's an uncomfortable silence that seems to last forever, and then, finally, Jesse clears his throat. "Um, have you ever heard of the Flamingo Kids?" he asks. Wait—why does that name sound familiar? Oh, right. Isn't that the band Samantha wants me to go see with her this weekend? I smile. For once, I am so glad that Samantha tried to involve me in one of her cocka-mamie schemes.

"Of course," I say, trying to impress him.

"Really?" He sounds as shocked as if I just said that I moonlight as a stripper. I don't know how it keeps happening, but I love playing the role of this mysterious, unpredictable girl to him. It really is fun.

"Uh-huh. They're playing at the Corridor this weekend. I'm going with Samantha," I add, just to send him over the edge.

"Wow. I had no idea you were into hardcore punk. You are full of surprises, aren't you?"

I swallow. Hardcore punk? Samantha never mentioned anything about hardcore punk. "Yes," I agree. "I am *full* of them."

"Well, I was going to ask you if you wanted to go with me. But since you're already going…"

I stare at the ball. *Oh crap. Crap, crap, crap.* I try to imagine me and Jesse in the front seat of his Cadillac—me snuggled up next to him while he steers with his left hand, his right arm draped around my shoulder—and I sigh. That would have been so much better than getting a ride with Samantha's housekeeper.

"Well, we could meet there," I offer, trying to salvage some shred of a date.

"Are you sure? I mean, do you think Samantha would care?"

"Samantha? No. Not at all. She'll be fine with it."

"Okay. Cool. So, I guess I'll see you there."

"Right. See you there."

When we hang up, I grab the ball and give it a huge kiss, right on the flat side of the clear plastic.

"Yes!" I say to it, as I jump up and down. "Yes! Yes! Yes!" I look up at the ceiling, the way my mom looked up at the roof of her car before. "Thank you, Aunt Kiki. Thank you sooooooo much!"

Twenty

So, you know, I was thinking about it, and I think you're right. I mean, maybe it would be good for me to go to the concert with you Saturday night."

Samantha doesn't say anything, and the phone line lets out a soft, crackling sound. I can just picture her—eyes narrowed suspiciously, head tilted to the side.

"Uh-uh," she finally says. "What happened? Why the sudden change of heart?"

"Nothing happened. I just think you're right. I should experience new things. Live a little. I might even have fun."

"I'm not retarded, Erin. Tell me what's going on."

I sigh. "*Okay*. Jesse Cooper asked me to go to the concert with him, and I told him that I was already going with you, and now I'm meeting him there. I mean, *we* are meeting him there."

Samantha snorts. "You're going out on a date with a guy who has a faux hawk?"

"It was never a faux hawk," I protest. "And anyway, at least Jesse puts some effort into his hair. Aiden always looks like he just rolled out of bed."

"That's a *look*," Samantha informs me. "It probably takes him forty-five minutes and a half a bottle of product to achieve that every morning. But whatever, I'm glad you're coming. It'll be fun."

"We'll see. Did you know the Flamingo Kids are a hard-core punk band?"

"Yeah. What did you think they were? Easy listening?"

I have to laugh. "I guess I didn't really think about it. But what does one wear to a hardcore punk concert?"

Samantha inhales excitedly. "Oh my God. We are so totally going shopping! Let's meet at the mall on Saturday. I know just where we should go. And afterward, we'll go back to your house, we'll have a little chat with the ball, and then I'll do your hair and your makeup before we go out."

"I don't know, Samantha. I don't think we need to get fancy or anything—"

"Yes, we do," she insists, cutting me off. "And besides, if you don't let me make you over, then I'll tell Jesse that you sleep in a Barry Manilow T-shirt." I roll my eyes to myself. This has disaster written all over it, but it's too late to turn back now. "So do we have a deal?" she asks.

I sigh loudly, to make sure she understands that I am agreeing against my will. "Yes. We have a deal."

If someone were making one of those feel-good teen movies about me and my two best friends—not that anyone would, considering that I have the Most Boring Life Ever, but let's just suspend reality for a moment and pretend that someone even more boring than I am actually did think my life was interesting enough for the big screen—then Samantha and me at Hot Topic right now would definitely satisfy the Teen Movie Dressing Room Montage requirement.

Just try to imagine a series of quick shots of the two of us in increasingly more ridiculous outfits (posing dramatically each time we emerge from the dressing room, of course), set to music by Demi Lovato or Ali & AJ, or, if there were a really clever music supervisor, a David Archuleta cover of a Flamingo Kids song.

"This is so much fun!" Samantha squeals, bursting through the door in her final getup: a tight-fitting black tank top, a pink and black pleated miniskirt, and black knee-high crew socks with three pink stripes at the top. She looks like a very, very naughty Catholic school girl, which I'm kind of guessing is the whole point. "I feel like we're in a movie," she adds.

I laugh. "I was just thinking the same thing."

She turns around to admire herself in the mirror. "This is it for sure. What do you think?"

"I think you will definitely get noticed."

She smiles. Apparently, that was the correct answer. "What about you? Is that what you're getting?"

I move next to her to get in front of the mirror. I'm wearing an orange T-shirt, a black and white plaid pleated miniskirt with a black studded belt, and a black sleeveless hoodie over the T-shirt.

"I don't know," I tell her, eyeing myself critically. "I feel like I'm dressed up for Halloween."

Samantha rolls her eyes and puts her arm around my shoulder. "That's good. You're not supposed to feel like yourself when you get dressed up."

"I know, but you look hot, and I just look stupid."

"No, you don't. You look like a punk rocker. You look like one of those girls." She points to a poster on the window of the store, showing three teenage girls with dyed hair wearing outfits similar to mine. According to the poster, they're in a band called Care Bears on Fire.

I hear a *ding* coming from my bag, and then another one coming from Samantha's.

"Lindsay," we both say at the same time, reaching for our phones.

OMG. The G/F & I r wearing same dress. Going 2 die…

"Here," Samantha says, snapping a picture of me with her phone. "This should make her feel better." She hands me the phone, then sticks out her chest, kicks up one leg behind her, and pretends to blow a kiss. "Take one of me too." I take the picture then type in a message, reading it out loud to Samantha as I write it.

"Wish you were here! Love and kisses from sunny Hot Topic!" I hit the send button and Samantha and I both crack up. A weird guy with six piercings in his face glances at us, annoyed.

"Seriously," she says. "I think you should get that. You look legit." She lifts up my hair and squints at me in the mirror. "With the right hair and makeup, it'll be killer."

I eye her skeptically. "Are you sure?"

Samantha puts her hands on her hips and gives me her most reassuring look. "Trust me," she says. "Have I ever steered you wrong?"

We're in line at TCBY in the food court when I hear the unmistakable screech of Megan Crowley.

"Oh my gawd, you guys, he was *not!*"

Samantha nudges me without turning around. "On your left. Three o'clock."

Slowly, I turn my head to the left, and I accidentally lock eyes with Madison Duncan, who immediately leans over to Megan and whispers something in her ear.

"Uh-oh," I say, turning back to Samantha. "They saw us."

Samantha's eyes sparkle and a devilish smile spreads across her face. "Don't worry, I've got this."

Within seconds, Megan, Madison, Chloe, and Brittany are behind us, vultures that have just come upon a carcass in the middle of the desert.

"Well, well, well, look who's here. Where's your stinky friend?" Megan asks.

Samantha looks at me, mystified. "Do you know what she's talking about?" she asks. "Because I have no idea what she's talking about."

I shrug and shake my head. "I don't know what she's talking about."

Megan gives us both a bitchy, sarcastic fake smile and then looks us up and down, stopping her gaze on our Hot Topic shopping bags.

"Hot Topic?" she asks, laughing. "I didn't know you were skater girls."

"Yeah," Chloe echoes. "There's a bunch of skater boys outside in the parking lot, you should go check them out. Maybe you'll find a boyfriend." Madison and Brittany giggle behind her as I roll my eyes, trying to think of a good comeback. But before I can say anything, Samantha tilts her head to the side and puts one finger on her chin, as if she just remembered something.

"Hey, Chloe, how are those lambs?" Samantha asks in a mocking tone. "I heard they were screaming, like, really loud. And gallantly too."

Chloe's mouth drops open. She looks stunned, but then her expression quickly gives way to one of anger. She puts her hands on her hips and glares at Brittany, who looks down at the floor.

"I can't believe you told *her* about that," Chloe whines.

Brittany clasps her hands to her chest with fake indignation. "What? I didn't tell her. The only person I told was Megan. I swear."

"Yeah, well, I told you not to tell *anyone*."

Megan puts her hand up and closes her eyes, and Chloe falls silent. When she opens her eyes again, they're black with anger, and her tone is seething.

"I don't know what you think you're doing, but you should tell Fart Girl that she'd better watch her back."

The email I got from Chris Bollmer flashes in my head and I can't help myself. I have to say something. "Maybe you should watch your own back," I warn her.

"I think my back is covered," she says, pointing at the three girls standing around her. "Come on. Let's get out of here. Losers."

As soon as they're gone, Samantha and I both burst out laughing.

169

"Did you see her face?" she screams. She has tears in the corners of her eyes and she dabs at them gently with her index fingers so as not to mess up her eye makeup. "And I love how Megan's got her back covered. Covered by three morons who couldn't keep a secret to save their lives." Samantha shakes her head, sadly. "I really wish Lindsay had been here for that."

"We'll call her. We'll tell her the whole thing." I hesitate before asking the question that's on my mind, but I need to ask it. "What do you think she meant, that Lindsay had better watch her back?"

Samantha waves the question away with her hand, as if it's meaningless. "She didn't mean anything by it. She was just trying to save face. Oh my God, that was priceless."

I laugh with her, but on the inside, my heart feels heavy. I'm not so convinced that Megan was just bluffing. In fact, it sounded to me like Megan was dead serious.

When we get back to my house, my mom is sitting at the kitchen table, with books and papers and legal pads spread out all around her.

"Hi, Dr. Channing," Samantha says when we walk in.

My mom looks up at us and smiles wearily. "Oh, hi girls. Did you have fun at the mall?"

"Yes," Samantha says, earnestly. "We spent hours in the bookstore, didn't we, Erin?"

I roll my eyes and ignore her. "What are you doing?" I ask my mom.

She sighs. "I'm teaching myself estate law. But it's slightly more complicated than I was anticipating."

"Let me guess, you couldn't find a lawyer who thought he could get Kiki's ashes back for you?"

"I couldn't find a lawyer who was even willing to try. But I'm not giving up. I will fight these people until the day I die if I have to. I will take them to court and represent myself."

Samantha looks at her, wide-eyed. "Well…good luck," she says.

"Thank you, Samantha. I need all the luck I can get right now."

⌒#⌒

"Your mom is crazy," Samantha whispers once we're upstairs in my room, safely out of earshot.

"She's not crazy. She's just upset. Don't you know that everyone grieves differently? Some people cry, some people eat, some people bury themselves in their work. And some people obsess and teach themselves to litigate."

Samantha makes a *she's crazy* face and moves her index finger in a circular motion near her head. "Does she know about the ball?"

"Noooo," I say. "Now *that* would make her crazy."

"Where is it, anyway? I want to ask it about Aiden."

I go into my closet and reach up to the top shelf, where I hide the ball and the papers and my notes.

"Here," I say. Samantha rubs her hands together.

"Come on. Let's do this."

I hesitate. "Let me show you the clues first," I say, picking up the letter that Kiki wrote. I sit down on the bed next to Samantha and explain to her what I've figured out. "I haven't figured out the first one yet, and this last one—'then it is time to choose another'—that must have to do with choosing the next person to give the ball to. But this one…" I put my finger on the third clue and tap the paper. "This is the one that makes me nervous."

Samantha reads it out loud. "'The future belongs to you alone. Other voices will be disappointed.'" She shrugs. "What's the problem?"

"I'm not sure. But don't you think it sounds ominous?"

"No. I think it sounds *obvious*. *Obviously*, you're the only one who can ask it a question. 'Other voices will be disappointed' means that the ball only recognizes your voice, or something. If anyone else asks it a question, it won't work. We already knew that."

"Right. And that's exactly why it makes me nervous. It's redundant. It already says that the future is for me alone, so why add the second part?"

Samantha rolls her eyes at me. "Come on, she thought it was important. She wanted to make sure that you really, really got it."

"I don't know. It just seems like a trick. Like, she wants me to think that that's all it means, but it really means something else. Crossword clues do that all the time."

"You're overthinking it," Samantha assures me. "This isn't a multiple choice test where they're trying to confuse you. Now come on. Let's do this."

I sigh. "Okay. But just for the record, this is against my better judgment."

"So noted. Now. Ask it if Aiden will ditch Trance at the concert to hang out with me. No, wait. Scratch that. Ask if it Aiden will ditch Trance at the concert to *hook up* with me, and then become my boyfriend." She glances at my boobs. "You can't be too specific with this thing."

I take a deep breath, then shake the ball. "Okay. Will Aiden ditch Trance at the Flamingo Kids concert tonight and hook up with Samantha, and then become her boyfriend?"

Samantha grabs the ball out of my hands and waits, breathlessly, for the answer.

"'Your karma shall make it so,'" she reads. "That means yes, right?"

I nod, laughing.

"Oh my God! It said yes!" She jumps up and down excitedly, clutching the ball in her hands, then hands it back to me. "Here, you have to ask it something too. Ask it if Jesse is going to kiss you!"

I smile at her. "No, I've got a better one than that." I shake the ball and bite my lip anxiously. "Will I kiss Jesse Cooper tonight and get to see his hot body?"

"Ooh, that's good," Samantha says. "But wait, does Jesse Cooper *have* a hot body? I can't tell with the clothes he wears…"

I close my eyes and picture him in the light blue T-shirt. "The hottest."

Twenty-One

Samantha's housekeeper, Lucinda, drops us off in the parking lot outside the Corridor, and I feel ridiculous the second we step out of the car. Everyone is wearing jeans and T-shirts and sneakers. I glare at Samantha as we walk toward the entrance.

"I feel like a hooker," I tell her, catching a glimpse of myself in a car window.

Before we left, Samantha gave us both smoky eyes and slathered our lips with Juicy Tubes lip gloss in Cherry Burst. She also back-combed my hair at the crown, and, just to make sure that I looked totally fake and plastic, she sprayed it with half a bottle of got2b 2 Sexy Voluptuous Volume hair spray.

"You look amazing," she insists. "Jesse is going to fall all over himself when he sees you."

A bottleneck is forming as we get closer to the door, and Samantha looks straight ahead, smiling confidently at everyone without focusing on anyone, seemingly oblivious to the fact that guys are literally stopping in their tracks to look at her. I watch her as she strides through the crowd: her back straight, her long legs looking even longer in the black platform boots that she put on over her knee highs, so that only the pink stripes show at the top. She's achingly pretty.

"Where are you meeting Jesse?" she asks as we wait in line to pay the cover.

"I don't know. He told me to text him when we got here. I just sent it." I glance around nervously as the crowd thickens. This is not my kind of scene. Everyone looks as if they've come straight from an MTV casting couch: tattoos, piercings, asymmetrical haircuts. Come to think of it, any one of them would have fit right in at my aunt's memorial service. I check my phone to see if Jesse has texted me back yet, and I feel a tap on my shoulder. I whirl around, and I almost bump my nose on a bright green Flamingo Kids T-shirt. I look up and find Jesse's sparkling blue eyes. He smiles at me, and my heartbeat quickens. I feel myself flush before I've even had a chance to think about it.

"Wow," he says, taking in my outfit. "You look...different."

"Yeah, well, you know me. Full of surprises." I feel an elbow in my ribs, and I realize that I've forgotten all about Samantha. "Oh, Jesse, you know Samantha, right?"

"Yeah. Hey." He nods at her, seemingly unfazed by her hotness, and looks right back at me. "Come on, let's go inside."

"But what about the line? And the cover?"

He smiles. "Don't worry. Just follow me." He turns back into the crowd, which seems to have grown even denser in the last minute and half, then reaches out behind him to clasp my hand. The tingling sensation I felt when he patted my hand in the museum comes right back.

"Hold on to her," he shouts, pointing his chin toward Samantha. "Don't get separated." I nod at him as I reach for Samantha's hand, and the three of us push our way, single file, through the throng of pierced, tattooed, hoodie-wearing Flamingo Kids fans. My feet get stepped on at least fifty times.

When we finally reach the door, Jesse cuts in front of about twenty people, walking right up to a big, hulking guy sitting on a bar stool. He's got a shaved head and a ring through his lower lip, and if I saw him on the street, I might cross to the other side. But Jesse leans in and the guy hugs him, slapping him on the back two times.

"Hey, man, good to see you," the scary guy says. "How many you got?"

Jesse holds up two fingers. "Plus two." The scary guy looks at me and Samantha, and lets his gaze linger on the expanse of bare leg between Samantha's knee socks and the bottom of her miniskirt. He looks back at Jesse and grins.

"Nice work, man."

Jesse gives him the same crooked smile that he gave to Lloyd when he left us alone in the snack shop at the museum, and whatever it is that's been moving around nervously inside my stomach all night does a double backflip.

Samantha leans in and whispers to me. "You're right," she says. "He does look cute with his hair like this."

I smile at her gratefully. I know it's silly, but there's nothing quite like getting a seal of approval from Samantha. I just wish Lindsay were here. Samantha and I called her earlier to reenact the scene with Megan at the mall (although we left out the part about how Lindsay should watch her back), and she barely even laughed. She sounded miserable. The new girlfriend keeps trying to get her to talk about boys. Ugh...

Scary guy pulls out three bright orange wristbands that say UNDER 21 in thick black lettering, and affixes them to our right hands.

"Have a nice time, girls," he says, winking at us. Samantha winks back, and I have to try really hard to not laugh.

When we get inside the club, Samantha disappears to go look for Aiden, and Jesse and I go to the bar to get some Cokes. There's an opening band onstage, and it's so loud that we both have to scream to hear each other. I sigh to myself. I know I'm trying to live a little, but I would so much rather be at a nice quiet dinner.

"It's really cool that you're here," Jesse shouts. "I was a little nervous to ask you, 'cause I wasn't sure if you'd be into something like this."

I take a sip of Coke through my straw. "I'm totally into it. I love this stuff."

He nods, and his eyes look just the slightest bit amused. But I can't tell if it's because he's pleasantly surprised by me, or because he knows that I'm a lying liar who lies. "So, do you ever go down to the pit?"

The pit? Am I supposed to know what that is?

"Um, yeah. I go down to the pit all the time."

His face lights up. "Cool. Me too."

Across the room I suddenly spot Samantha, standing by herself and looking crushed. "I'm gonna go grab Samantha," I tell Jesse. "Don't go anywhere, okay?"

He raises his eyebrows. "Sure. But don't be too long, the band's going on soon and we should get a good spot."

I promise him that I'll be right back, and when I get to Samantha I put my arm on her shoulder. Her eyes are wet and glassy.

"Are you okay?"

She shakes her head and stares longingly at the corner of the room. I follow her gaze and there's Aiden, right at the end of it. He's trying to steady Trance, who is stumbling in her black heels and holding a beer in her hand.

"Maybe you were right about the ball," she says, not taking her eyes off of them. "Maybe it really doesn't work for anyone but you. I mean, he didn't even look at me. I got myself all dressed up for him, and he didn't even look at me. He just asked me to get a wet paper towel. For *her*."

I glance back over at Trance. Aiden is trying to take the beer from her, but she's pushing him away, yelling at him.

"He's an idiot," I tell her. "There are a million guys in here who would kill for you to just say hi to them."

Finally, Samantha turns to look at me. She's smiling and her eyes are bright again, as if the hurt she was feeling never even happened. I sometimes wish I could trade places with her, just to understand how it is that she makes everything look so easy. She grabs my hand.

"Come on. Let's go find Jesse. You're on a date, remember?"

Jesse leads us down toward the front of the club, and we elbow our way through all of the people crowding around the stage until we're almost at the very front. Everyone is pushed up against each other, so close that I feel like I need to turn my face upward and gasp just to be able to get some air. Somehow, Jesse manages to bend his arm and reach into his pocket, from which he pulls two small neon orange cones.

"You brought earplugs, right?" he asks us.

Samantha and I look at each other. Earplugs? I do a quick inventory of the people around me, and there are bright orange dots everywhere. I smack myself on the forehead.

"Shoot. I think I left them in the car."

Jesse gives me that same, semiamused smile again, and digs four more orange cones out of his pocket.

"Here," he says, handing them to us. "I always bring extra, just in case."

I push them in just as the lights go down and the place erupts into deafening screams. A few seconds later, there's a horrible thrashing sound coming from the stage. I push the earplugs in a little harder, wishing that they were the noise-canceling headphones that my dad likes to take on airplanes. As the lights go back on, I see four guys dressed a lot like everyone in the audience, jumping around on the stage, singing and playing electric guitars and drums. Jesse's whole body is bouncing to the beat, and he's mouthing the words to the song. He sees me looking at him and he grins at me. But part of me wishes the song would just end so I can hear myself think…

The music comes to a screeching halt.

"We are the Flamingo Kids!" screams the lead singer.

Everyone in the audience screams back at him. It's a wall of noise, madness. I look over at Samantha, and she screams too, raising her fist up in the air. The lead singer holds the mic close up to his mouth and yells into it again.

"We love our fans! And we *really* love all of you brave souls down here in the mosh pit!" He points to all of us standing just below the stage, and I can feel the color draining out of my face as I realize that this is what Jesse meant when he asked if I like to go down into the pit. "Just be careful, please! We don't want anyone getting trampled tonight!" With that, he runs over to the drummer and jumps up into the air. "One, two, one two three four…" The drummer taps his drumsticks together and the amplifiers explode once more, causing everyone to start thrashing themselves against each other, their hoodied heads moving in time to the music.

Um…did he just say *trampled*?

I start to feel panicky as someone steps on my foot and someone else elbows me in the back. *Oh my God*, I think. I can just see the headline: GIRL WITH HIGHEST GPA DIES IN MOSH PIT: DIDN'T EVEN LIKE PUNK MUSIC.

The music, by the way, is horrible. Not that I would ever admit this out loud (in fact, I would deny it even if under threat of having my fingernails pulled out with a pair of pliers), but I would take Barry Manilow over this any day of the week. Jesse keeps stealing glances at me, though, presumably to see if I'm enjoying myself, so I just keep smiling and dancing. (Well, not dancing exactly, but moving as much as one can possibly move when one is sharing six inches of floor space with sixty other people…and basically trying to appear as if I am actually here for the music, and not, in fact, because I want to impress a cute guy.)

After a few more songs, Jesse taps me on the shoulder. I stop my pretend head-banging to see what he wants. His mouth is moving, but with the noise and the earplugs, I can't hear the words. It looks like he's saying "do you love me?" but that can't possibly be right. I mean, it is only our first date.

"What?" I shout.

"Do. You. Trust. Me?"

Ohhhh. Do I *trust* him? That makes more sense. Actually, that doesn't really make sense at all. Why would he ask me that now? Why would he ask me that here?

But it's too loud for questions, so I just nod. He smiles, then bends down. I feel his hands around my calves, but I can't see what he's doing because there are too many people swarming around us, filling the space that his body had previously occupied. The next thing I know, I feel myself being lifted up off of the ground. Jesse is hoisting me up by my legs, and then some random guy with a hoop stuck through his eyebrow grabs hold of my shoulders, and the two of them raise me up so that I'm lying down above them, parallel to the ceiling.

"What are you doing?" I scream. "Put me down!" I scream it at them over and over, but they can't hear me because everyone else is screaming too.

Someone else is holding my legs now. I turn my head from side to side, still yelling desperately, when I spot Samantha and Jesse. They're looking up at me, smiling, as if they could care less that I'm thrashing around like a scared caged animal. I watch, helpless, as Samantha reaches into her purse and pulls out her cell phone.

"Stop moving!" Jesse yells.

He balls his hands into fists and crosses his arms in front of his chest, indicating that I should do the same. From the serious look on his face, I understand that he's trying to help me. I realize suddenly that no matter how much I scream, I'm not getting out of this. I swallow hard and lie still, crossing my arms just like he did. Jesse nods reassuringly.

"Just relax!" he shouts. "Trust the crowd!"

I peek at the swirl of body piercings and tattoo sleeves and crazy hairdos. I'm supposed to trust *them?* Terrified, I try to shake my head at him, but I'm momentarily blinded by the flash from Samantha's camera phone. I blink and blink, and when my eyes clear, Samantha and

Jesse are no longer in my line of vision, and I'm slowly making my way above the mosh pit, as hand after hand grabs onto my legs, my butt, my back, my head. I breathe deeply, trying not to think about what would happen if they dropped me.

Just relax, I repeat to myself. *Trust the crowd.*

I close my eyes and concentrate on relaxing, and the first thing that comes to mind is my aunt Kiki. She would have loved this. Actually, she probably did this. Probably more than once. And in spite of the terror, I can't help smiling as I picture her lying on her back, screaming with joy as people pass her along, relishing the idea that total strangers would care enough to keep her safe. And just like that, my shoulders unstiffen, my neck untenses, and I go with it.

I open my eyes and look out, and it's like being in the treetops, except that all of the trees are actually people's heads. I turn my head to the other side, toward the stage. I have a perfect view. The guitar player is on his knees, his head bowed down, and I can see the sweat dripping off of his shaggy bangs as he plays. The lead singer is jumping around like a maniac, his eyes closed, and I wonder how it is that he doesn't bump into anything.

I look up at the ceiling and I exhale. I have never felt so alive.

When I reach the edge of the crowd, a guy with short spiky hair and tattoos covering his entire neck gently lowers me to the ground. He raises his hand up, palm open, and I high five him.

"That was rad," he says.

I beam at him, and as he disappears back into the crowd, Jesse and Samantha appear by my side.

"Oh my God, that was so awesome!" Samantha squeals. "I can't believe you did that!"

Jesse laughs. "You are officially the coolest girl I have ever met." He looks me right in the eye, but I look away, not wanting him to see how flattered I am by such a designation. Especially since just a week ago I was Just a Boring Girl from AP Art History Class with Whom Jesse Is Being Forced to Work. "Hey, would you guys want to meet the band?" he asks. "'Cause RJ, the guy at the door, he slipped me four backstage passes when we came in."

Samantha cocks one eyebrow. "Did you say *four* backstage passes?"

"Yeah."

Samantha looks at me, her eyes shining. I know exactly what she's thinking.

"We'll be right back," she says to Jesse. "Don't move."

"I really don't think you should do this," I caution—but it's too late; Samantha has seized my arm and plunged me back into the crowd. "He was such a jerk to you before!" I yell. "What makes you think he's going to be any nicer?"

Samantha's eyes are laserlike in their focus as she drags me to the other side of the club, toward Aiden and Trance. "Don't you see?" she shouts back. "This is it! This is the ball's doing. It has to be."

"But what if he says no?" I shout to her. I can't help it. Even after Jesse, even after everything, I'm still skeptical. It's just how my mind works.

Samantha looks at me solemnly. "He won't," she mouths.

We approach Aiden and Trance, who are sitting on a ledge along the side wall of the club. Aiden is furiously playing air guitar, mouthing the words to the song that the band is playing, and Trance has her arms crossed in front of her. She looks pissed off.

"Hey, Aiden!" Samantha yells to him. He doesn't hear her, so she taps him on the shoulder. When he sees that it's Samantha who has interrupted his guitar solo, he rolls his eyes. I suddenly wish I had a pair of gardening shears to cut off that stupid messy hair of his.

"I'm not giving you a ride home, so don't even ask," he yells over the music.

"I didn't come over here to ask you for a ride," Samantha shouts. She leans in toward him and cups her hand over her mouth, talking directly into his ear. His eyes widen, and he nods, then puts up one finger as he turns away from her to talk to Trance. Samantha grabs my arm excitedly and jumps up and down behind his back.

I watch as Aiden puts his hand on Trance's leg and leans into her ear to explain the situation. From the look on Trance's face, I can already tell that this is not going over well. Aiden points at me and Samantha, and Trance suddenly leaps up from where she's sitting and starts screaming at him. I can't really hear what she's saying, but I can see her gesticulating toward Samantha, and it's pretty obvious what's going on.

She gives Aiden the finger, then grabs her bag and storms off.

My heart sinks. Of course Aiden is going to run off after her, and poor Samantha is going to be devastated. But to my surprise, he just stuffs his hands into the pockets of his jeans and watches her walk away, then turns back to Samantha and shrugs.

"Screw her," he says, more to himself than to either of us. "Come on, let's go."

Twenty-Two

The lead singer of the Flamingo Kids—I think Jesse said his name is Eric—is prancing around the stage, screaming into the mic (I wouldn't call it singing, exactly), less than ten feet from where we're standing in the wings, our backstage passes hanging from our necks. This is by far the coolest night of my entire life. I can't believe I almost didn't even come. I can't believe I thought I would prefer Barry Manilow to *this*.

Eric glances over in our direction, then quickly looks back again, as if to make sure that he'd really seen what he thought he'd seen. Which is, of course, Samantha: a vision in Hot Topic and knee-high boots. He crosses the stage and looks over a third time, and I notice that this time he catches her eye, causing the left side of his mouth to turn up into a little one-quarter grin before he turns back out to the crowd. I think Aiden must have noticed, too, because he immediately puts his arm around Samantha's waist and whispers something in her ear that makes her giggle.

As soon as the show is over, the other guys in the band leave the stage on the opposite side, but Eric makes a beeline for us. Well, not for us. For her. And now he's standing here, bare-chested and sweaty, his damp brown hair falling over one eye, his dark brown eyes dilated and wide with adrenaline. He has great swirling tattoos covering almost his entire torso, and across his chest it says "Pink Flamingos" in heavy Gothic letters. His body is long and lean, muscled but not bulky. He looks sinewy and hard. He looks like the kind of guy who would get you grounded until you're thirty.

A guy with an earpiece rushes over and hands him a towel and a cup of ice water. He downs the water in one long gulp, without ever taking his eyes off of Samantha. Instinctively, Aiden pulls her closer.

"I'm Eric," he says, completely ignoring Aiden, and me and Jesse for that matter.

"Samantha," she says, ignoring Aiden as well.

Eric nods. "Well, *Samantha*. What'd you think of the show?"

Samantha sticks her tongue in her cheek and looks him right in the eye, unblinking. "It was pretty good, but I would have ended on a better-known song. You should always leave your audience wanting more."

Eric raises his eyebrows, and he looks surprised by the criticism. But then his mouth slowly breaks into that one-quarter grin. "That's funny. My drummer said the same thing." He narrows his eyes at her just a little, looking more intrigued than ever. And who could blame him? Even I'm amazed by her coolness and confidence. Plus, she has Aiden right where she wants him. I suddenly have the feeling that I'm in the presence of a master, and I watch, wide-eyed, waiting to see how she's going to manipulate this situation to her advantage.

"These are my friends," she says, suddenly. "Erin, Jesse, and Aiden. Jesse's a huge fan."

My mouth drops open. She knows that Aiden is a huge fan too. Aiden is the only reason that she even wanted to come, and she's acting like he's not important. She's acting like he's not even here. Like she doesn't even notice that he has his arm wrapped around her like a python. Although I'm starting to think that that's kind of the point.

"Rock on, man," Eric says. He makes a fist with his hand and holds it out toward Jesse, who fist bumps him back. "You want me to sign your shirt?"

Jesse looks like a kid on Christmas morning. "Yeah. That'd be awesome."

Eric motions to the guy with the earpiece, who is still hovering nearby. He quickly produces a black Sharpie from his front pocket and hands it to Eric. Jesse turns around and bends forward slightly, and Eric leans on his left shoulder, writing with the Sharpie on his shirt. When he's finished, he hands the pen back to the guy with the earpiece, then looks back at Samantha.

"Me and the guys were thinking about going to an after-party at a club downtown. Do you want to come?"

An after-party? At a club? I wonder how old he thinks she is. She definitely could pass for eighteen, but twenty-one? I don't think so. I hold my breath as I wait to see how she's going to get around this one.

"I don't know," she says, wrinkling her nose. "I think I'm in the mood for something mellower tonight."

Eric's eyes dart back and forth from Samantha's face to Aiden's hand curled around her waist, and it's obvious that he's having trouble figuring out the situation.

"I can do mellow," he says with a shrug. "But I gotta know first, are you with this guy or what?" he asks, nodding toward Aiden.

Apparently he's finished making small talk and if it's not going to happen with Samantha, then he wants to hurry up and find someone who it is going to happen with before all the rest of the groupies take off. Samantha tilts her head, as if she has to think about it.

"I don't know," she answers. She tosses her hair and then slowly turns her face toward Aiden. "Am I with you?"

Aiden smiles. "Hell, yeah."

Samantha turns back to look at Eric. "I guess I am."

Eric raises his eyebrows. "Good for you, man," he says to Aiden, giving him a grudging nod of respect. Then he looks pointedly back at Samantha. "We're playing here again this summer. In case, you know, you're ever not with him."

Samantha smiles coyly. "Good to know."

Outside, the full moon is hanging so low in the sky that it looks like a prop in a school play: a wooden cutout painted iridescent silver, suspended from the sky by invisible nylon cords. The four of us walk out to the parking lot together, Aiden and Samantha slightly ahead of me and Jesse. Aiden has his arm draped across Samantha's shoulders, and Samantha is laughing and squealing. Every few seconds, Aiden pulls her toward him. To be honest, their PDA is making me feel a little uncomfortable with Jesse right next to me, sort of like how it is when I'm watching a make-out scene in a movie with my parents. Except...

"What is that about?" Jesse whispers to me after their, like, fifteenth kiss. I roll my eyes and shake my head.

"It's a long story. Not even worth your time."

When we finally get to Aiden's car, Aiden pushes Samantha up against the passenger side door and makes out with her, his hands traveling up and down the sides of her body. *Ew.* I clear my throat loudly. Aiden stops kissing Samantha and gives me a sheepish grin.

"Right," he says, reality dawning on him. "You guys came together, so you're gonna need a ride home, aren't you?" I nod at him, and Samantha grabs onto him by the belt loops of his jeans. "That's cool. Not a problem."

I will admit that I am slightly surprised by this. I was definitely expecting him to throw a tantrum about having to give me a ride.

"It's all right," Jesse says, stepping in front of me. "I can take her home." Aiden looks at the two of us as if it has just occurred to him that we might be together, and he shoots me a concerned, big-brother-ish stare.

"Is that cool with you?" he asks me.

Again, not the Aiden I thought he was, and I can't help but wonder if maybe I've got him all wrong, and maybe Samantha isn't crazy for liking him so much.

"It's fine with me," I answer. "I just need to talk to Samantha for a second. Alone."

Aiden steps back and bows a little, holding his hands out as if he's making way for the queen. I grab Samantha by the arm and pull her away from the car.

"Can you believe this?" she whispers giddily. "That ball is amazing. It totally worked! He ditched Trance to hook up with me, just like I asked!"

I sigh. "Samantha, I will admit that he is being particularly nice to us right now, but are you really sure you want to do this? Just remember, he hasn't technically broken up with Trance. They only got into a fight."

She looks at me like I'm crazy. "Are you kidding? He's going to forget all about Trance. And don't forget, it's working for you too. You're going home with Jesse now, so you're going to get to kiss him. And see his hot body, remember? It's *perfect*." She plants a huge lip-gloss-sticky kiss on my cheek and starts to walk back toward Aiden, but I stop her.

"There's just one more thing."

"What?"

I sigh. I hate that I feel like I need to be Samantha's mother. It's really not a healthy dynamic for a teenaged friendship. But her own mother just seems so incapable of doing the job, so…

"Listen, just be careful, okay? Don't do anything that you might regret in the morning."

Samantha looks at me like I'm a lost cause and shakes her head, annoyed.

"Thanks a lot, Captain Buzzkill. Way to ruin the moment. Do you want to tell me how babies are made too?" I must look as hurt as I feel, because Samantha immediately leans in and gives me a hug. "Sorry," she says.

"I didn't mean that. I'm just so excited about everything that's happening, and, you know, I mean this in the nicest way, but you're always so serious and responsible, and it's kind of a downer. I mean, you just crowd-surfed! Go with that. Take a breather from being the voice of reason for once. Even if it's just for tonight."

"Okay," I say, trying to be peppy but still stinging.

Aiden honks his horn impatiently.

"Coming!" she yells, as she runs back to the car. She opens the passenger door and slips in, and Aiden leans over and kisses her again, grabbing the back of her hair. Samantha puts her head on his shoulder as he starts the engine, blowing me a kiss as they drive away.

"Are you okay?" Jesse asks, once we're in the front seat of his car, heading toward the highway. Now that we're alone together, a heavy awkwardness has settled in, and the small space between us in the car feels more like a gulf. I so badly want to sidle up next to him, the way Samantha did with Aiden. I want to fall against him and breathe him in, and I want to feel his heart beating under his T-shirt, fast and hard, like mine is. But it just seems too contrived now. Plus, in spite of the earplugs, my ears are still ringing from the concert, and my head is throbbing from replaying Samantha's words over and over and over again in my mind.

"Yeah. Why?"

Jesse chuckles. "I don't know. You're just clutching the door handle, and you like you're going to be sick any second."

I look down at myself; I *am* clutching the door handle. God, I am such a dork. I remove my hand from the door and slide over—slightly—toward him. I remember a romance novel that Samantha once stole from her mom about a housewife and her hot gardener. I didn't quite understand what the narrator meant about the "sexual tension" that was always between them, like when she was sunbathing by the shimmering pool, caressing her smooth, tanned legs with oil, while he was kneeling just a few feet away from her, plucking the soft petals of the fading blooms with his strong, nimble fingers. Oh my God, it was the cheesiest thing ever. But boy, do I understand it now.

"Sorry," I say. "I'm fine." Jesse looks up suddenly, like he's just had an idea.

"Hey, what time do you have to be home?"

I glance at the clock on the dashboard. It's ten-fifteen. "Eleven-thirty. How come?"

He smiles. "I want to show you something."

A few minutes later, we pull up to an old, run-down, rambling white house with an enormous wrap-around porch. The paint is peeling off of the wood and the floorboards are littered with rusting chairs and a couple of swings that hang from the rafters. Above the doorway is a white wooden sign that reads, "The Mansion House Inn, est. 1923," in a neat, fading script. I can't imagine what we're doing here.

"What is this?" I ask as he turns off the car headlights.

He smiles secretively. "You'll see."

We both get out of the car and he motions for me not to slam my door, so I close it as quietly as I can.

"Come on," he whispers. "Follow me."

We tiptoe around the perimeter of the house, until we come to a flimsy-looking wire fence. We follow it for about fifty yards, and then Jesse stops. He crouches down and puts his hands against the fence, feeling for something.

"Here it is." He pulls on the wire, and a section of the fence opens out toward us, revealing a hole just big enough for a person to crawl through. He holds it back with one hand and puts his other hand out, motioning for me to go through. "After you."

Warily, I examine the hole. "I don't know. Isn't this trespassing?"

Jesse laughs. "That's right. I forgot that you were a rule-follower. Do you remember the time in fourth grade when Joey Forlenza said he was going to steal our lunch money? Remember how fat he was? I told you to run. But you wouldn't do it, because there was a rule that no running was allowed in the hallways. And he got you, and he stole your lunch money, just like he said he would."

I shake my head. "I don't remember that…"

Jesse nods, still laughing. "Yeah, you do."

I can feel my face turning red. I'm glad that we're outside, in the dark, so that he can't see.

"Trust me," he says, motioning to the fence. "It will be totally worth it."

"The last time you told me to trust you I ended up being passed around a mosh pit on my back."

"And you had fun, didn't you?"

I hesitate, not wanting to admit it. As I contemplate the hole, I hear Samantha's voice echoing through my head again. *Take a breather from being the voice of reason for once. Even if it's just for tonight.*

Okay, fine, I think. *But just for tonight.*

I get down on my hands and knees and crawl through the hole, pretending not to hear Jesse as he cheers me on, softly clapping in the night.

We make our way down a fairly steep embankment. After I trip on a tree stump and nearly kill myself, Jesse takes my hand to help keep me steady.

"Where are we going?" I ask him for the thousandth time, and for the thousandth time he tells me that I'll see.

Finally, after at least ten minutes of me clutching onto Jesse's hand for dear life, we reach the bottom. In the moonlight, all I can see is something that looks like steam, rising up from a pile of rocks. It's beautiful.

"What is this place?"

"It's a hot spring," he tells me, still holding onto my hand even through we're on stable ground now. "It's one of the only ones on the entire east coast. It used to be a popular swimming hole in the 1800s. In 1884 they closed it to the public and put a sanitarium here. Doctors thought that sitting in the hot water could cure arthritis, so people came from all over the country for treatment. In the 1920s it was shut down and turned into an inn that's been run by the same family ever since. But now the family is down to one old lady in her nineties, and she stopped taking in guests about fifteen years ago. And what's crazy is that hardly anybody remembers that the hot spring is even *here*." He bends down and picks up a stone, then tosses it into the water, where it lands with a soft *pling*. "I'm sure the second she dies, some developer will rush in and turn it into a health spa or a fat farm or something stupid like that."

I shake my head in awe. "How do you know all of this? And more importantly, *why* do you know all of this?"

He shrugs. "I don't know. I'm just interested in history, I guess. I like knowing about what things were like before

I was here to see them for myself." He unclasps my hand and bends down to untie his shoes. "Come on," he says. "Let's go in."

"Go in? There?"

"Yeah. The water's, like, a hundred degrees. Think of it as the original Jacuzzi."

I stare at him like he's crazy as he kicks off his shoes. *Oh God*, I think nervously. Is he going to get undressed? Is he expecting *me* to get undressed? Because I'm not. *No way, Jose.* I quickly turn around so that my back is to him, but I can hear the fabric of his T-shirt rubbing against his skin as he lifts it off, and I almost faint as I hear the *ziiiip* of his jeans.

"You can turn around," he says, but I stay where I am and shake my head, too nervous to say anything. Too nervous to breathe, even. "It's okay," he laughs. "I'm not naked or anything. Jeez. What kind of a guy do you think I am?"

Finally, I exhale. Well, that's a relief. For a second, I wasn't sure *what* was going on. Slowly, I turn around to face him…

I let out a little laugh. His boxers have red chili peppers all over them, and the chili peppers are wearing dark sunglasses and smiling huge, toothy smiles.

"Come on," he says, stepping into the water. "You have to come in. If you're going to trespass, you might as well take full advantage of the property."

There's a part of me that wants to go in so badly it hurts, but a boy swimming in boxers is not the same as a girl swimming in her bra and underwear. Especially when the girl wearing the bra doesn't have anything to fill it with.

"That's okay," I tell him. "I'll just wait here. You have fun."

He dunks his head under the water, then pops back up again and leans his elbows on a rock next to where I'm standing.

"Please?"

I hear Samantha's words echoing in my head again: *Thanks a lot, Captain Buzzkill.*

"I don't think so, Jesse. I'm sorry."

He bats his eyelashes dramatically. "Pretty please? With sugar on top? I promise I won't look, if that's what you're worried about."

You just crowd-surfed at a punk rock concert. Go with that.

I don't answer him. Instead, I start undoing my studded belt.

"Yes!" he says, pumping his fist. "I knew you had it in you."

"Just turn around," I order, dropping my skirt to the ground and pulling off the sleeveless hoodie, then the T-shirt, and then, finally, removing my shoes. I dip my toe into the water. It really is like a Jacuzzi.

"Can I turn around now?" he asks, once I've slid into the water up to my neck.

"Yes. You can turn around now." He turns, slowly, and faces me, his black hair slicked flat against his head, his blue eyes blue even in the dark. He reaches out and puts his hands on my bare shoulders, and my whole body trembles.

"So, you've never been to a punk concert before, have you?"

Uh-oh. I guess my head-banging wasn't all that convincing. I press my lips together and shake my head in mock shame. Jesse smiles.

"And you don't really like the Flamingo Kids, do you?"

I shake my head again, trying not to laugh. "How'd you know?"

"Um, let's see…the outfit was the first tip-off. Not that you didn't look good, but most people don't get quite so dolled-up for a concert at the Corridor. But I knew for sure when you said you like the pit. No girls like the pit."

"That's a little chauvinistic," I tease.

He raises his eyebrows and grins. "Oh, really? So you did like the pit, then? Should we go back for our second date?"

"Okay, fine. I hated the pit. I felt like I was in a bad movie, in one of those rooms where the walls are closing in all around me."

We both laugh, and then his face turns serious again.

"It's funny, you haven't really changed at all in the last two years, but somehow, you've changed completely," he murmurs. "Do you know what I mean?"

I nod. "I could say the same thing about you." I lift his right hand off of my shoulder and turn it over, so that I'm looking at his wrist. I study his tattoo in the moonlight. It's some kind of a word, but it's not written in English. It looks like Hebrew maybe, or Arabic.

"What does it say?" I ask.

"It says 'truth.' It's Hebrew."

"What does it mean?"

He smiles. "It means that I should never forget who I am. That I should always do what feels right, and not what everyone else thinks I should do." I trace over it with my fingers. His skin feels soft and raised just the slightest bit along the edges of the ink. He lifts his wrist out of my hand and puts his fingers under my chin, tilting my face up toward his. He looks so deeply into my eyes that I feel like he must somehow know everything that's going through my mind. And then all of a sudden my eyes are closed, and he's kissing me, and I'm kissing him back. *This is amazing*, I think. *Everything is falling into place, just as the ball predicted.*

After a minute or so he pulls back and looks at me, brushing a piece of my hair away from my face. "That was so much better than it was in Jeff DiNardo's closet."

I look back at him, totally shocked. So he does remember!

"I thought you'd forgotten about that."

He shakes his head and widens his eyes. "Are you kidding? I've thought about that kiss every night for the last two years." This time, my eyes are the ones that get wide. Jesse Cooper has been thinking about me? For the last two years? God, I'm stupid. No wonder he was so weird at the museum. He probably thought I was a horrible person for not talking to him all of this time, just because he had changed his look. Just because he was living his life according to his tattoo.

"But what about Kaydra?" I ask.

"What about Kaydra?"

"Well, I don't know. I thought you two were…I mean, she's really pretty, and she was flirting with you at the museum and everything."

"First off, she's, like, twenty, and second of all, she's not my type. You're my type. And I've missed hanging out with you. A lot."

Jesse leans in and kisses me again. His mouth tastes soft and sweet and delicious, like a ripe strawberry in the middle of summer. So I'm his type. I didn't even know I *was* a type. But I like the way it sounds.

"We should get going," he says, when we finally come up for air. "It's almost eleven."

I know he's right, but I so do not want to leave. I make a mental note that when I get home, I need to ask the ball if my parents will extend my curfew.

Twenty-Three

The next evening, Lindsay is lying on my bed, her hands crossed behind her head, relaying the horrible details of the weekend with the Girlfriend. Or the G/F, as I've come to think of her, given all of the texts that Lindsay sent yesterday while she was at her dad's.

"Seriously, she was so annoying. She kept acting like we were friends or something. Like we're the same age. She even asked me if I wanted to go hang out with her at *the mall*. And the worst part is, my dad thinks that it's awesome. He's, like, 'Oh, Lindsay, isn't this so great, it's like having a big sister.' And I'm, like, 'Yeah, dad, except she's your girl-friend, remember?' If this goes anywhere she could be my *stepmom*." Lindsay shudders. "Ugh. Could you imagine?" She lifts her head up when I don't answer and looks across the room at me. "Erin?"

I quickly snap myself out of my daydream about me and Jesse, kissing in the hot spring last night.

"No," I say dramatically, even though I'm not exactly sure what it is I'm supposed to be imagining, since I kind of tuned her out there for a minute. But it doesn't matter. I can tell from her tone that it's something bad. "It would be *awful*."

Satisfied, Lindsay lies her head back down. "I know, right? I mean, what does he even have to talk to her about? My little sister is smarter than she is."

"I kissed Jesse Cooper last night," I blurt out, unable to contain myself for another nanosecond.

Lindsay sits straight up. "You *what*?"

"I kissed Jesse Cooper. In a hot spring." I close my eyes and sigh. "It was amazing." I proceed to tell her the whole story from the very beginning, from asking the ball if I would get to see Jesse's hot body, all the way to my kiss. Lindsay's mouth is hanging open, getting wider and wider with every detail.

"Okay, let me get this straight. You *crowd-surfed* in a mosh pit? And you climbed through a hole in a fence on private property? And you took off all of your clothes and went swimming in your bra and underwear?" She gapes at me. "Who are you? And what have you done with Erin?"

I laugh. "I know, right? It's like something came over me last night, and I just went with it. It's like I was someone else completely."

I don't tell her about what Samantha said to me in the parking lot. My feelings are still too raw for me to talk about it. Although, I suppose I should thank her, really. I mean, if she hadn't said what she did, I might never have crawled through that hole in the fence and into the best night of my life.

"It's your aunt," Lindsay says, matter-of-factly. "I'll bet you she's channeling her spirit through you. I've heard of that happening before."

"Okay, I don't necessarily think that she's channeling her spirit, but it's funny you say that. I kept thinking about her all night. How I was doing the kinds of things that she would have done."

Lindsay has a goofy smile on her face, and she's looking at me like a proud parent. "Do you know what you are?" she asks.

"No. What? And why are you looking at me like that?"

Her smile widens. "*You* are not boring. Not anymore."

I tilt my head to the side as I think about this. She's right. I mean, how could anyone who goes to a concert wearing Hot Topic and crowd-surfs in a mosh pit and illegally trespasses on private property be boring?

"Thanks, Linds," I say, beaming back. "I think that's the nicest thing anyone has ever said to me. Only, how do I turn that into an essay about why I should get picked to go to Italy?"

"Hmmmm," she says. She looks up at me, blank-faced. "I have no idea. But what about Samantha? Did the ball work for her? Did she hook up with Aiden?"

This is an excellent question. I must have texted her ten times last night when I got home, and I've been calling her all day, but she's not responding to anything. Which, I think, can only mean one of two things: Either a) things went really well and she can't talk because she and Aiden are still making out, or b) things went really, really badly and she doesn't want to talk to anyone at all. Given the circumstances, it could have gone either way.

Before I can answer Lindsay, my cell phone rings. "Maybe this is her," I say, reaching for it. "I haven't even spoken to her yet." But when I look at the caller ID, my stomach flips over, just like it did last night. It's Jesse.

"Hi," I answer. Lindsay raises her eyebrows—*is it her?*—and I shake my head. I mouth that it's Jesse and she smiles and bites her lip.

"Hi," he says. "I had a really good time last night. I think it was one of the best nights I've ever had. I mean, can you believe the lead singer of the Flamingo Kids signed my T-shirt?" I'm silent. That wasn't exactly what I thought he was referring to. "Kidding," he says with a laugh, and I laugh back, relieved. "But seriously, do you want to know what he wrote?"

"Yeah. I meant to look last night but I forgot."

"It says, 'To Jesse, you have hot friends. Eric Anderson.'"

Hot *friends*? Plural? I can feel myself blushing a little as I think about what I was wearing last night.

"I'll let Samantha know," I tell him. "Not that she'll care."

"Yeah, right. Did she hook up with Aiden? Have you talked to her?"

"No. Not yet. She's not answering my texts or phone calls or anything. Lindsay and I were just sitting here saying that we're a little worried."

"Hi, Jesse!" Lindsay shouts enthusiastically.

"Hi, Lindsay," he says back.

"He says hi," I tell her, and she giggles.

"You told her everything, didn't you?" he groans.

I try to keep my voice serious. "No. I didn't tell her anything. We've just been talking about our math homework."

Lindsay bursts out laughing.

"All right. I'm obviously intruding on your girl time. Go back to pillow fighting or whatever it is you do. I'll see you tomorrow at school?"

"Yes, definitely. And Jesse?"

"Yeah?"

"I had a really good time last night too."

I hang up the phone and Lindsay screams.

"Oh my God, you two are soooo cute! I love this! I can't believe you have a boyfriend!" She looks at me, her eyes twinkling. "Aren't you glad now that you listened to me about the ball?"

"Yes," I admit to her. "I am. I am *so* glad that I listened to you about the ball." I pause, turning around to face my closet. Suddenly, a thought occurs to me. I whirl back around to look at Lindsay.

"Actually, would you mind looking at the rest of the clues with me? I think I just realized something. I think I won't be ready until I've figured out what all of the clues mean."

"Ready for what?"

"I'm not sure, exactly. Just, my aunt's friend, the one who gave me the ball, she said I should call her when I'm ready. I didn't know what it meant before, but I'm starting to get an idea."

Before I even realize what I'm doing, I throw open the closet, grab the ball from the shelf, and spread out the papers on my desk. Lindsay hunches beside me to pore over them.

"'Absolute knowledge is not unlimited; let the planets be your guide to the number,'" Lindsay reads. "What do you think that means? What's the number?"

"I don't know. But what about the word '*unlimited*'? If something is not unlimited, then that means it has to have a limit. So, absolute knowledge has a limit?"

Lindsay nods, like all of a sudden she gets it. "It ends," she states confidently. "I think it means that eventually the ball isn't going to work for you anymore. Look at the last clue. 'You will know more when no more is known; then it is time to choose another.' I think it's saying that when the ball stops working for you, you have to choose someone else to give it to. Like how your aunt chose to give it to you."

"But my aunt died," I counter. "It didn't stop working for her. She died. And she left it to me." A serious thought occurs to me, and I turn sideways to look at Lindsay's face. "Do you think I'm going to die when the ball stops working?"

"No," she says adamantly. "No way. Think about it. Your aunt would not have left you the ball if she thought it would bring you harm. She would never have done something like that."

"Well, she did stop speaking to me. She must have been angry with me about something."

"Angry enough to want you to die? I don't think so."

"Okay, but maybe she didn't know that would happen." I can feel my voice rising as the pieces of the puzzle start coming together in my head. "Think about it. She died in a freak accident, right? Maybe it had something to do with the ball. Maybe when the ball had run its course with her, she suddenly got struck by lightning." I feel panicked, and I slump in my chair. "Oh my God. That's what happened. It makes too much sense for it not to be true."

Lindsay shakes her head again. "No. It doesn't make any sense. If she didn't know what was supposed to happen, then how could she have written a clue about it?"

I think about this for a second, and then I exhale, relieved. "You're right," I say. "Of course you're right. But—"

Lindsay pats me on the back before I can go on. "You shouldn't worry so much. The ball is working. It's bringing you everything you want. Your aunt obviously left it to you because she wanted you to improve your life." She grins. "And it definitely has improved."

My cell phone rings again.

"Ooh! Maybe that's Samantha. Or maybe it's Jesse calling to tell you that he loves you, and he wants to father forty children with you."

I roll my eyes at her, even though I'm blushing. "It was just a kiss."

"Yeah, well, that's what Sleeping Beauty probably thought, and the Prince married her, like, on the spot. And…" She doesn't finish.

"What?" I ask.

"And they just had *one* kiss."

But it turns out that it's not Samantha or Jesse calling. It's Chris Bollmer.

"Chris?" I say, frowning into the phone.

Lindsay moves her hands back and forth and shakes her head, letting me know that I shouldn't tell him that she's with me.

"Have you seen Lindsay?" he asks, his voice filled with anxiety.

"No," I lie. "I don't know where she is. Have you tried calling her?"

"She blocked my number. I can't get through."

"Really?" I ask, remembering how he hacked through my email filter. "You've figured out that getting-through problem before, haven't you?"

"It's important," he says, ignoring my accusation. "I just wanted to warn her."

"Warn her about what?" I ask. Hearing this, Lindsay rolls her eyes.

"Check your email." He pauses, then lowers his voice to a hiss. "You should have listened to me."

"What? Chris, what are you talking—?"

But it's too late. He's already hung up. Lindsay looks at me, waiting for an explanation.

"He said he wanted to warn you about something. He said I should check my email."

She sighs. "Okay. Here we go again."

Lindsay stands over my shoulder as I click on my inbox. Nothing.

She exhales loudly. "There is something seriously wrong with that guy. I mean, does he think this is funny? Like I don't have enough stress in my life."

"Wait a second," I say, remembering the email filter yet again. "Maybe there is." I go into "Unknown Sender" alerts and, sure enough, there's someone who's been trying to email me. The sender is listed as "anonymous." Hmmm. I click on it to allow the message, and it pops into my inbox.

"Here it is."

I click on the message, and within seconds my entire screen is taken up by an enlarged picture of Lindsay in her bra and underwear. Someone Photoshopped a red cape around her neck that appears to be floating out behind her, and they've rotated the picture onto its side so that it looks like she's flying. At the top it says, "The Amazing Adventures of Fart Girl." Underneath, there's a caption that reads, "Incredibly propelled by the power of natural gas!"

So *that's* what Megan meant when she said that Lindsay had better watch her back. I knew she wasn't bluffing. But I never thought she'd go as far as this. She must have *planned*. She must have hidden her phone in the locker room and snapped a picture when Lindsay wasn't looking. How else could she have gotten Lindsay in her bra and underwear?

Lindsay puts her hands over her eyes and starts to cry.

"How many people got it?" she asks, her voice barely a whisper.

I click on the recipient list, and my heart sinks when I see that it was sent to the entire tenth grade. "Not that many," I lie.

"How many?" she asks, her voice stronger this time.

I sigh, not wanting to tell her but knowing that I have to. "She sent it to the whole grade." I click on the sender again, to see if it will give me any other information aside from "anonymous," but it doesn't. *Smart*, I think to myself. Now nobody can prove it came from her.

Lindsay looks up and angrily wipes the tears from her eyes, like she's pissed at them for even being there.

"I'm going to kill that bitch," she says, and I look at her, surprised.

That sounded so weird coming from her mouth. First of all, Lindsay never curses, and second of all, Lindsay wouldn't hurt a fly. Literally. If a fly gets into her house, she tries to trap it in a jar and then takes it outside and sets it free.

"She is awful," I say, trying to calm her down with my usual let's-just-agree-and-she'll-get-over-it routine. But this time, it doesn't seem to be working.

"Get out the ball." Her voice is deep and the words come out almost like a growl. I look over at her, half expecting to see that her irises have turned red, like she's a vampire from *Twilight*.

"What? Lindsay, I don't think you should do anything rash right now. Let's just think about this. We could go to the principal. We could tell your mom. We could tell *my* mom. She would know what to do." But Lindsay is in no mood for rational.

"Get it," she demands. Her tone is hard and forceful, like it was the other day with Megan. Like it used to be in third grade, when she was mean and bossy. Obediently, I get the ball down from the top shelf of my closet, and I hold it protectively against my chest.

"I don't think this is a good idea. We don't even know what happened to Sam—"

"Yes, we do," she yells, interrupting me. "Aiden ditched Trance and hooked up with her, just like she asked. You saw them making out. You saw her get in the car with him."

"Yes, but I don't know what happened after they left. For all I know, Aiden could have dropped her off on the side of the road, and she could be missing."

"For all you know, the two of them could still be in his bedroom!"

I purse my lips, unconvinced. There's just something about that clue—"other voices will be disappointed"—that's bothering me. And the fact that Samantha hasn't called me yet isn't making me feel any better about it. Lindsay sits down on my bed and wipes her eyes. "Erin, I have never asked you for anything big in my life. But you are my best friend. Don't you want her to stop doing this to me?"

"I do," I say. "Of course I do."

"Then do this for me. Please. I'm begging you. You can't ask it for Samantha to hook up with some guy but then not do this for me."

I feel my will break as soon as I look into her watery blue eyes. Poor Lindsay. She shouldn't have to go through this. And besides, she's right. Why should everyone else be happy except for her? Why should I get to be on cloud nine about kissing Jesse while seminaked pictures of her are being emailed around the school? I'm her best friend. If I have a way to help her, then I need to help her. Anyway, even if I'm right about that clue, how bad could it be? It's not like things could get much worse for her than they already are.

I sit down next to Lindsay on the bed and put my arm around her back.

"Okay. What do you want me to ask?"

Twenty-Four

I spot Jesse waving at me from across the cafeteria, and as I make my way toward him, I notice that my entire body is all tingly and nervous, and I realize that I have a huge, stupid smile pasted on my face that I can't seem to get rid of, or even make smaller, no matter how hard I try. But then again, so does he, so I feel a little bit less stupid. But just a little.

"Hi," he says, giving me a light kiss on the cheek. Of course, my face instantly turns into a furnace, and knowing that I'm turning red only makes me blush that much harder. But hello, I just got kissed *at school*. I look around to see if anyone saw, and I notice that Maya Franklin is staring at me, her mouth hanging open. I smile at her, trying not to gloat. (Okay, maybe I didn't try all that hard.) I'm definitely feeling cooler than I have ever felt in my life. With that one little kiss, I just officially joined the elite ranks of the boyfriended.

"Is this seat taken?" I ask. Jesse is wearing jeans and an orange T-shirt with a picture of a wizard in a cape and a pointy hat catching a football. Below it is a caption that reads, "Fantasy Football." I swear, he's so cute I can't even stand it.

He grins at me. "Yeah, it's for my girlfriend." *Oh my God, he just called me his girlfriend.* In my head, I jump up and down. "So where's your posse?" he asks, as we sit down next to each other.

I sigh. "Lindsay is hiding out in the bathroom because she was too embarrassed to come into the cafeteria today."

Jesse's face turns serious. "I saw that email. Is she okay?"

"Not really. She's pretty upset about it."

"She shouldn't be," he says. "Everyone knows that Megan is insecure and that she tries to hide it by being ridiculously mean."

"Yeah, well, try telling that to Lindsay."

He nods. "What about Samantha?"

I shake my head. "I don't know. I haven't seen or heard from her since Saturday night. I know she made it home after the concert, because I called her house last night and her mom said that she couldn't talk. But I'm really starting to worry about her. It's not like her to go AWOL."

Jesse reaches over and takes my hand. "You're a good friend," he says.

I smile at him as the now-familiar lightning bolts shoot down my legs. "So, last museum trip today," I say, trying to change the subject. I don't want to talk about Lindsay and Samantha anymore. I'm afraid I might say something that I shouldn't. "Have you thought about which painting we should choose?"

Jesse pauses. "I don't know…but I think the time period should definitely be modern. Something post–World War II, for sure. Maybe even something from this decade. I think it'll really round out our presentation." As he's talking he looks up, as if he's just noticed something, and I turn around to see what it is that's caught his eye.

It's Samantha.

She's wearing black jeans, a black T-shirt with extra-long sleeves that almost entirely cover her hands, and a pair of huge dark sunglasses that dwarf the rest of her face. If I didn't know better, I'd think she was in mourning. Something is different about her, though. I try to figure out what it is, and then I realize: she looks short. Well, as short as a five-foot, eight-inch person can look. I look down at her feet and notice that she's wearing black flats. Yup. That's what it is. Samantha never wears flats. She says they make her calves looks stubby. I get a sinking feeling in my stomach. If Samantha is wearing flats, then something must be really wrong.

"Are you okay?" I ask. "Didn't you get any of my messages? I've been so worried about you."

She plops dramatically into the chair next to me, and rests her chin on her hands.

"I'm sorry. I got grounded. They took away my cell phone and my laptop. I wasn't allowed to leave my room the whole day yesterday."

"Grounded? For what?"

Samantha pushes her sunglasses up on top of her head and rolls her eyes. "I didn't get home Saturday night until three in the morning. My mom wouldn't have even noticed, but Lucinda ratted me out."

"Who's Lucinda?" Jesse asks.

"Her housekeeper," I tell him. "She's lived with them since before Samantha was born."

"She always says she loves me like I'm her own child," Samantha grumbles. "Some love. I mean, it's not like I just showed up three hours late. I called her. I called her and I told her that I got a ride and that she didn't need to pick me up. I told her to just go to bed. But she was sitting in the living room with the lights off when I got home, all angry and tapping her foot and cursing at me in Portuguese. And then the next morning she told my parents."

"What were you doing until three in the morning?" I ask, mystified.

She sighs, pulling her sunglasses back down over her eyes. "It's a nightmare. I don't even want to talk about it."

"Are you kidding? You have to tell me what happened!" I lower my voice. "I need to know."

"Okay, fine. I went home with Aiden, you know that. So anyway, we got to his house, and he goes in through the front door so that his parents know that he's home, and he tells me to go around the side of the house to the basement window. So I wait there for him for, like, ten minutes while he kisses his mom good night or something stupid like that, and then he opens the window and tells me to climb through. Climb through! In platform boots!"

Jesse and I sneak a glance at each other and he flashes an amused smile. With my eyes, I tell him, *welcome to my world*.

"So anyway, his *bedroom* is down there, which I totally did not know. I mean, I thought it was, like, a rec room or something, with a couch. But the next thing I know we're in his bed, fooling around, and he's telling me how hot I am and how sexy I am, and how he wants to be with me and go out with me, blah, blah, blah, and then suddenly, Trance is crawling through the window, screaming at him that he's a bastard."

Oh my God. That really *is* a nightmare. "So what happened?"

She hesitates. "You can't tell anyone."

"Who am I going to tell? I only talk to you and Lindsay!"

"Not you. Him." She points at Jesse.

"I won't tell anyone," he says, holding up two fingers. "I swear." She looks at me for verification.

"He won't," I insist. "He's very trustworthy."

Samantha chews on a dark purple fingernail as she considers it. "I need you to tell me something embarrassing," she says finally.

Jesse looks confused. "I'm sorry, what?"

"Tell me something embarrassing about yourself. So I have leverage, in case you ever think about going informant on me."

Jesse looks at me, flabbergasted. "Is she serious?"

"Unfortunately, she is."

Jesse rolls his eyes upward, trying to think of something. "Okay…how about this: I listen to Barry Manilow sometimes. I actually think 'Copacabana' is kind of a good song. Is that embarrassing enough for you?"

Samantha and I both stare at him, fish-eyed, and Samantha giggles. "Oh my God, you two are made for each other."

Jesse looks at me for an explanation, but I wave my hand at him. "Forget it," I say quickly, before Samantha can explain. I turn back to her. "Can you finish the story now, please?"

"Okay. Where was I?"

"Trance was crawling through the window, calling Aiden a bastard…"

"Oh, right. Anyway, so Aiden starts yelling at me to get the hell out of his room, like it had all been my idea. Like I had jumped him against his will. And I'm, like, are you kidding me? Did you not just have your hand down my—?" She looks guiltily at Jesse. "Sorry."

"Don't worry about offending me," he says.

I can't stand it anymore. I blurt out my own ending. "And then Trance told him to go to hell and she left, right?" I ask anxiously. "And he apologized to you, and told you that he wanted you to be his girlfriend?"

Samantha and Jesse both look at me like I'm crazy.

"No," Samantha says. "He told me to get out and never speak to him again, and he got down on his hands and knees and begged Trance to forgive him. And then I walked two miles in those stupid boots, until my feet were, like, one giant blister, and when I couldn't take the pain anymore I sat down on a bus bench and called a taxi."

My shoulders droop and I hunch over in my seat. Oh. Well, I guess that explains the flats, at least.

Jesse clears his throat and stands up. "I'm…um, gonna get a bottle of water," he stammers. "Do you want anything?"

"No thanks." I try to smile, but I feel dizzy and sick to my stomach. He tilts his head and looks at me like he's trying to figure out what's wrong, and as his eyes search mine, I manage to eke out a small fake grin.

"Okay," he says, unconvinced. "I'll be right back."

When he's gone, Samantha lowers her voice to a whisper.

"You can spare me the 'I told you so,' but I think you were right about that clue," she admits. "It must be some sort of defense mechanism, so nobody can force you to ask it things against your will. Remember how it said that other voices will be disappointed? I think it means that if you ask a question for someone else, it's going to backfire on them. I mean, think about it: it's almost like the ball did to me exactly what I had wished on Trance. Like, I asked it if he would ditch her to hook up with me and become my boyfriend, and it worked. But then he ditched me to hook up with her, and now he's her boyfriend again."

I close my eyes as I try to process this. "So, you're saying that if someone tries to make me use the ball for them, then whatever they wish on someone else is also going to happen to them?"

Samantha nods. "That's what it seemed like to me."

My heart jumps into my throat, and I push my chair back so hard that the metal legs make a loud, screeching noise on the cafeteria floor.

"I've gotta go," I say frantically. "I've got to go find Lindsay."

"Why?" she asks. "What's going on? Erin!"

I ignore her as I speed-walk toward the door of the cafeteria, but before I'm even halfway across the room, I see the principal, the vice principal, and Mrs. Newman, the geometry teacher, standing in the doorway, scanning the room with serious, stern looks on their faces.

I freeze. *Oh no*, I think. *Oh no*.

Samantha catches up to me and grabs the back of my shirt. "What is going on?" she asks. "Why are you acting so weird?"

I don't answer her. I just keep my eyes on the three adults in the doorway. Suddenly, Mrs. Newman points across the room, and I watch as they walk determinedly through the cafeteria. Samantha has seen them too by now, as has most everyone else, and the volume level suddenly drops. We watch as they stride to the far corner of the room, heading straight for Megan Crowley.

"Oh my God," Samantha whispers. "You didn't."

I blink, hard, trying not to cry as I nod to her that I did.

Twenty-Five

I can't find Lindsay before the bell rings, and when I walk into physics the whole room is buzzing about how Megan Crowley was escorted out of the cafeteria by the principal, the vice principal, and Mrs. Newman. I quietly sit down at my desk, trying to eavesdrop on what people are saying about it.

"I heard it was drugs," says Lizzie McNeal. "Someone told me that she's been growing pot in her basement for two years."

"No, I heard she was running a gambling ring out of the garage where they keep the driver's ed cars," says Cole Miller. "High stakes poker. Twenty bucks a hand. And I heard that Brittany Fox, Madison Duncan, and Chloe Carlyle were the dealers. And that they wore bikinis."

"That's stupid," argues Matt Shipley. "She got busted giving a blow job to a basketball player in the boys' locker room. I heard she does it every day after third period."

"Well, either way, she's outta here," Lizzie replies. "She'll definitely be suspended. Maybe even expelled."

Just then Mrs. Cavanaugh walks in, and everyone scatters to their desks.

"Good afternoon. Take out your homework and pass it forward, please." She picks up a piece of chalk and turns to the blackboard. "Today we are going to start a new unit on wave-particle duality. Based on your reading over the weekend, can anyone tell me what wave-particle duality is?"

Mrs. Cavanaugh's voice sounds like it's light years away from me. All I can hear is Samantha. *It's almost like the ball did to me exactly what I had wished on Trance.*

Oh my God. I have to warn Lindsay. I have to.

I bend down and take a pencil out of my backpack, and pick up my phone at the same time, pushing it up my sleeve. Mrs. Cavanaugh glances at me, and I make a big show of switching pencils and putting the old one away. When she turns back around to write on the board, I slide the phone out from my sleeve and rest it on my upper thigh, then lean over the desk, just like Samantha showed me in the cafeteria. I pretend to be taking notes with my right hand, and with my left hand I push the buttons on the phone.

911. U have 2 leave school. Now. Will explain l8r.

I glance up at the board, but Mrs. Cavanaugh isn't standing there anymore. My eyes dart from side to side, looking for her, and I realize that everyone is staring at me. Slowly, I turn my head to my left.

"Give me the phone, please," Mrs. Cavanaugh says quietly.

I swallow, and my skin gets as hot as if I've just spent a summer's day at the beach with no sunscreen. Without saying anything, I hand Mrs. Cavanaugh my phone. She glances at the text message that I haven't finished sending yet, then slips my phone into the pocket of her sweater. "I'll see you in detention after school."

When class is over, I wait for everyone to leave, and then I go up to Mrs. Cavanaugh's desk. My heart is pounding in my chest, but I don't feel like I'm going to cry this time. I feel hardened, somehow, like a criminal with prior convictions.

"Yes?" she asks. Her tone is cool, like she's angry with me.

"Um, I just wanted to apologize for what happened today. I know I told you that it wouldn't happen again, but this really was an emergency, I swear. Not that that's an excuse or anything. I just wanted to tell you that I'm sorry."

Mrs. Cavanaugh purses her lips and looks down her nose at me. "No, it's not an excuse. I'm disappointed in you, Erin. I gave you the benefit of the doubt last time, and you took advantage of me."

"I know," I say. "I know, and I'm really sorry." I hesitate, scared to ask her what I came for. But I have to. "Um, about detention today. I know I have to do it, but is there any way that I could do it tomorrow instead? Or Wednesday? It's just, I have this presentation for AP Art History that's due Wednesday morning, and I'm supposed to go to the museum after school today with my partner to work on it, and it counts for, like, thirty percent of our grade."

Mrs. Cavanaugh appears unmoved by my predicament. "Detention isn't meant to be convenient, Erin. Your homework is not my problem. It's yours. And you should have thought about it before you violated the rules. I'll see you after school *today*. End of discussion. And you can have your phone back at the end of the week."

Of course. Because things weren't already bad enough.

I find Jesse in the hallway before last period.

"Where have you been?" he asks. "I've been calling you all afternoon."

"Mrs. Cavanaugh took my phone," I tell him. "And even worse than that is she gave me detention. For today."

Jesse's face drops. "But you can't today. Did you tell her we need to go to the museum?"

"She didn't care. She said detention isn't meant to be convenient."

Jesse looks up at the ceiling. I can tell he's annoyed with me. "Why were you texting in class? That's so stupid."

"I know. But I swear, it was an emergency. I have to find Lindsay. Have you seen her anywhere?"

"No. But what's going on? You were acting weird at lunch, and then you ran off without even saying good-bye when I went up to get water. Are you mad at me about something?"

I can feel my eyes welling up with tears. I want to just fall into his arms and tell him everything, but I can't. First of all, he wouldn't even believe me, and second of all, it would take hours to explain this mess. Hours that I do not have right now.

"No. I'm not mad at you at all. You have to believe me, this has nothing to do with you. I just really have to find Lindsay." I start walking backward, still talking to him as I go. "We'll go to the museum tomorrow, I promise. And if I have to stay up until midnight working on the presentation myself, I will. I have to go." I turn around and run down the hallway before he can get a word in, trying to hold back my tears.

I finally find her in the parking lot after school.

"Oh my God," Lindsay whispers to me. "Did you hear? She got escorted out of the cafeteria. She cheated on a test or something. I heard she's going to be expelled." Her face is ghostly white, and she looks like she's been crying.

"Lindsay, I have to tell you something. It's important."

She looks past me like she doesn't even hear me, and I notice that her hands are shaking. "I thought it would feel good," she says. "I thought I would be happy. But I'm not. I feel horrible." Her voice catches, and her eyes fill up with tears. The blue of her irises seems duller, almost gray. "I've totally ruined her life. For real."

"Lindsay, listen. I talked to Samantha. She figured—"

"Hey, Lindsay," says Chris Bollmer, interrupting me as he approaches. He's wearing the same black hoodie that he always wears, but he looks different, and after a second or two, I realize that it's because he's smiling. I don't think I've ever seen him smile before. "Did you hear about Megan Crowley?" he asks, not even trying to hide the glee in his voice. "I was in the principal's office when they brought her in. I heard the whole thing. She's been stealing math tests off of Mrs. Newman's computer all year long. She knew her password and everything." He laughs. "You must be pretty happy, huh?" I glance at Lindsay's gray watery eyes and tear-stained face, and I wonder if he's looking at the same person that I am.

"No, Chris," Lindsay barks at him. "I'm not happy, okay? Why don't you just go drink some more of your haterade and leave me alone."

Chris's smile disappears and his face turns dark. "You said we could be friends if Megan ever left school. And now Megan is leaving school, so you should be my friend."

Lindsay's words come out loud and harsh, like she's pressed the Caps Lock button on her voice. "Get this through your head, Chris: I am not your friend. I don't want to be your friend. Okay?"

Chris gives her a scary glare, the same one he used on Megan when she was teasing them in the cafeteria.

"You don't want to do this, Lindsay," he warns.

But Lindsay just throws up her hands, exasperated. "Yes, I do. Look, I get it that you thought we had something in common because of Megan, but now Megan is leaving. So we really don't have anything else to talk about. Now please, I'm trying to have a conversation here."

Chris narrows his eyes and stuffs his hands into his pockets, then turns and walks away, muttering something under his breath that I can't quite hear.

I stare at Lindsay, shocked.

"Don't you think that was kind of harsh?" I ask.

She looks at me as if to say that I can't be serious. "It's not like he takes a hint," she answers, defensively. "Didn't you hear him?"

"He's just trying to be nice to you. You didn't have to be so mean."

Lindsay's eyes fill up again, and she gets a hurt look on her face. "I'm not mean! God, don't you think I'm feeling bad enough today? Do you really have to take Chris Bollmer's side?"

I can see that this is going nowhere, and I still haven't even told her about what happened to Samantha.

"I'm sorry, okay. I just—listen, this isn't important. I need to tell you something. Samantha didn't hook up with Aiden on Saturday night. I mean, she did, but, well, in the middle, Trance showed up, and Aiden kicked Samantha out. Anyway, the point is, I was right about that clue. It's not okay for me to ask things for other people. It backfires on them." I swallow hard and look down at the floor. "It's going to backfire on you."

Lindsay looks confused. "What do you mean, backfire?"

I have a knot in my stomach, and I'm scared to tell her. I know she's going to freak out. I take a deep breath and exhale. "Okay, follow me here for a second. Samantha said it seemed like what she asked to happen to Trance also happened to her."

"What do you mean?"

"I mean, Samantha asked if Aiden would ditch Trance at the concert, hook up with her, and then become her boyfriend."

"And?"

"And, what happened was that he *did* ditch Trance and hook up with Samantha, and he *did* say that he wanted to be her boyfriend. But then afterward, he ditched Samantha to hook up with Trance, and now he's Trance's boyfriend again. So you see, Samantha got what she asked for, but then she also got to be on the other end of it too."

Lindsay's face turns red as she follows the logic. "So, you're saying that because I asked for Megan to get kicked out of school, then I'm going to get kicked out of school also?"

I close my eyes and nod.

"Are you kidding me?" she yells, her Caps Lock voice turned on again. "How could you do this to me? This is all *your* fault!"

"*My* fault?" I ask, turning on a Caps Lock voice of my own. "How is this *my* fault? You're the one who ordered me to get the ball. You're the one who cried and begged me to ask it for you."

"You should have stopped me! You knew you didn't know what the clue meant! You knew it wasn't right! And you did it anyway! You treated me like a guinea pig. Like one of your stupid science experiments!"

I just stare at her, too stunned to say anything. I can't even believe that she's turning this around on me. I knew it was a bad idea, but I *told* her that. I put my hand on her arm. "Lindsay," I say calmly, trying to smooth things over.

She shakes my hand off of her. "No! Don't touch me." She picks up her bag and runs off, leaving me standing there, alone. The tears are welling up in my eyes again. I can't believe this. Lindsay and I have been best friends for ten years, and we've never been in a fight before. Not once. First detention, then Jesse, and now this. I look up at the sky.

Thanks a lot, Aunt Kiki, I think. *Your stupid ball is ruining my life.*

I turn around and walk back inside, trying to calm myself down as I make my way to the detention room.

Being not boring is so totally overrated.

Twenty-Six

Lindsay isn't at school the next day. After homeroom, Samantha and I meet outside of our lockers.

"Being grounded sucks," she complains. "I'm, like, a full twenty-four hours behind in the news cycle. And I never realized how much I rely on technology as a way of not having to talk to my mother. I swear, that woman is driving me crazy. She keeps asking me if I had sex on Saturday night."

I'm drinking from a bottle of water, and I almost choke mid-sip as she says it. I can't imagine my mother asking me if I had sex. I can't imagine my mother even *saying* the word sex. "What did you tell her?"

"I told her that I can't remember because I did too many drugs." We both laugh. "Seriously, though, have you talked to Lindsay?" Samantha asks. "What did she say?"

I sigh. "I talked to her after school yesterday. She said it's all my fault and that I should have stopped her, and then she ran away. And I couldn't go after her because I had to go to detention. Which was horrible, by the way. Everyone in there was a repeat offender except for me, and they were all staring at me like I was from another planet. I felt like that song from Sesame Street. *One of these things is not like the other*," I sing.

"Please don't sing," Samantha requests, glancing around to see if anyone heard me. "What about after? Did you call her when you got home?"

"No," I say indignantly. "She *screamed* at me. In a Caps Lock voice. *She* should have called *me* last night."

"You're so stubborn," she says, shaking her head. "You told her she was going to get kicked out of school, for God's sake. You know she always takes things out on people when she's upset."

"I know, but you weren't there. This wasn't like normal. She was really mad at me. She actually thinks this is my fault."

Samantha lowers her voice. "Well, can you fix it? I mean, can't you ask the ball to undo what it did?"

"I don't know." I did think of that last night. I sat with the ball in my hand for almost an hour, daring myself to ask it. But I was too scared. What if it backfired again? I kept thinking about what Lindsay had said, about me treating her like a science experiment. "I didn't want to do anything without talking to Lindsay first."

"Well, then talk to her. Let's go to her house after school today. I'll go with you."

"I can't. I have to go to the museum with Jesse. Our Art History presentation is due tomorrow, and I couldn't go yesterday because of detention. Plus, he keeps saying that I'm acting weird, and he thinks I'm mad at him…" I let my sentence trail off because I can feel a lump of self-pity forming in my throat, and I don't want to start crying right before first period. "Everything suddenly became a huge mess."

"All because of the ball," Samantha says sympathetically.

I nod at her.

"This is why people like me should not venture outside of the box," I say, recovering my voice. "It's just too unpredictable out there."

At lunch, Samantha and I sit with Jesse again. But it's different today, knowing that Lindsay is mad at me, and that Jesse is annoyed with me. The three of us are more or less silent as we eat. The awkwardness between me and Jesse is back again, and it feels like it did when we were in the car Saturday night, after the concert. When we met up in the cafeteria, there was no kiss on the cheek like yesterday.

A few tables over, Brittany Fox, Madison Duncan, and Chloe Carlyle are huddled together, their faces serious. I wonder if they're even upset about Megan getting kicked out of school. I wonder if right now they're trying to decide which one of them should be boss now that Megan is gone.

"What are you thinking about?" Jesse asks me suddenly.

I look up, surprised by the sound of his voice, and I can tell from the look on his face that he's trying to make things normal between us again. I give him an embarrassed smile, and hook my thumb over in the direction of Megan's groupies.

"I was just wondering which one of them is going to be the new Megan," I say. Jesse and Samantha turn around in their chairs.

"Twenty bucks says Brittany," Samantha wagers.

Jesse shakes his head. "I don't know. I'm putting my money on Madison," he says. "Brittany's the obvious choice, but I like an underdog."

Samantha laughs, then leans forward conspiratorially. "I heard Megan's denying everything. She says she never touched Mrs. Newman's computer. But apparently, Mrs. Newman has proof. Megan emailed the tests to an account that was supposed to be anonymous, but Mrs. Newman was able to trace it back to her. Incidentally, it was the same account that Megan used to email that picture of Lindsay to everyone."

Jesse's eyes widen. "How do you know this?" he asks, amazed.

Samantha beams, pleased that she's impressed someone new with her ability to score prime gossip.

"She's an information ninja," I tell him.

"That's right," she confirms. "And do you know what else I heard? I heard that Megan is having some kind of allergic reaction to all of the stress, and she's broken out in huge red hives all over her face."

Jesse shakes his head in wonderment. "Amazing," he declares. "If only you could apply that gift to something useful."

"I know," she laments. "People say that to me all the time."

When lunch is over, Jesse and I steal a moment alone together outside the cafeteria.

"Are we cool?" he asks. "Because I feel like there's a tension between us or something."

"I know. I'm sorry. I'm just upset because Lindsay and I got in a fight, and because I got detention, and I still haven't written my essay for the Italy trip, and we have to work on our presentation, and I'm just so stressed out. But it's not you, I swear. You're the only good thing in my life right now."

He smiles and his eyes crinkle at the corners, just the tiniest bit. It reminds me of my dad's eyes, and I wonder if my mom's stomach used to flip over like an omelet every time he looked at her, the way mine does whenever Jesse looks at me.

"Just relax," he says, resting his hand on the waistband of my jeans, just above my right hip. "Everything will work out." He leans down and kisses me gently on the forehead. "I have a dentist appointment during last period today, but I'll pick you up at your house at three-thirty and we'll go to the museum. And then I was thinking we could get some pizza and work on the presentation. Does that sound good?"

"It sounds amazing."

After school, I call Lindsay on her cell phone. She doesn't answer, so I leave a message.

"Lindsay, it's me. Listen, I'm really sorry about yesterday. I know you're freaked out, but please don't be mad at me. I've been thinking, maybe we can ask the ball to undo everything. Maybe it will work. But I don't want to do it without talking to you first. I know you're not a science experiment. You're...you. So please call me, okay?"

When I hang up, I stand in front of the full-length mirror on my closet door and examine myself.

I'm wearing old jeans and an even older T-shirt, and my long, boring brown hair is hanging limply against the sides of my face, causing me to look like a Cocker Spaniel, except that Cocker Spaniels are cute and I'm...I sigh.

Even I know that this is not an acceptable way to go out with one's boyfriend, even if it is just to go to the art museum and Nick's Pizza.

I go into my closet and change into ten or twelve different outfits, finally settling on a pair of black leggings, a white tank top, and a dark gray ripped V-neck boyfriend T-shirt that Samantha left here the last time she slept over. I slip on a pair of silver ballet flats and a long silver necklace to complete the ensemble, then spend five minutes teasing my hair a little at the crown. I put some clear gloss on my lips and rub some blush onto my cheeks, then stand back to take myself in.

Not bad, I think. Samantha would definitely approve.

The phone rings and I glance at the clock: three seventeen. I look at the caller ID: it's Lindsay. Thank God.

"Hi! Where were you today? We missed you."

"Erin, it's not Lindsay. It's me, Carol."

Oh. Why is Lindsay's mom calling me?

"Sorry," I say quickly. "I saw the caller ID and I thought it was her."

"So she's not with you?" she asks. I can hear an undercurrent of worry in her voice.

"No. Why? What's going on?"

"I don't know. I was hoping you could tell me. I don't know where she is. She left this morning to go to school, but then the school secretary called this afternoon and said that Lindsay didn't show up today. And Erin, she said that Lindsay is in some kind of trouble, and that the principal would like to see both of us first thing tomorrow morning. She wouldn't say why. Do you know anything about this?" Her voice breaks. "I won't be mad at her, whatever it is. I just want to make sure she's okay. Do you know where she is?"

My heart begins to pound wildly. It's happening. It's really happening. I glance at the ball, sitting innocently on my desk. I should have asked it to undo all of this yesterday, before it was too late.

"I don't know what's going on," I lie. "But I think I might know where she is. But listen, Mrs. Altman, let me go find her, okay? I promise I'll call you as soon as I have her."

"Are you sure? I could drive you, it would be faster."

"No. Really, it's better that I do this myself."

I hang up the phone and look at the clock again. Three twenty-one. Damn. I pick up the phone and dial Jesse's cell phone number. Come on, come on, pick up.

"Hey, this is Jesse. Wait for it…"

Damn.

"Jesse, it's me," I say after the beep. "Listen, there's been a little emergency and I have to run out for a few minutes, but I'll meet you at the museum. Sorry." I hang up and quickly stuff the ball into my backpack, then run down the stairs. My mom is at the table, poring over legal books, just as she has every afternoon since my aunt died.

"I'm going to Samantha's," I tell her. "Don't wait for me for dinner, I have to work on a project. Love you, 'bye!" I'm out the door and on my bike before she even has a chance to look up.

By the time I get to Samantha's house, I'm sweating and the hair around my face is damp and frizzy. I stand in front of the massive wooden double doors and ring the doorbell impatiently. After two seconds, I ring it again, and then a third time. Finally, Lucinda opens the door. She's huffing and out of breath.

"Erin!" she shouts, exasperated. "Why do you ring the bell so much? You know this house is big and my legs are not so long. It takes me time."

"Sorry," I say. "Can I talk to Samantha?"

Lucinda cocks an eyebrow at me, just like Samantha does. I wonder if she learned it from Samantha, or if Samantha learned it from her.

"Samantha is in her room. She's grounded, you know."

I widen my eyes innocently. "Didn't she tell you about the school project?"

Lucinda eyes me suspiciously. "What school pro-yect?" she asks in her thick Portuguese accent.

"We have a research project due in English tomorrow. We're supposed to go to the library today."

She thinks about this for a minute, then nods. "Anyone else, I would not believe, but I know you and you are a good girl. I bet you don't come home three hours late and scare your mama half to death." She turns around and calls up toward the staircase. "Samantha! Erin is here to work on the pro-yect!"

I hear footsteps above, and then Samantha emerges at the top of the stairs.

"The project, riiiight," she says, as she walks down the steps. "Sorry, I thought that was tomorrow. But I can go now. Not a problem. It's not like I have anything else to do, right, Lucinda?"

Lucinda wags her finger at her. "That's not my fault, lady. You're the one who come home three hours late, not me."

Samantha blows her a kiss. "Later, Lucinda!" she yells as we walk out the front door.

Once we're outside on the front porch, Samantha narrows her eyes at me. "Isn't that my shirt?" she asks.

"Didn't I just get you out of your house?" I shoot back.

"Yes," she concedes, looking me up and down. "But I want it back. It's cute." She rubs her hands together excitedly. "So where are we going? I thought you had to meet Jesse at the museum."

"I do," I say wistfully. "But first we have to make a stop at Ye Olde Metaphysical Shoppe."

She raises one eyebrow. "Seriously? Why?" I tell her about the phone call from Erin's mom, and she nods understandingly.

"Come on, get your bike," I urge.

"Nah," she says. She reaches into her purse and pulls out a set of keys. "I think I'll drive."

I stare at her. "You don't have a license," I remind her.

"Actually, I do. I've had it for three months. I just didn't tell anyone because I didn't want Aiden to stop driving me to school. But that ship has sailed, so…" She pushes a button on her key chain and one of the automatic doors on the three-car garage opens to reveal a red BMW convertible with a white leather interior.

"You're kidding," I say with disbelief. "You didn't drive *this* because of *Aiden?*"

Samantha shrugs. "What can I say? I was under hotness hypnosis."

I open the passenger side door and get in, the smell of new leather overpowering my nose. "Well, thank God you snapped out of that."

Twenty-Seven

"You realize you're not going to make it to the museum, right?" Samantha asks. We're inching along the main road in town, one of a long snake of cars waiting to get past the construction on the side of the road, where a crew is feverishly working to repair a burst water main.

"I know. This is a nightmare." Instinctively, I reach into my bag for my cell phone, groaning as I remember that Mrs. Cavanaugh still has it until Friday. "Can I have your phone? I have to call Jesse. He's going to be so mad at me."

But Samantha shakes her head. "I'm grounded, remember? No cell phone."

Oh my God. I feel disconnected, like a baby whose umbilical cord has just been cut. I throw my hands up in the air in frustration. "How did our parents ever get through high school without cell phones?"

"I know. Could you imagine? It's so primitive. I mean, they actually had to, like, make plans and stick to them, or else their friends would think they flaked." She nudges me, one hand on the wheel, and smirks. "Kind of like what Jesse is going to think about you."

"Thank you. That helps." The traffic is making me feel trapped and panicky, and I'm trying to focus on breathing in through my nose and out through my mouth, the way our P.E. teacher taught us to do when we had our unit on yoga first semester. But the alarms going off in my brain don't seem to be responding to the increased flow of oxygen. "You don't understand," I tell Samantha. "It's not just about Jesse. Our presentation is *tomorrow*. If I don't work on it tonight, I will never get an A minus, and I have to get an A minus or else my GPA won't be high enough to qualify me for the Italy trip."

Samantha shrugs. "So then, get yourself an A minus," she says, like it's nothing.

"Did you not hear what I just said?" I move my hands around like I'm speaking sign language. "I can't get an A minus if I don't work on the presentation."

"Uh, yes you can." She glances at my backpack, which is lying on the floor between my feet, and suddenly I understand what she's getting at.

A slow smile spreads across my face. "You are a genius."

Samantha sighs, like she's heard it a million times before. "I know. And someday, the world will know too."

I unzip my backpack and take out the ball, giving it a

quick shake. I take a deep breath, exhaling slowly, and then stare at the window.

"Will I get an A minus on my AP Art History presentation tomorrow, even if I don't work on it tonight?" I press my lips together as I wait for the answer to make its way through the pink, sparkly liquid.

It is inevitable.

I kiss the ball, making a loud *mwah* sound. Samantha looks at me, giving me her famous one-eyebrow raise.

"Looks like all is forgiven," she says.

"Maybe." I wag my finger at the ball, imitating Lucinda. "But screw up one more time, lady, and I'm going to put you in a yuicer!"

We both giggle, and finally the traffic begins to break up in front of us, like a giant hairball getting pulled, slowly, out of a clogged drain.

Samantha and I enter Ye Olde Metaphysical Shoppe to the sound of a tinkling bell. The place is (not surprisingly) deserted. The walls are lined with dark bookshelves bursting with spiritual and self-help books, and spread out around the store are display tables crowded with (real) crystal balls, stacks of tarot cards, candles and incense sticks, aromatherapy fragrances, potions, primitive wooden masks, statues, and dolls...including one that looks just like the

Megan Crowley voodoo doll that Lindsay bought. In the back of the store, close to the counter, are shelves lined with dozens of different kinds of crystals and stones and jewelry, each claiming to heal various physical and spiritual ailments.

I shake my head. I feel like I have now taken up permanent residence in Weirdville.

"Hello?" I call. "Is anyone here?" I try to peek behind the counter, into the back room, but there's a long, beaded curtain blocking the view. I look at Samantha and shrug. "Maybe they're in the bathroom," I suggest.

We walk around the store, taking everything in.

"Listen to this," I say, grinning as I read a label under a stone called eudialyte. "'Promotes energies of sound waves to help with clairaudient abilities; a tuning fork of transmissions. Activates the fourth chakra, dispels jealousy.'"

Samantha joins me. "Oooh, look at this one," she says, picking up a light blue crystal. "It's kyanite. It opens the brow and throat chakras." She stands back and holds her arms out and away from her body, then closes her eyes and tilts her head back, balancing the crystal in the middle of her forehead. "Tell me, do my chakras look open to you?" I laugh as she places the crystal back on the shelf. "I just want to know one thing," she says. "Where do they keep the eye of newt?"

"Eye of newt is locked behind the counter," says a familiar voice behind us. We whirl around, and there, in front of me, is Roni, my aunt Kiki's best friend. "You can imagine how hard it is to come by, and we don't want anyone trying to steal it," she adds with a smile.

"Where did you—? How did—?" I'm so surprised to see her that I can't even complete a full sentence.

Samantha stares at me, her face crinkled with confusion. "Do you two *know* each other?" she asks.

I nod, still not quite recovered enough from the shock of it to speak.

"I'm Veronica," Roni says, holding out her hand to Samantha.

Finally, my voice lands back in my throat. "*You're* Veronica? I thought you said your name was Roni."

"My friends call me Roni. But at the store, I go by Veronica. It sounds more…you know, *metaphysical.*"

I can't tell if she's making fun of me or not, the way she emphasizes that last word. I can't believe any of this. *I've* been making fun of Veronica to Lindsay for almost a year, and the whole time she was best friends with my very own aunt.

"So you know Lindsay," I say. "Did you know she's my best friend?"

Veronica/Roni nods. "Not at first, but as Lindsay came in more and more and as she opened up to me about her life, I figured it out. Lindsay had no idea, of course, but Kate was thrilled about it. She used to pump me for information about you all the time. Kate, that is."

"She did?" I feel a sadness creep over me when she mentions Kiki's name. If she wanted to know about me so badly, why didn't she just call me?

"Wait a minute," Samantha interjects. "I'm sorry to break up your little reunion, but we came here looking for Lindsay. Have you seen her?"

Veronica/Roni points toward the curtain behind the counter just as Lindsay steps out from behind it.

"I'm here." Lindsay's face is bright red, and she looks down at the floor.

"Oh my God," I say, so relieved to see her that I almost start to cry.

"I'm sorry," she says, hurrying forward and giving me a hug. "I didn't mean what I said yesterday. I was just so upset."

"I know," I say, squeezing her in return. "It's okay. But your mom is worried sick about you. You have to tell her you're okay."

"I just talked to her. She told me that the principal's office called. They said I'm in trouble. It's the ball backfiring on me, isn't it? Do you think they're going to kick me out for cutting school today?"

Samantha makes a snorting sound. "No way. I cut school all the time. All they do is call your parents and then your mom promises to buy a new scoreboard for the football field or whatever, and that's it. It's really not a big deal." We all look at her, not really sure what to say, and then she blinks, realizing what just came out of her mouth. "But, I mean, I know other people who cut, and the worst that happens to them is a few days of detention. If you're going to get kicked out, it has to be for something more serious than that."

"Lindsay told me what happened," interrupts Veronica/ Roni. "With the ball."

"Okay. So can we fix it?" I ask eagerly.

"I think so," Roni says. Lindsay and I both close our eyes and let out a sigh of relief. "But you might have to use more than one question. How many do you have left?"

"Have left?" I look over at Lindsay to see if she knows what Roni is talking about, but she makes a don't-look-at-me face.

"You didn't figure out the clue?" Roni asks, surprised.

"I figured out all of the clues. Sort of. The only thing I didn't get was the part about the number. I just don't understand what that means."

"It means you only get eight yes answers," Roni explains. "'Let the planets be your guide to the number.' There are eight planets. Gosh, and Kate thought that one was the most obvious."

Of course. I groan. "How could I not have gotten that?"

"It's kind of ironic, isn't it?" Samantha asks, grinning. "I mean, for someone who's supposed to be so good at math, that's the one clue you miss?"

Lindsay shoots Samantha a look, and the grin disappears from Samantha's face.

"So how many have you asked?" Lindsay wants to know.

"I don't know. I didn't realize there was a limit. I wasn't keeping track." I hold up my fingers and start listing the questions that have come true. "Let's see, first there was Spencer Ridgely, then there was the one about my English paper…"

"Your boobs," Samantha adds.

"My boobs," I repeat, avoiding Roni's eyes as I stick a third finger up in the air.

"What was next?" Lindsay asks. "Samantha's question about Aiden?"

"Ummm, actually, there was one I didn't tell you guys about. There was one about Jesse asking me out on a date."

Samantha's mouth drops open.

"The concert? That was the ball?" I nod sheepishly, and Samantha gives me an I-can't-believe-you-didn't-tell-me-that look.

"Okay," Lindsay says impatiently. "Let's not get off track here. So there was Jesse, then Aiden," she says, holding up five fingers.

"Then Jesse again," Samantha reminds me. "Something about a kiss and a hot body?"

I blush as Veronica/Roni looks over at me, her eyebrows raised.

"That's six," Lindsay counts. "And then the one I asked about Megan. That's seven." She exhales. "Whew. We still have one left."

I look guiltily at Samantha, and she moves her eyes in Lindsay's direction, letting me know that I'd better say something.

"Um, actually, there might have been one more," I say.

Lindsay's face crumples. "What? What one more?"

"Well, you see, I was supposed to go to the museum with Jesse today, but I blew him off to come here instead. Only, my AP Art History presentation is due tomorrow, and since I didn't go to the museum I won't be able to get a good grade on it, and if I don't get a good grade then I can't go on the Italy trip...so when we were in the car I asked the ball if I would get an A minus on my presentation tomorrow." *The Italy trip*, I think, regretfully. *I didn't even get to ask it about the Italy trip*.

Lindsay blinks several times.

"I'm sorry," I say. "I had no idea it was the last question. I never would have asked it if I had known."

Lindsay shakes her head. "I know," she croaks. "It's not your fault. It's just that now there's no way to fix this. I'm going to get kicked out of school no matter what. And I don't even know what I did."

Roni puts her hands on her hips and looks at me. "Do you know what?"

I narrow my eyes at her. This is all her fault. If she had just talked to me when I called her and answered my questions, none of this ever would have happened.

"No," I say, my voice rising in anger. "I do not know what. But I'll tell you what I do know. I know that my best friend's life is a mess because of me. I know that the first boyfriend I've ever had is going to break up with me because I completely blew him off. I know that I've missed out on the chance to ask the ball the only question that I even cared about. Plus, my mother is a total wreck, and my aunt stopped speaking to me for a year and then left me a stupid ball that's completely ruined my entire life. But aside from that, no, Roni, or Veronica, or whatever your name is…I do not know *what*."

Roni nods sympathetically, and her eyes get glassy. "I think you're ready," she whispers.

Twenty-Eight

There's a surprisingly large room in the back of the store that is decorated like a cozy lounge area. There's a couch covered in dark purple velvet with lots of plush, comfy accent pillows, a chocolate-colored wood table with a few chairs around it, and on the floor is a huge, shaggy area rug that makes your feet feel like they're stepping on cotton balls. Roni explains that the store often hosts psychics, tarot card readers, and palm readers, and sometimes they have speakers and book signings back here, as well.

She tells me to take a seat on the couch, and then she disappears into a tiny office. When she comes out, she's holding two envelopes, along with a small black lacquer box inlaid with mother-of-pearl. One of the envelopes has my name on it, and the other has my mother's name. Both of them are in Kiki's handwriting.

"What's all this?" I ask.

"Kate's ashes," she says, pointing to the box. "Well, half of them, anyway. I kept the other half. They're for your mother. Kate wanted me to sit down with her and explain everything, but she was so agitated at the funeral, I knew she wouldn't listen. Then she called me a few times, but all she did was yell and threaten to sue me, and there was just no getting through to her."

I sigh. "My mom can be kind of difficult that way."

Roni smiles. "So I've heard. Anyway, I'm just going to give them to you, and you can give them to her. It's not what your aunt wanted, but I can't hold on to this negative energy anymore. It's really messing with my chi."

"And what about this?" I ask, holding up the envelope with my name on it.

"It's for you," she says. "Go ahead and read it."

I carefully open the envelope and take out three pieces of lined sheet paper, all filled with Kiki's handwriting. I feel a lump form in the back of my throat before I even get past the *Dear Erin* part.

Dear Erin,

If you're reading this, well, then, I suppose I'm gone, and you've figured out how to use the Pink Crystal Ball that I left you. So congratulations. (About the second part, not about me being gone.) Let me first say that I'm so sorry that I didn't get a chance to see you and talk to you over the last year. I never had children, but I have no doubt that I loved you the way I would have loved a child of my own. Which is why staying away from you was one of the most difficult things I have ever done in my life. I hope that after you read this you will understand why it was necessary.

Erin, I was diagnosed with a rare form of cancer just over a year ago. I met with several of the area's top doctors, and all of them agreed that I had six months to a year to live. I tried several treatments recommended by the holistic medical community, but none of them were strong enough to stop the spread of the tumors. I could have undergone chemotherapy and radiation, but the side effects are so unpleasant and debilitating, and there was no guarantee that they would work, or even that they would prolong my life by any significant amount of time. So I declined traditional treatments, and decided that I would rather spend the time I had left living my life to the fullest and dying naturally.

Erin, the reason I didn't tell you is because I knew that your mother would never have accepted this. Her mind is too rational, too logical, too different from my own. As a doctor, she would have insisted that I explore every medical option available, and I did not want to spend my precious, precious days arguing with her about it. I considered telling you and asking you not to share the information of my illness with her, but I didn't feel that it was fair to put you in that position. Instead, I made the impossible choice to cut off contact.

Some of the best days of my life, Erin, were spent on my front porch with you, solving puzzles together. But there were so many other things that I wanted to teach you about life, which is why I chose you to receive the Pink Crystal Ball.

You see, I wanted to open your eyes to the world the way that I see it. Full of possibilities and opportunities, and twists and turns, and not all laid out for you in little boxes, the way your mother sees it. Don't get me wrong: I love your mom. She's my sister, and a piece of my heart has always and will always belong to her. But I feel like she's missed out on so much of life because she can never see beyond those little boxes. It would be such a terrible shame if the same thing happened to you.

But you are a logical mind too. I knew that if I left you an explanation and a clear set of instructions for how to use the ball, you would have laughed it off as your crazy aunt Kooky (yes, I know about your father's nickname for me) just being kooky again. So I wrote the clues for you, knowing that you would not be able to resist a good puzzle, and knowing that as you saw your wishes coming true, you might really start to believe.

I hope that in using the ball you got some things that you really wanted, and I also hope that you made a big fat mess of everything. Because if there's anything that I would want you to take away from this experience, it's that life is at its best, and most interesting, when it's messy. Always remember that, Erin. It will serve you well, I promise.

I love you more than you can ever know, and I'm truly sorry if I caused you any pain over the last year. I hope you can understand and forgive me, and know that wherever I am in the afterlife, no matter who or what I become, I will find you, and I will look out for you always.

Much love,

Aunt Kiki

The tears are streaming down my face when I put the letter down.

Roni sits down next to me and hands me a tissue. I notice that she's crying too. She puts her arm around me and pulls me close, and I don't try to pull away from her. Just knowing that she was my aunt's best friend, knowing that she hurts as much as I do, is strangely comforting, in a way. We sit together like that for a few minutes while we both get out all of our tears, and then, finally, Roni turns to look at me.

"She asked the ball if she would die in that field," she tells me. "It was her final question."

So that's what she was doing out there in the middle of a storm. I try to imagine Kiki holding the ball, asking it if she will get struck by lightning.

"But why?" I ask.

Roni shrugs. Enveloped by the couch, she looks small and frail, and suddenly, I realize that she must have been there too, just like Samantha and Lindsay were there with me when I asked most of my questions. I revise the picture in my head, imagining Roni crying as she sat next to Kiki, imagining the discussions they must have had about it. I can picture Roni arguing and pleading with her not to ask the ball to end her life, and I can picture Kiki, stubborn as ever, telling her that nothing she says is going to change her mind. Poor Roni. I try to think about how I would feel if I lost Samantha or Lindsay, and just the thought of it makes me shudder.

"She knew the end was coming, and she didn't want to be a burden to anyone. Not that she would have been. But she didn't want to suffer. And this was easier than swallowing a bottle of pills, or sticking her head in an oven." She glances at me, a guilty look on her face. "Sorry. I didn't mean to be insensitive."

"It's okay," I tell her. "I can handle it."

Just then, Samantha's head pops out from behind the curtain. "Um, sorry to interrupt, but it's getting kind of boring out here. I mean, there are only so many things that I can make fun of before the amusement starts to wear off."

I smile at her, more appreciative than ever of my blunt, sarcastic best friend, and of her particular knack for knowing exactly when to interrupt a conversation. Because if I'm being totally honest, I'm not really sure that I *can* handle much more of this.

"That's okay," I say. "We're finished anyway."

As soon as I say it, Lindsay's head pops out too. "Finally," she adds. I let out a laugh. I'm so lucky to have her too. Even with all of the drama and the healing crystals and the voodoo dolls, there's nobody else I would rather have as my best friend. Nobody.

Lindsay looks at Roni crying, and at the letter in my hand, and the box on the table. A flicker of concern appears in her eyes.

"Are you two okay?" she asks. I glance at Roni, unsure how to answer. But she smiles at me, and somehow, I can tell she's thinking that I have great friends.

"Yes," she says, putting her hand on top of mine. "We're fine."

Lindsay nods. "Good. That's good." She hesitates, then finally asks what she's obviously been dying to know. "You didn't happen to discuss how you're going to get me out of being kicked out of school tomorrow, did you?"

I turn to Roni. "Are you sure I only get eight questions?" I ask. "I mean, isn't there a way to get just one more?"

She shakes her head. "Eight is the limit. But listen, you have to remember, the ball is just a tool. It doesn't control your destiny. *You* do."

As soon as I hear the word "destiny," the image of a man being eaten by a giant eagle flashes across my brain.

"Like Prometheus," I say absentmindedly. What was it that Jesse said? *Prometheus represents the triumph of the human spirit over those who try to repress it.*

Suddenly, I have an idea.

"Samantha, you said the ball did exactly to you what happened to Trance, right?"

"Yeah. Why?"

"Well, then maybe it's going to do the same thing to Lindsay. Maybe Lindsay is going to get kicked out of school for stealing tests, just like Megan did."

"But I didn't steal any tests," Lindsay argues.

"I know. But I'm starting to think that Megan didn't either." They both look at me quizzically. "Look, with every single thing that has happened, there's been a logical explanation. My boobs grew because of an allergic reaction to the dim sum. Jesse asked me on a date because we had a really good time at the museum. Aiden ditched Trance because Samantha had an extra backstage pass to meet the Flamingo Kids. And Spencer Ridgely said I was smexy because of that short skirt that I was wearing."

"No," Samantha says, shaking her head vehemently. "I wear short skirts all the time, and Spencer Ridgely has never said anything to me. I'm sorry, but that was just plain old magic."

I have to smile. "You're never going to let that go, are you?"

"Nope. Not ever."

I roll my eyes at her playfully. "Okay, whatever. My point is, everything that's happened can be explained somehow."

Samantha nods, catching on to my idea. "Right. And so can this. We just need to figure out what the logical explanation is, and then we need to stop it from happening."

"But how do we do that?" Lindsay asks. "We don't even know for sure what's going to happen."

"I think I have an idea," I say. "Lindsay, do you still have your voodoo doll of Megan Crowley?"

Lindsay nods. "Yeah, I keep it in my bag." She narrows her eyes at me. "What are you going to do?"

"You're just going to have to trust me. I think I know how to fix this, but I'm going to have to do it by myself. If I tell you, it will never work."

Twenty-Nine

I climb the front steps of Megan Crowley's house as Samantha's BMW peels out of the driveway. I watch Lindsay's hair, blowing out behind her. They turn the corner and her hand sticks up in the air, palm open, in a gesture of good-bye—and good luck.

I reach into my backpack for a red pen and quickly draw small dots on the face of Lindsay's voodoo doll before shoving it back into my bag. I knock on the door, and heavy footsteps approach as I nervously shift my weight from side to side on the straw welcome mat.

"Can I help you?" Megan's father asks, looking down at me. He's a big, tall, scary-looking dad. The kind of dad who would answer the door with a shotgun to greet his daughter's boyfriend.

"Um, hi, I'm Erin Channing. I'm a friend of Megan's. I was wondering if I could talk to her?"

Her dad frowns. "Does this have anything to do with that cheating nonsense?" he asks gruffly. "Because she didn't do anything. I know Megan, and she is not a cheater."

"No," I lie. "I just wanted to see how she's doing, and to let her know that everyone misses her at school."

His face softens a little, and he opens the door to let me in. "She's in her room. Top of the stairs, first door on the left."

⌒✳⌒

"Who is it?" Megan asks when I knock on the door.

"It's Erin Channing. I need to talk to you."

"I don't have anything to say to you," she shouts though the door.

Great. I knock again.

"Megan, please open the door. I have some information that I think you'll want to know."

There's a long pause, and then the door unlocks from the inside with a *click*. I push it open and walk into her room, which is typical-looking enough, except for the fact that there are posters of cats and dogs and kittens and puppies and bunnies and horses papering the walls, so that only a few patches of the purple paint color underneath are visible. *Okay*, I think. *I definitely was not expecting that.*

Megan is sitting on her bed, dressed in worn-looking sweatpants and a stretched-out T-shirt. Her hair is a mess and she's not wearing any makeup. Her eyes are bloodshot. Dotting her face are red splotchy hives, just like Samantha reported.

She eyes me as I look around at the animal posters.

"I want to be a vet," she explains defensively. "But if this goes on my record, I'll never get into a good college, and then I'll never get to go to veterinary school." She sniffles a little and wipes at her eyes, and I'm surprised that she's acting so vulnerable in front of me. I'm also surprised to learn that she wants to be a vet so badly. I guess I never considered that bullies have dreams too.

"By the way, I didn't steal those tests," she announces. "I was set up. And I wouldn't be surprised if Fart Girl had something to do with it, so you can tell her that my parents are hiring a lawyer."

"I'd appreciate it if you would call her Lindsay," I say. "And I know you didn't steal the tests. But you weren't set up either. There *is* another explanation."

Megan looks confused, hopeful, and suspicious all at the same time.

"Oh, yeah? And what's that?" she asks.

"Magic."

Megan's eyes well up with tears and she turns her back to me. "Okay, Harry Potter. Did you come here on a broomstick? You're not funny," she says, her voice breaking. "If you only came here to get back at me, then you can leave."

"I'm not joking." I take the voodoo doll out of my bag. "Look at this," I say, holding it up.

Megan crosses her arms in front of her chest and turns around, and from the impatient look on her face I know that she's expecting to see a snake jump out of a can, or some other stupid practical joke. But I just hold the doll, and try to muster the most serious face possible. I need for her to believe what I'm about to say, because if she doesn't, then my entire plan is worthless. My heart is pounding so hard I can hear it in my ears.

"And what is that?" she asks, irritated.

"It's you." She recoils the tiniest bit, and something in her expression changes, just slightly. "It's you," I repeat. "See the hair? And the cheerleading outfit? And do you see these dots on its face? Lindsay put them there three days ago. And look at that, you have dots on your face that look just like them."

Megan's eyes widen, and I can tell that I've got her attention now.

"I don't believe that. She can't make that happen." But her voice sounds unsure, like she's trying to convince herself of it.

"Actually, she can do a lot of things. Have you ever heard of Ye Olde Metaphysical Shoppe? It's run by a woman who claims she's a witch. It's where Lindsay gets her supplies. It's where she learned everything." Megan bolts up and grabs the phone by her nightstand.

"Okay, well, if she did this, then I'm going to tell. I'm calling the principal right now."

"Really?" I ask, fighting with every ounce of concentration I have to appear mildly amused. "And what are you going to say? That Lindsay Altman put a spell on a voodoo doll that made math tests appear in your email? Do you think he'll believe you?"

Slowly, Megan puts the phone back down. "No," she says. "Because it's ridiculous."

"I know," I say sympathetically. "I know it sounds that way. I thought the same thing, at first, too." I lower my voice to just above a whisper. "But it's real. I've seen what she can do."

Megan crosses her arms. "Oh, please."

I shrug. "Make fun of it all you want, but just think about it. Do you think it's a coincidence that this happened right after you sent out that email to our entire class? She wanted you kicked out of school. She wanted revenge." I pause for dramatic effect, and I watch Megan trying to process what I'm saying. I can see in her eyes that she's not sure whether to believe me or to kick me out, so I continue, hoping to capitalize on her confusion. "You're lucky, though, because she feels bad about it. She's such a good person, that after everything you've put her through, she still doesn't want you to suffer. Personally, I think she should just let you rot.

But Lindsay said no. She asked me to come here to tell you that she's willing to make things right for you again."

Megan looks skeptical. "She can get me back into school?"

"She can," I say. "But only on three conditions. First, you're going to send out an email to the entire tenth grade, publicly apologizing for all of the mean things you've said and done to her over the last two years."

"Wait a minute," Megan argues. "She's not exactly innocent, you know. She did something pretty bad to me too. She *humiliated* me."

I stare at her. "Megan, that was *seven* years ago. And yes, she humiliated you, but it was one day. You've been humiliating her for two years. I think you're even."

She seems to thinks about this, as if the idea has never before crossed her mind. She sits back down on her bed.

"What else?" she asks.

"Okay, well, second, you're going to call Chris Bollmer, and you're going to apologize to him too. And third—and listen carefully now, because this is important—you're going to personally guarantee that no one ever calls Lindsay 'fart girl' or even says the word 'fart' in Lindsay's presence ever again." I shrug, like it's no big deal. "If you can do that, then she'll make all of this go away."

Megan studies me for a minute, thinking it over. She's still not sure, I can tell.

"How do I know you're telling me the truth?" she finally asks. "How do I know she can really make these things happen?"

"You don't," I say, as I open the door to her bedroom and start to walk out. "That's the thing about magic. You either believe in it, or you don't. It's up to you."

When I get home, my mom is still sitting at the kitchen table, surrounded by legal books, just as she was when I left. I pull out a chair across from her and sit down. My body goes limp as soon as my butt hits the cushion, and I realize how physically—and mentally—exhausted I am. It's been (to say the least) an emotionally draining twenty-four hours. And it's not over yet. Not even close.

I reach into my backpack and take out the box and the envelope with my mom's name on it.

"Hi, honey," my mom says distractedly. But then she looks up and sees my face, and she frowns. "Is everything okay? You don't look like yourself."

"Mom, there's something I need to give you." I put the box and the letter on the table, and when she recognizes Kiki's handwriting on the envelope, she gasps.

"What's this?"

I let out a long sigh. "I ran into a friend of Aunt Kiki's today. It's a long story, but she asked me to give you these.

It's Kiki's ashes. Well, half of her ashes. She kept the other half." I swallow hard, trying not to think about how upset she's going to be when she reads her letter. I didn't open it, but I assume that it explains everything, the same as mine did. "And I think you'll want to read the letter. There was one for me too."

A tear falls from my mom's eyes before they even have a chance to redden. It's as if I'm witnessing some sort of miraculous event dreamed up in a sci-fi movie: Uber-Rational Cybernetic Organism Experiences Emotion. I know she gets emotional and irrational (emphasis on the latter), but for some reason that lone teardrop makes me happy. My mom's love for Kiki is so deep that she has no control over it. I sit and watch her as she opens the envelope and begins to read. She smiles a few times, and even laughs once, and I wonder what Kiki could have written that was so funny.

When she puts the letter down, the tears are coming like rain, splashing onto the legal books on the table beneath her. She looks up at me and smiles through them, and puts her hand on top of mine.

"Thank you, honey," she manages. "Thank you for doing what I couldn't." She takes a shaky breath and lets it out slowly, wiping the tears away with the back of her hand. "I'm just so glad to know that I didn't do anything. You have no idea how that's been haunting me, thinking that she died angry with me…" She pats my hand two times. "This means so much to me. Thank you."

"So no more digging through pictures in the guest room at two in the morning?"

She looks down sheepishly. "You heard that?"

I nod, eyeing the mess on the table. "Yeah. And as a sleep-deprived American teenager, I respectfully request, Counselor, that you refrain from engaging in such activities going forward."

She laughs and pushes aside the books and yellow pads with her forearm. "I guess I won't be needing these anymore."

"Thank God. I liked you much better as a pediatrician."

"You know something? I liked me much better as a pediatrician too." She looks at her watch, realizing how late it is. "Have you eaten yet? Do you want me to make you something?"

"No, that's okay. I'm not that hungry. And besides, I still have a ton of homework to do."

Upstairs in my room, I check my email. There's an alert that a new sender has been trying to contact me, BlackCrow16.

I click to allow the message, then open it.

Dear tenth grade class,

I'm writing to tell you two things. First of all, I would like to make it known that I did not steal any tests. I strongly believe that, in the next few days, my name will be cleared and I will be invited back to school. Second, I would like to sincerely apologize to my classmate, Lindsay Altman, for the mean and crude jokes that I have made at her expense over the last two years. I realize now that my actions were wrong, and I am truly sorry for any hurt that I have caused her. Lindsay is a very nice person, and she does not deserve the treatment that she received from me.

I hope to see you all again soon.

Sincerely,

Megan Crowley

So she bought it after all. Or maybe she didn't. Maybe she just figured that she didn't have anything to lose by trying. Either way, it worked. One down, one to go.

I click on "write message," and begin composing an email to Chris Bollmer. When I'm finished, I fill in the subject line: *I know things too.*

I hold my breath as I hit the send button, then let it out, exhausted.

Two down. Only one more thing to do.

I pick up my phone and dial Jesse on his cell, my stomach doing different kinds of flips from the ones it usually does when Jesse is involved. It goes straight to voicemail.

"This is Jesse. Wait for it…"

I wait for it, but when the beep comes, I have no idea what to say. What could I possibly say? I hang up.

I pull the covers up over my head, not even bothering to get undressed. It's dark and warm and comfy, and I already know that tomorrow, it's going to be very hard for me to get up. If I even sleep at all...

Thirty

Samantha and I both glance anxiously at Lindsay's empty desk during homeroom the next morning.

She and her mom arrived at school just before the first bell rang, and I saw them in the hallway outside the principal's office, waiting for their appointment to start.

Lindsay took me by the arm and pulled me in the opposite direction, wanting to know if I had fixed everything. But I didn't know what to tell her. I hadn't heard back from Chris Bollmer last night, and I hadn't seen him yet this morning, so I didn't (and still don't) know if the second half of my plan worked or not. But I didn't even have a chance to tell her that much, because the secretary called Lindsay and her mom in before I could open my mouth. She kept her eyes glued to me as she walked into the office, silently pleading with me to help her, and now. I just can't get that picture of her out of my mind. The image of Lindsay's panicked face will be seared on my brain for all of eternity.

"I'll see what I can find out," Samantha says once homeroom is over and we get outside into the hallway.

"Okay. Let me know as soon as you hear anything."

"I will. Did you talk to Jesse? Is everything okay?"

I tell her about how I hung up on his cell phone last night, and she winces.

"Yeah, I'm gonna say that that probably wasn't the way to go on that one," she murmurs.

I hang my head. "I know. I'm such an idiot. I just didn't know what to say. And now I have to do the presentation blind. I don't even know what painting he picked for our third example…How am I going to talk about a painting for ten minutes when I don't know anything about it?"

Samantha raises her eyebrows. "Well, it's a good thing you're getting some help from our little round friend, or you would definitely be giving up your GPA title."

"I know, I know." My mind starts racing again. "You should have seen Maya Franklin when I got detention in physics the other day. She was practically foaming at the mouth. But really, I'm worried. If *we're* in control, does that mean the ball can't pull this off? I mean, what could possibly happen that is going to make me suddenly know all about a random piece of art?"

Samantha shrugs. "Osmosis?"

When I walk into AP Art History, Jesse won't even look at me. I brace myself as I march over to his desk to apologize.

"Jesse, I'm so sorry. Please, you have to let me explain. I didn't have a cell phone, and Lindsay disappeared and her mom called me and I had to go find her..." I let my sentence trail off as it becomes obvious that Jesse isn't going to respond. He just sits there, quiet and withdrawn. After a few torturous seconds, he hands me a yellow folder without looking at me.

"Here's the work I did. Good luck."

I wish he would have yelled at me. I wish he would have called me horrible names. Anything would be better than this. I sit back down at my desk. I can't believe I messed this up so badly.

I flip through the folder, trying to calm myself down.

You have to focus, I tell myself. *You need to relax.* Jesse typed up note cards on *Prometheus Bound* and *The City*, more or less paraphrasing the discussions we had about them at the museum. I anxiously turn to the next page, looking for the third piece. When I see what it is, my heart almost stops. For a second, I feel light-headed, like I'm going to faint.

I can't believe this. The piece he picked is *Camo-Outgrowth*, my aunt Kiki's favorite poster. The one with the globes covered in camouflage that hung above her dining room table. The one that we used to talk about every time I went to her house.

So *that's* how the ball is going to pull this off.

"Jesse, Erin, are you ready?" Mr. Wallace asks.

We both say that we are, and we stand stiffly in the front of the room, not making eye contact with each other.

"Tell me, Erin, which three pieces did you pick?" Mr. Wallace asks. I rattle off the names and artists of each piece, and Mr. Wallace nods. "Very interesting," he says, making notes on a pad in front of him. "All right then, go ahead, please. Tell us how spirituality is represented in each of them."

I pause so that Jesse can take the lead with *Prometheus Bound*, since that was, after all, his choice. He looks nervous, and he stammers a bit as he reads from his note cards without even looking up. I can see the sweat forming on his brow. *What's happening to him?* I wonder. *Is this because of me?* He's mumbling and his words are all over the place, so I jump in and try to rescue him.

"I think the point Jesse is trying to make is that Prometheus *is* spirituality. In stealing the fire from the gods, Prometheus came to represent the triumph of the human spirit over those who would try to oppress it." Mr. Wallace smiles appreciatively, and I move on to discuss my interpretation of *The City*. Out of the corner of my eye, I notice that Jesse's hands are trembling.

"The third piece we've chosen is Thomas Hirschhorn's *Camo-Outgrowth*," I reiterate. "Jesse, do you want to start on that one?"

Jesse shuffles through his folder, trying to compose himself. "Yes, um, thanks. Like Erin said, we chose *Camo-Outgrowth*, which is, um, a modern, uh, sculpture about how we as a, um, society, are obsessed with, uh, war."

Mr. Wallace looks confused. I glance at the note cards Jesse outlined last night. They're so detailed and so carefully outlined, but he's obviously frazzled by the whole situation. I feel horrible. This is all my fault. When he pauses, I jump back in.

"I also think that this piece is a comment on society's fascination with war in the twentieth century. The repetitiveness of the globes symbolizes how pervasive war has become. The camouflage, I think, can also be interpreted as just how oppressive war can be on the human spirit, causing it to go into hiding, in a way. If you really think about it, when taken as a whole, the three pieces we chose come full circle. *Prometheus* represents the triumph of the human spirit over the gods who would oppress it; *The City* shows how spirituality can be lost in the machine age; and *Camo-Outgrowth* says that war can turn men into machines if they're not careful, allowing the oppressor to ultimately win." I exhale, exhausted. Talk about channeling my aunt Kiki. I don't even know where that stuff came from.

Mr. Wallace stares at me, and the whole class bursts into spontaneous applause. Well, the whole class except for Maya Franklin, who is scowling to herself. (Ha!)

"Very well done," Mr. Wallace mutters. "You—"

The bell rings, cutting him off.

"Tomorrow, we'll hear from Emily and Phoebe," he continues in a hurry. "And don't forget, applications for the Italy trip are due in my office by tomorrow afternoon at 5:00 p.m.!" he shouts, trying to make himself heard over the din of everyone packing up their things. "Erin, Jesse, please stay for a moment after class, would you?"

When everyone has gone, Mr. Wallace motions for us to sit down with him at the table in the front of the room.

"I have to say, I was very impressed with the pieces that you two chose. They were original and unexpected. But I was disappointed in the overall presentation. It seems clear to me, Jesse, that you were unprepared, and it was quite obvious that Erin did the majority of the work. I'm afraid I'm going to have to factor that into your grades."

Jesse's mouth drops open and his face flushes a bright red.

"Mr. Wallace," I try to explain, but before I have a chance to say anything, Jesse picks up his bag and races out of the room.

"Jesse, wait!" I yell. I try to run after him, but I'm stopped by a throng of seniors entering the classroom for next period. I finally push my way through them and into the hallway, but I'm too late.

He's gone.

I slide down the wall outside of the classroom—and just like my Mom, the tears come. I never wanted it to be like this. I replay yesterday afternoon in my head like it's a scene in a movie—riding in Samantha's car, taking out the ball, asking it the completely wrong question. I shouldn't have asked if *I* would get an A minus on the presentation. I should have asked if *we* would get an A minus on the presentation. Stupid, stupid, stupid.

I don't know what to do. If I tell Mr. Wallace the truth now, I'll never get to go on the trip. But if I don't tell him, then Jesse won't get to go either. I put my head in my hands, trying to think of an answer or solution. But this time, none appears.

⌀

Luckily, today is a Wednesday. On Wednesdays, my last two periods of the day are free periods. Well, technically, seventh period is a free period, and sixth period is an optional physics study hall/review. But today, I'm opting to go home instead.

My mom has put Kiki's ashes on top of the mantle, and I take the black lacquer box and carefully put it inside my backpack. The ball is still inside it from yesterday too, and I shove my sweatshirt in between them so that they won't bang against each other, and then head out into the backyard.

There's a huge oak tree in the far corner of our property. When I was a kid I used to go there all the time: sometimes to think, sometimes to read a book, sometimes to play, sometimes just to get out of the sun on a hot summer afternoon. I haven't been there in years, but for some reason it's the only place where I want to be right now.

I take out the box and place it gently on the ground next to me, and then I take out the ball and turn it over in my hands as I lie back against the thick base of the tree trunk. It's cool and breezy and calm, just like I remember it.

Essays are due for the Italy trip tomorrow. I've heard that the Committee of Tenth Grade Teachers is going to meet after school to go through them. And still, I don't know what I'm going to write about.

I stare at the ball. I can't believe I didn't get to ask it for the only thing I really wanted. I shake it halfheartedly.

"If I tell Mr. Wallace the truth, will I get picked to go on the Italy trip?" I whisper. I watch as the octagonal dipyramid spins through the pink liquid, finally settling on an answer.

Your future is obscured. You must ask again.

Right.

I put the ball down and pick up the box with my aunt Kiki inside. It's so weird to think that she's actually in there. Now I understand why my mom wanted the ashes so badly: it's so much easier to feel close to her when she's right there with you.

"What should I do, Aunt Kiki?" I say to the box.

I run my index finger over the mother-of-pearl design and, out of nowhere, a monarch butterfly lands on my leg.

"Whoa," I say out loud.

The butterfly flutters its black and orange wings, seemingly oblivious to the fact that I'm not a flower. It flies up a few feet and I watch as it flits around above me in the tree leaves. I'm just about to close my eyes as it flies back down, landing on my arm. It's maybe two feet from my face, and I watch it as it watches me with its unblinking eyes. It seems like its staring at me, waiting for me to do or say something.

My heart pounds. "Aunt Kiki…Is that you?"

At the sound of my voice, the butterfly flies up and away, and I watch it until it's gone so far that I can't see it anymore. I look at the black box and laugh at myself. I can't believe I just talked to a butterfly. And I really can't believe I thought that a butterfly might be my aunt Kiki reincarnated. The old me would never even have considered something like that. Not for a second.

The old me, I think.

Right.

Does that mean that there's a new me?

Suddenly, I have an idea. I open up my backpack and take out a notebook and a pen, and the words begin to pour out of me, like they're writing themselves.

Dear Committee of Tenth Grade Teachers,

I used to think that I was an open-minded person. I thought this because I didn't discriminate against people based on their race, color, or religion. I didn't shout people down because of their political views. I wasn't offended by people who pierced or tattooed their bodies, or who dyed their hair purple. And yet, while I tolerated differences in others, I still always judged them. In my head, I categorized different people as weird or wrong or too popular for their own good, while I was normal and right. But I realize now that simply tolerating differences doesn't make a person open-minded.

In the last two weeks, I've met a lot of new people and have been exposed to a lot of new beliefs and ideas. At first I dismissed them, just as I always have. These people and their ideas seemed crazy and illogical. Most of all, they seemed strange. But over time, I began to see that maybe they weren't. My mind started to open—for real—and I began to see that maybe *I'm* the one who is strange. In always being so fixed and rigid in my thinking, maybe *I'm* the one who is wrong. And it occurred to me that this is what art is all about: being open to the world around you, and being willing to try to understand things that don't always make sense right away.

A wise person once tried to convince me to view the world as being full of possibilities and opportunities, and twists and turns, instead of allowing it to be all laid out for me in little boxes. Now I see that she was right.

To conclude, I believe I would be an excellent candidate for the Art History trip to Italy because I very much want to learn new things and to be influenced by new ideas and to take advantage of all of the possibilities and opportunities that the world has to offer. I hope that you will decide that I am worthy of such a privilege.

Sincerely,

Erin Channing

"You see, I told you she would be here."

I look up, startled to hear Lindsay's voice. She and Samantha are walking toward me. (Well, Lindsay is walking. Samantha is stopping and starting in a sort of limp-hobble because her three-inch heels keep sinking into the grass.)

"What are you doing out here?" Samantha asks, semi-distracted. "It's all dirty and there are, like, bugs and things." She swats at the air around her face, and then smirks at my white jeans. "I'll bet you anything you have grass stains on your butt."

"I wrote my essay," I say proudly, holding up my notebook. "I finally figured out what to write about."

Samantha rolls her eyes. "Um, that's great. I'm really happy for you. But don't you want to know if your best friend got kicked out of school today or not?"

Oh my God.

I was so wrapped up in my presentation and my fight with Jesse and my essay for the trip, I forgot all about Lindsay.

"Of course! I'm so sorry! What happened? Tell me everything."

Lindsay plops down next to me on the grass, while Samantha takes off her sweater (it's an old one, I notice) and carefully lays it down, gently lowering herself on top of it. Once she's sitting, she kicks off her shoes, and her whole body seems to unstiffen at once.

"Well, it was *so* crazy," Lindsay begins. "My mom and I are in Mr. Baker's office, sitting across from his desk, and he starts explaining that they've uncovered a cheating ring. And then he says that Megan Crowley was in charge of it, but they have evidence that I was helping her. And I swear to God, if I hadn't been so scared I would have just burst out laughing at how clueless he is, to think that *I* would help Megan Crowley with *anything*. I mean, it's like the teachers have no idea what goes on in that place every day. None."

"So what happened?"

"So, I'm just about to lose it and start swearing on my mother's life that I had nothing to do with it, when the secretary opens the door and says that she urgently needs to speak to Mr. Baker. So he goes outside to talk to her, and then a minute later he comes back in and his face is all red, and he apologizes. Like, ten times. He looks all sheepish and says there seems to have been a misunderstanding, and I should go back to class and forget this ever happened. And my mom and I are, like, what? But when we leave the office—mind you I'm shaking from head to toe and I can barely even walk—who do I see waiting outside Mr. Baker's door?"

"Chris Bollmer," I answer.

Lindsay and Samantha both look surprised.

"How did you know that?" Lindsay asks. I smile and raise my eyebrows.

"Magic," I tell her.

Thirty-One

Samantha gives me a ride back to school, and I walk into the Art Department office just as Mr. Wallace is packing up his things. "Hello, Erin," he says, looking pleasantly surprised to see me. "Your ears must have been burning, because I was just telling some of my colleagues about how impressed I was with your presentation today. Your interpretation of *Camo-Outgrowth* was quite sophisticated."

I blush and nervously shift my weight from side to side.

"Thanks, but, um, I actually need to talk to you about that. The presentation, I mean."

Mr. Wallace blinks behind his glasses as he sits back down in his chair. "Okay. Go ahead."

I swallow back the lump in my throat, using all of my composure to keep the tears from coming. "Okay. This is really hard, but, well, I know it seemed like Jesse wasn't prepared, but he really was. I think he was just nervous or something."

Mr. Wallace nods sympathetically as he strokes at the little goatee on his chin like it's a pet.

"But this was an oral presentation," he reminds me. "Part of your grade was based on your ability to present the material to the class."

I sigh. I can see that Mr. Wallace isn't going to make this easy for me. "I understand. But he was also really upset with me, and I think that may have affected his presentation also."

Mr. Wallace raises an eyebrow at me. "Why was he upset with you?"

I keep picturing the tattoo on the inside of Jesse's arm: Truth. Truth. Truth. It repeats itself over and over and over.

"Because I didn't show up for our last trip to the museum last night. And I didn't help him work on the presentation at all. Jesse did everything. I mean, not everything. I went to the museum the first two times and I helped pick the first two paintings. But he picked *Camo-Outgrowth* on his own." I swallow and look down at the floor. "It was just a coincidence that I already knew that piece really well."

Mr. Wallace leans back in his chair, his eyes unreadable. "I see," he says. He strokes his goatee again and lets out a long sigh. "Well, Erin, I appreciate that you told me the truth. But you didn't complete the assignment. Each person was supposed to visit the museum three times, and you only went twice." He shakes his head regretfully. "I was going to give you an A minus, but based on this information, I'm going to have to lower that by at least a full grade."

A full grade. That brings me to a B minus, which would bring my average in the class down to a B plus. Which means I won't qualify for the trip. My eyes begin to sting.

"I'm disappointed in you, Erin," Mr. Wallace continues. "And not just because you didn't do the work. I'm disappointed that you let your partner down."

There's a pesky teardrop, just like the one my mom shed. I don't say anything back to Mr. Wallace. I just fumble through my backpack, looking for the essay. I went through a lot of blood and sweat (and yes, tears) to write that thing—okay, maybe just a little bit of sweat and not so much blood, but still—there's no way I'm going to just throw it away. He'll have to do that himself.

"Here," I manage to say, lying it down on the desk. "Not that it really matters anymore." I turn around and walk out of the office, leaving Mr. Wallace alone with his goatee.

At nine o'clock that night, a green jellybean sails through my window.

What the hell?

I get up from my math homework and pick it up off of my carpet. As I'm examining it, I hear a *plink* against my window, and then a red jellybean comes flying through, hitting me on the back. It has to be Samantha. She probably snuck out of the house and wants me to accompany her on a road trip to God knows where. Las Vegas, probably.

I lean out the window, ready to yell at her, but then I stop. It's not Samantha. It's Jesse.

"What are you doing?" I ask in a stage whisper.

"I'm trying to hit you with Jelly Bellies," he stage-whispers back, grinning. "I nailed you with that cinnamon one."

"I'm coming down," I tell him. "Meet me on the side of the house, by the laundry room door."

I grab a pile of dirty clothes out of my hamper and tiptoe down the stairs, hoping that my parents won't hear me. I wince as one of the treads creaks under my weight.

"Erin, is that you?" my mom yells from her bedroom.

"Yeah," I call back. "Just taking some stuff down to the laundry room."

I make it the rest of the way uninterrupted and quickly dump the clothes on top of the washing machine. I'm beyond baffled. Jesse is done with me, but now here he is, acting like everything is okay. Here he is, *grinning* and throwing Jelly Bellies at me. I wonder if maybe the Flamingo Kids turned him onto drugs, or he suddenly came down with short-term amnesia and he can't remember anything from the last twenty-four hours…I run my hands over my hair and open the door, realizing too late that I'm wearing my Barry Manilow T-shirt.

"Hi," I say, trying not to blush.

"Hi," he says. "Is that a Barry Manilow concert T-shirt?" he asks.

"You like 'Copacabana,'" I remind him defensively.

He laughs. "Yeah, but I didn't go to the concert."

I cross my arms in front of my chest to cover up Barry's face. "Did you want something?" As soon as the words are out of my mouth, I regret them.

He looks at me with those blue, blue eyes, and my heart aches inside my chest like it's a rotten, throbbing tooth.

"Yeah," he says. "Mr. Wallace called me. He told me what you did. He's giving me a B plus."

"So, is your GPA high enough for the trip?" I whisper, staring at the floor.

"Yeah. By about a tenth of a point." He puts his hand under my chin and tilts my face up, the way he did that night at the hot spring. Just thinking about the night at the hot spring makes my legs go weak, and I feel like they're going to buckle underneath me. "But he told me that he's giving you a B minus." He looks at me searchingly. "Why did you do it?"

I shrug, trying to pretend that it's no big deal, even though I know that he knows that it is. "It was the right thing to do. And besides, you deserve to go to Italy more than I do. You had a much better reason."

Jesse leans in and kisses me.

"I was really hoping that we'd be able to go together," he says.

Now the tears are escaping, rolling down my face, but screw it—I wrap my arms around him and bury my head in his soft yellow T-shirt, my cheek pressed against him. "Me too," I choke, barely able to get the words out.

We stand there, hugging each other for a few minutes, while I cry and cry, letting out all of my tears: the ones for letting him down, the ones for not being able to explain why, the ones for embarrassing him in front of the whole class, the ones for not being able to go to Italy, the ones for him going to Italy without me. Finally I pull back from him.

"I'm sorry," I say. "For everything."

He wipes my wet cheeks with his fingertips, brushing my tears away into the ether. "It's okay. I don't know what's going on, but I know you were doing something to help Lindsay, and I get it. Friends come first. It's how it should be." He stands back. "Hey, speaking of Lindsay, did you hear about Chris Bollmer? He confessed that he hacked into Mrs. Newman's computer and made it look like Megan Crowley had stolen those math tests. And he said that he'd been trying to frame Lindsay too. He was mad at her for not, like, bowing down before him after Megan got kicked out. Anyway, Mr. Baker expelled him. But then the police came. They're talking about charging him for breaking into the school's computer system, and he might have to go a juvenile detention center. Can you believe that?"

"No," I say, both shocked and pretending to be shocked by the news. "That's crazy."

"Actually, that not's even the craziest part. The craziest part is that when he was telling his story to the police, he kept saying that there was a magic ball that was going to get him if he didn't come clean."

My heart thumps so loudly I'm worried Jesse can hear it. "Wow," I say. "That really is crazy. Lizzie and Matt and Cole must be having a field day."

Jesse rolls his eyes. "You have no idea."

I bite my lip. I feel kind of bad for Chris. I mean, he's getting what he deserves—he did hack into a school computer and frame other people for doing it—but still. I can't help but think about Megan wanting to be a vet. It makes me wonder if Chris had dreams for his future too.

"I should get back inside," I say. "I don't want my parents to think that I'm actually doing laundry or anything. They might start expecting it from me."

Jesse laughs. "Okay. I'll see you tomorrow?"

I lean in and give him a light peck on the cheek. "Yes. I will definitely see you tomorrow."

Thirty-Two

At lunch the next day, things are totally back to normal. Or, as Samantha likes to text, back to the way things were BTWAB (Before Things Went All Bizarre). Samantha and Lindsay and I are sitting at our usual table. Meanwhile Megan, Chloe, Brittany, and Madison huddle together at a table on the other side of the cafeteria. I see Jesse walk in through the side door, and I wave to him across the room. He waves back and heads toward us, giving me a kiss on the cheek as he reaches our table.

Okay. So maybe things aren't *totally* back to BTWAB.

The whole room is buzzing with the news about Chris Bollmer. Everywhere you turn, someone is talking about him or Lindsay or Megan's email about Lindsay. It's, like, *the* gossip event of the century. It could have its own Barbara Walters Special (with Lizzie, Matt, and Cole as cohosts, natch).

"I still can't believe everything worked out," Lindsay whispers, squirming in her seat. Her dimple is back. It's the first time I've seen it in a while.

Samantha arches an eyebrow and gives me a knowing look. "It *is* pretty amazing. But it would be so much more amazing if we knew what you said in that email to Chris Bollmer."

Just as I am about to remark that I have no idea what she's talking about, Megan and her posse stride up to our table. A few people at the table next to us nudge each other, and like a crowd doing the wave at a football game, a hush spreads out across the room. I look around at the sudden quiet, and once again, I see hundreds of eyes watching, waiting to see what is going to happen next.

Lindsay freezes, and the old fear creeps into her face. I give Megan a look, warning her with my eyes not to do anything stupid.

But Megan simply smiles.

"Hi, Lindsay," she says brightly.

Lindsay looks around, not sure what to do. I know exactly what she's thinking. She's thinking that she can't believe Megan actually called her by her real name.

"Um, hi?" Lindsay says. It comes out as a question, like: *Do you really expect me to be nice to you after two years of torture, just because you apologized to me in an email?*

"I just wanted to say how relieved I am that that lunatic isn't at school anymore," Megan continues. "For both of us." She looks around, lowering her voice so that the whole room doesn't hear, and when she turns back to us, I can see just the slightest hint of worry in her eyes. I smile to myself. So she does believe it. She really does believe that Lindsay has magic powers. I *love* that.

"Also, I wanted to say that I hope there are no hard feelings between us. I mean, I think it would be nice if we could be friends. Like, why not, right?"

Lindsay gives Megan a you-can't-possibly-be-serious look, and Samantha covers her mouth with both hands.

"I'm pretty happy with the friends I have," Lindsay answers. "But thanks anyway."

"Oh," Megan says. The fake smile that she pastes onto her face doesn't do much to hide her shock. "Okay, well, I'm around…" She doesn't finish. She just lowers her head and slinks off, her groupies following her back to their corner.

"Oh my God," Samantha hisses, finally letting go of her mouth. "That was so amazing! You were like, 'Sorry, bitch, TTYN!'"

Jesse turns to me, a puzzled look on his face.

"Talk to you never," I translate.

Lindsay lets out a loud, satisfied sigh. "I've been waiting for that. You don't know how long…"

Jesse raises his milk carton.

"Well then, I propose a toast," he says quietly, as the rest of the cafeteria processes what just happened. "To Lindsay."

Samantha and I raise our cartons to touch his.

"To Lindsay," we all whisper together.

As lunch winds down and people start throwing their stuff away and going off to their lockers, I notice that Samantha is transfixed on something on the other side of the room. I follow her eyes. It's Aiden.

"I was able to fix everything but you and Aiden," I say to her. "I'm sorry."

She breaks her gaze and turns to look at me.

"*Au contraire, mon frère*," she says. "Aiden got fixed all by himself. Trance broke up with him last night. Turns out she's been cheating on him for months with some guy in community college, and she finally told him. He came crawling back to me with his tail between his legs this morning."

I'm not sure if I want to be happy or barf. "So…are you going out with him now?"

Samantha laughs, like I've just said the most ridiculous thing ever. "Oh please. I told him to try digging through a different trash can. I mean, is he kidding? Like I would go out with him after the way he treated me?"

I lean in and lower my voice, so that Jesse won't hear me. "But maybe it was the ball," I remind her.

"Ball, schmall," she whispers. "He treated me like crap, and that's that. I've moved on. Aiden is *so* last week." She glances longingly at him again.

"Really?"

"Okay, maybe not *really*, but he doesn't need to know that." She giggles. "I'll torture him for a few months. It'll be fun. Maybe I'll even go out with that singer from the Flamingo Kids. He did say they were coming back, remember?"

I groan. "Please, no more concerts. My hoodie is officially retired."

Jesse taps me on the shoulder. "What are you guys whispering about over there, huh?"

Samantha smiles at him brightly. "Oh nothing. Erin was just saying how she can't wait to go to another Flamingo Kids concert."

Jesse laughs. "You're lying."

Samantha laughs too, and I give her the evil eye.

"You suck," I whisper to her.

"You wouldn't have me any other way," she whispers back.

Jesse and I hold hands as we walk down the hallway to AP Art History. "I don't know if I can face Mr. Wallace," I admit. "Do you think he hates me now?"

"Not possible. No one could hate you. Besides, what you did took a lot of guts."

We pause outside the doorway and he gives me a long kiss on the mouth, right in front of everyone. "It's so hard for me to concentrate in there, knowing that you're just two rows behind me, and I can't touch you," he whispers when he's done.

"Well, it's worse for me. I have to just sit there, staring at the back of your head. Talk about distracting."

He kisses me again, but we're suddenly interrupted by Maya Franklin.

"First of all, you two should get a room. And second of all, Erin, I heard about your B minus. That's really too bad."

I swallow. "Yeah, well, congratulations. I guess you're number one now."

Maya pretends to think about it for the first time. "Oh, wow. I am number one, aren't I? Gosh, I hadn't even realized that…"

The bell rings. We take our seats, and I have to suffer through Phoebe and Emily's presentation. Yawn! And I'm not being a hater or anything. It's just that, compared to ours, it's awful. It's unimaginative and predictable, and… well, for lack of a better term, it's inside the box. Even though I don't feel like crying, I can't help but be pissed. My B minus is so undeserved.

I try to distract myself by staring at Jesse. I look at every part of his body, trying to remember which parts I've felt and what they felt like. The back of his neck, his shoulders, his lower back…all of a sudden he shifts in his seat, lifting his left heel up off of the ground so that the bottom of his Converse is exposed.

I see you looking.

I try to stifle a laugh. He turns his head around and gives me a quick wink.

When the bell rings, everyone claps for Emily and Phoebe. Mr. Wallace stands up at the front of the room, yelling his announcements over the noise, just like he did yesterday.

"Tomorrow we will hear from Christian and Maya, and don't forget, Italy applications are due in my box by five o'clock today! Also, Erin Channing, would you please stay for a moment after class? I need to talk to you."

Jesse and I exchange worried glances, and he signals that he'll meet me in the hallway when I'm done.

I wait as Carolyn Strummer corners Mr. Wallace with a question about the Italian Renaissance, and my heart is pounding as he gives her what might possibly be the longest answer in the history of answers. What could he want with me? Maybe he thought about it and decided that a B minus wasn't low enough. Or, maybe he's decided that lowering my grade isn't enough, and he's going to give me detention. Again. My hands get clammy as I consider all of the possibilities.

Finally, Carolyn leaves the room and Mr. Wallace waves me up to his desk. My strategy is to beat him to the punch on whatever he's going to say. I'm hoping that if I show him that I know he went easy on me, he'll be less inclined to punish me anymore.

"Mr. Wallace, I just want to tell you that I know you could have been a lot harder on me, and if you feel like you need to do more, I totally understand."

Mr. Wallace furrows his brow. "Erin, I didn't ask you to stay so that I could lay more consequences on you."

"You didn't?"

The faint hint of a smile crosses his face. "No. I asked you to stay because I read your essay last night. For the Italy trip."

I don't understand. He must know that I don't qualify with a B minus on my presentation. So why would he read my essay if I'm not even eligible to go on the trip?

"But why?" I ask.

"Well, I was impressed with what you did for Jesse. If you remember, one of the things we're looking for is character. And what you did yesterday really proved to me what a strong character you have. So I was curious to see what you wrote." He sighs. "I have to tell you, I was skeptical about this idea. I told the principal not to get his hopes up. I told him that it would probably be just a bunch of kids who only want to go because they think it will beef up their college applications. But it seems I underestimated you. Your reason for wanting to go is exactly what we were hoping for."

"But I got a B minus," I hear myself remind him. "My grade in the class will never be an A minus now. I'm disqualified."

He nods. "I know. And the B minus stands."

My heart sinks. For a minute there, I thought he was going to reinstate my original grade.

"So that's it? You just wanted to tell me how great my essay was, and how sorry you are that I'm going to miss out on the trip?"

"No," he says. "I wanted to tell you how great your essay was, and I wanted to offer you some extra credit work that could bring your GPA back up to an A minus."

I stare at him for a moment, speechless.

"Do you have anything to say?" he asks.

"Really? Really? Oh my God. Thank you, Mr. Wallace. Thank you so much! You have no idea how much this means to me."

He laughs and hands me a thick folder. "Don't get too excited. You haven't seen the work yet."

"I don't care. Whatever it is, I will do it. I will write essays in Italian—I mean, first I'd have to learn Italian, and then I would write the essays, but whatever. I just want to go on this trip." I pause for second. "But what's the work?"

"I'd like you to write a ten-page paper discussing the role of superstition and magic in artwork from the Renaissance period."

I stare at him, waiting for him to tell me that this is a joke, that Samantha and Lindsay put him up to this. But he just strokes his goatee, and I realize that it's not a joke at all. He's dead serious.

A smile spreads across my face.

"I can do that," I tell him confidently.

"That's good, because you have to turn it in before we make our announcement on Monday."

When I get outside in the hallway, Jesse is waiting for me. I jump up and down.

"What? What is it? What happened?"

I tell him the news and he gives me a huge hug, lifting me off the ground and spinning me around in a circle.

"We're going to Italy!" I squeal. "And I'm still going to have the highest GPA in tenth grade!"

Jesse laughs, but then suddenly his face turns serious.

"What?" I ask him. "What's wrong?"

"Well, *you're* going to Italy. But how do we know that they're going to pick me too?"

I think about this for a second, and then I shrug.

"We don't, really." I tell him. "But I just have a feeling, the same way that you had a feeling not to get on that boat with your mom and your brother."

Jesse gives my hand a little squeeze. "You know what?"

"What?"

"So do I."

Epilogue

Lindsay and Samantha and I sit in a circle on the floor of my bedroom. In the middle is the Pink Crystal Ball, along with the rules, a black felt-tip pen, and the scroll with the list of names on it. I unroll the scroll, pushing it flat against the floor and holding it down with the side of my knee. At the bottom is my aunt's name—Kate Hoffman, carefully written in her neatest handwriting—but this time, no lump forms in my throat when I look at it.

I pick up the pen and sign my name directly underneath hers, then roll the scroll back up and place it back in the middle of the circle. I look at Lindsay.

"Are you sure about this?" I ask her.

She nods solemnly. "Yes. I'm sure. Samantha needs this more than I do. I mean, you heard her, her parents hate each other. She needs to do something." Lindsay's mouth breaks into a grin as she rolls her eyes. "Besides, my father's girlfriend can wait. It's not like she's going anywhere."

"Thanks, Linds," Samantha says. "I'm always amazed by how nice and unselfish you are. Although, now that

I've seen your dark side in action, I have to say, I kind of like it."

"Okay," I say, anxious to move things along. "Can we do this please?"

But Lindsay holds up her hand insistently. "No," she says. "There's something we need to do first."

Samantha and I glance at each other.

"What do we need to do?" Samantha asks.

But instead of answering, Lindsay closes her eyes. She takes hold of my right hand and Samantha's left hand, and with her eyes still shut, she motions with her chin for Samantha and me to close the circle. Samantha and I roll our eyes at each other and begrudgingly take hold of each others' hands.

I start to tell Lindsay that she's being kind of dramatic, but she shushes me loudly before I can get the words out, and then she begins to talk in a low, serious voice.

"Today, we three are bound forever by a mystical force. And in recognition of the gift we have been granted, we swear that we will use the magic ball for good and not for evil. We swear that we will follow the rules of the ball as they have been written. And we swear that we will never, ever speak of it to anyone outside of this room." She pauses dramatically then says my name in such a loud, bold voice that it startles me.

"Erin Channing. Do you swear?"

I feel like I should say I do, but that seems wedding-ish and inappropriate. As I'm considering an alternative answer, Lindsay opens her eyes to see what's taking me so long.

"Swear!" she whispers at me, forcefully enough to be kind of scary.

"I swear," I say quickly, and Lindsay closes her eyes again.

"Samantha Burnham. Do you swear?"

"I swear," Samantha repeats solemnly.

"And I, Lindsay Altman, also swear to uphold these promises." She pauses again, letting her words hang in the air for a moment before continuing with her—I don't even know what to call it—her spell? Her ritual? Her weirdness.

"Today, we three are sisters in magic." Her voice is slowly getting louder, and as she speaks, she raises her arms up, bringing my arm and Samantha's arm with hers into the air as her words come to a crescendo. "Today, we three shall forever be known as…the Secret Society of the Pink Crystal Ball."

I drop my hand.

"Seriously?" I ask. "The Secret Society of the Pink Crystal Ball? Don't you think that's a little, like, seventh grade?"

Lindsay looks offended and opens her mouth to protest, but Samantha beats her to it.

"I love it," Samantha says. "I've always wanted to be part of a secret society. It's like the Masons. Or like Skull and Bones at Yale." She gives me a you-are-such-a-loser look. "And it's not seventh grade," she snips. "It's cool."

"Okay, fine," I say. "The arbiter of cool has spoken. We're the Secret Society of the Pink Crystal Ball. Now can we please just get on with this?"

Lindsay smiles, and I can tell that she's satisfied to have Samantha on her side for once. "Yes," she says. "Let's begin."

"Finally," I say, fully aware of my stubborn need to always have the last word.

I pick up the ball, holding it gently between my hands. Then I close my eyes and give it a shake. I have no idea if I'm doing this right, but I thought about it for a long time, and I couldn't come up with any other way to do it. I inhale, then slowly let out my breath.

"I choose...Samantha Burnham." I open my eyes and place the ball into Samantha's outstretched hands. She pulls it toward herself greedily, and already I can see the wheels turning in her head.

"Why," she asks, noticing my look of concern, "are you looking at me like you're my mother?"

"Because I know you, and I don't like what you're thinking. We just swore that we're going to use the ball for good and not for evil and that we're going to follow the rules, and here you are, ten seconds later, with that mischievous look on your face."

She waves her hand at me like I'm being ridiculous. "I am perfectly aware of the rules. I get it. Nothing past twenty-four hours, don't ask questions for other people, blah, blah, blah. Now stop worrying so much. It's going to be fine."

"So have you thought about what you're going to ask it?" Lindsay wants to know.

"Well, I can tell you that I'm not going to ask it for good grades and G-rated kisses, that's for sure." She looks down at the ball and shakes her finger at it. "You, Mr. Ball, are about to see some *real* action."

Oh no, I think to myself. *I've created a monster*.

"What does that mean, *real action*?" I ask, nervously. "We agreed that you get to be next so that you can fix the situation with your parents. And I don't see how that involves real action."

"Oh my God. You look like you're about to start convulsing. Will you please relax? Did you learn nothing from your experience with this ball? You need to *lighten up*." She overenunciates the words *lighten up* and says them extra slowly, like she's talking to someone who doesn't speak English. She looks at Lindsay. "And to answer your question, yes. I have my first question all prepared." She gives us a Miss America smile, then holds the ball out in front of her and closes her eyes. She sits in that pose for what feels like ten minutes.

"All right," I say impatiently. "I can't take it anymore. Let's hear it."

"Okay, okay. Hold your horses. My God, have you never heard of the dramatic pause?" I roll my eyes while Lindsay giggles, and finally, she gives the ball a shake.

"Tell me, Pink Crystal Ball," she says, in a hushed, theatrical voice. "Will I, Samantha Burnham, be discovered by a Hollywood director who will cast me in a major production?"

I groan. "What does that have to do with your parents?"

"Um, excuse me, but what did kissing Jesse Cooper have to do with you becoming less boring? And please, do not interrupt the ball while it is performing its magic."

We all move in close to look at the ball, and the pink liquid seems to melt away as the acrylic die floats up to the surface.

Samantha lets out a squeal as the answer appears, a slow smile spreading across her face.

It is your destiny...

Acknowledgments

People often imagine the work of writing to be a solo affair: an author sitting for hours in a room, alone, with nothing but a computer and the sound of birds chirping outside the window. In my case, if you substitute the birds for really loud kids, a barking dog, and a phone that rings all day long, I suppose you'd be right. But while writing may be a lonely pursuit, creating a book is not, and there are many people I need to thank for helping to turn my writing into a book.

Thank you to Barbara Zitwer, my agent of many years, for encouraging me to give the Young Adult genre a try. You were right! Thank you to Dan Ehrenhaft, my gifted editor, for your ability to see what was missing, for the gentleness of your criticisms, and for your patience and understanding during a tough year. Thank you to Todd Stocke, Kristin Zelazko, and Kelly Barrales-Saylor at Sourcebooks for jumping in at the eleventh hour and providing me with all of the support I needed, and to the publisher, Dominique Raccah, for being so incredibly flexible and supportive. Thank you to Rusty Weiss for your counsel, your wise advice, and your ability to make your emails sound both friendly and hostile at the same time. Thank you to Amy Keroes, my friend, de facto public relations consultant, and editor at mommytracked.com, for reading multiple drafts and for sending me your thoughts in real time. Thank you to all of my friends for being so helpful and supportive in trying to spread the word about this book— the mom network is unbelievable! And of course, thank you to my wonderful family. Thank you to my husband, Michael, for listening to me ramble as I try to work out ideas in my head, for being my biggest critic (in a good way), and for not taking it personally when I yell at you for criticizing. I love you to death. Thank you to my daughter, Harper; you have been my muse since before you were even born. I would never have had the idea for this book if you and I had not been lying on your bed together, playing with a "magic" ball. And thank you to my son, Davis, for understanding when mommy has to work, and for being so proud that I'm a book writer.

About the Author

Risa Green writes a weekly column for www.mommytracked.com, and her prior adult novel, *Notes from the Underbelly*, was made into a television series. She is originally from the Philadelphia area and now lives in Los Angeles with her husband, their two children, and their dog.